Sign up for our newsletter to hear
about new and upcoming releases.

www.ylva-publishing.com

OTHER STORIES IN THE
L.A. METRO SERIES

WOUNDED
Souls

RJ NOLAN

Ylva

ACKNOWLEDGMENT

I would not be able to write a novel like this without the help of a wonderful group of people. But without my loyal readers, who have supported and encouraged me, it would all be for naught. So a big thank you to all my readers.

As always to ETJ. Your love and support keep me going every day.

To Pam. We made it through another book together. It just wouldn't be the same without you. Your dedication and support are greatly appreciated. Thank you.

To my critique partner, Jae. Thank you for keeping me on track and for your encouragement and help along the way.

To Jennifer. Thank you for adding your expertise to the book and suggesting such great exercises.

CHAPTER 1

LOGAN GAVE ONE LAST LONGING glance at the crowded beach before turning away. After she had arrived in LA that morning, the lure of the sand and surf had been too tempting to ignore. Despite the wind and chilly weather, apparently a lot of people had decided to enjoy the ocean and the impending sunset. She retraced her steps along the trail, back across the point, toward the parking lot. When she'd spotted the tiny parking area earlier, she had hoped that translated into a fairly unpopulated beach. No such luck.

As she veered to the right, following the trail, she noticed a smaller, less used path that she had not seen on her way to the beach. There was a sign on the trail, but it was too far away to read. She smiled when she reached the sign. It simply said *beach* with an arrow pointing in the exact opposite direction she had taken before.

What the heck, it was worth a try. She slapped her thigh and called to her companion. "Come on, Drake."

He glanced up from whatever smell had enticed him from her side. For a moment, he looked as if he was going to balk. A shake of his leash, which made the tags on his collar jangle, convinced him otherwise.

The trail narrowed and then ended at the top of a stairway. Logan looked down and hesitated. The stairway to the beach was narrow and steep. From what she could see, the beach below looked empty. She eyed the stairway again, which sported a handrail on each side. It was too tempting.

"Don't worry, boy. We'll take it slow and easy. Let's go."

Halfway down, she glanced back to see how he was faring with the steps. He grinned at her, his tongue lolling.

When they reached the bottom of the steps, her gaze swept the secluded cove. There was not a person in sight. *Perfect.* She settled onto the sand and leaned back against the cliff wall, letting the sound of the surf wash over her. She patted the sand next to her. The big dog settled down by her side. "Well, Drake, this is it. We made it all the way across country, from the Atlantic to the Pacific." She stroked his head where it rested on her thigh and sighed. "I just wish I knew where we go from here." There was one thing she was sure of: there was no going back to Boston.

The sun sank into the ocean, painting the sky with vivid hues of orange, red, and purple. As the sky darkened, her thoughts meandered through all of the places they had been in the last two years.

A sudden low growl from Drake made Logan jump.

A stranger was almost on top of them. The rapidly fading light and the sound of the incoming tide had shrouded the stranger's approach.

Logan's heart slammed against her ribcage like a trapped bird trying to escape.

Drake leaped to his feet and planted himself between the stranger and Logan.

The stranger skidded to a halt. She backpedaled, almost tripping in her haste to put some space between them.

Logan scrambled off the sand and grabbed the flashlight off her belt. Her thumb hovered over the button that would turn the ordinary looking flashlight into a stun gun.

"Sorry about that. Didn't see you there."

At the sound of the woman's voice, the tension left Drake's body, but he remained in place in front of her. It took a long moment before Logan made her thumb move off the stun gun's button. She returned the flashlight to the holder on her belt. Blowing out a breath, she berated herself for letting her fears get the better of her. Her hand strayed to her chest.

"I rarely come across anyone here," the woman said. "Most people prefer Point Dume Beach on the other side of the promontory. And not too many people want to take on those steps, even in the daylight. So this little cove is usually pretty deserted."

Which was exactly why Logan had chosen it. "No problem."

"Anyway, I'm sorry I startled you. I should've had my light on." She pulled out a flashlight and turned it on.

Even with the added light, the only things it illuminated clearly were the woman's gray sweatpants and red running shoes; her face remained shrouded in shadow.

Her solitude gone, Logan gave up on the beach. "Drake. Side." The big dog immediately moved to her side and pressed his shoulder to her thigh. "Good boy."

As soon as Drake moved, the woman took several steps backward, giving him a wide berth.

While the woman had given her a fright, she didn't like to see anyone afraid. Logan hugged Drake's head to her side for a moment. "Great Danes really are gentle giants. He won't bother you."

The woman nodded, but her body language said she wasn't convinced. "Have a good evening," she said and with a wave continued down the beach.

"We better head back to the campground, boy. Probably going to be a long drive in traffic." She glanced down the beach where the other woman had gone. She was already lost in the darkness. Logan turned in the opposite direction and headed back toward the stairs.

Her thought turned to tomorrow and having to meet the head of the ER department. She scowled. What made the woman think LA Metro's ER was so special? No use worrying about it now. She'd find out soon enough.

CHAPTER 2

DALE RUBBED HER ACHING THIGH. Every step she took caused pain to throb through her leg as she made her way down the corridor toward Jess McKenna's office. It just figured that she had chosen last night to push herself by going to Pirate's Cove before work. Even after three years, she still felt the need to prove to herself that she could do anything she used to.

The night in the ER had started out quietly but had turned chaotic when the fog had rolled in and covered a large swath of I-5, causing a multiple-vehicle pileup. It hadn't helped any that the other ER doctor had once again been unable to see her share of patients. Dale knocked on Jess's door and opened it when Jess called out admittance.

"What are you still doing here, Dale? After the kind of night you had, I thought you'd be out the door as soon as you could. Is there a problem with the turnover?"

"No. Everyone's been taken care of. I need to talk to you about Gretchen...again."

A frown marred Jess's face before her usual all-business expression reappeared. She motioned toward the chair in front of her desk. "Have a seat."

Dale sank into the offered chair. She reached out to rub her thigh and stopped herself just in time. "Look, I sympathize with what she's going through. I know she can't control when she has morning sickness, but it's causing problems. We were overwhelmed last night with incoming from the pileup on I-5. Riley and Craig had already taken patients to the OR. It was an all-hands-on-deck kind of thing. We had a bilateral flail chest, and

Gretchen bolted from the room in the middle of putting in a chest tube. I had to talk the resident, who took over for her, through the procedure while I got the guy intubated and inserted a chest tube on the patient's other side." Dale raked her fingers through her hair. "I know I said I'd take up as much slack as I could, but this has been going on for two months now. We need help on the night shift."

"I understand, and I'm working on it." Jess pulled over a file from the corner of her desk. "I don't want a repeat of what happened with the last guy."

Dale scowled as she remembered what a fiasco that had been. The guy had been an abrasive jerk who did as little work as he could manage in between alienating as many patients as possible. "I'm with you on that one. But what choice do you have but to take who the agency sends?"

"I've already talked to Dr. Tate. This time, I'm going to review the applicants' past work history." She tapped the file in front of her with one finger. "If they want the part-time position, they'll have to work with me for a few days before I agree to the hire."

Dale's already abundant respect for Jess went up another notch. She knew Jess cared about the ER, but getting the new Chief of Staff to agree to going well beyond the normal procedure for hiring a physician for a limited-time position must have been a hard sell.

"Not to be too pushy or anything, but do you think you can get us some help by the end of the week?"

"I'll see what I can do. I've got an applicant coming in this morning."

"Great." Dale grinned at the prospect of getting some much needed help. "Thanks."

Jess shook her head. "Don't thank me yet. I'm going to put this woman through her paces before I agree to the hire." She held up her hand to stop Dale's protest. "I know you need help, but it would be better to take a couple of extra days and be sure we've got someone really good than to have to go through this again in a week."

Dale sighed. "You're right. And thank you for understanding about the situation with Gretchen."

Jess's office door swung open, and her wife, Kim, stepped into the room. "Oh, sorry. Didn't realize you were busy." She started to back out the door.

"Wait," Jess said as she rose from her chair, a glowing smile lighting her face. She glanced at Dale. "We all set here?"

"We're good. Thanks again." Dale smiled at Kim in passing. "Have a good day." As she closed the door on the pair, she couldn't help envying them. How wonderful it must be to not only have a wife but one that you worked with every day. She shook her head. *Dream on.*

Logan stopped outside the entrance to LA Metro's ER. The dark, thick clouds that blotted out the sun matched her mood perfectly. "Time to go face the new boss," she muttered with a scowl. Having to pass muster with the department head was not the usual procedure for locum tenens work. The company she worked for specialized in providing physicians to fill short-term positions all over the country. Normally, the hospital hired the company, and as long as the physician met the criteria for the hire, you got whoever the company sent.

Why couldn't LA Metro be like every place else? She had been tempted to refuse, but there were no other offerings in the area, and she needed to work. If she wanted the job, she just had to suck it up. "Fine, let's get this over with."

She marched up to the ER front desk. The area was fronted with thick glass like the teller area of a bank. A small grill was inset into the glass, along with a slot for passing papers back and forth. She leaned in close to the glass. "I'm here to see Dr. McKenna."

The clerk looked up from the computer screen. "Which one?"

What? Logan frowned. "The head of the ER, Dr. McKenna. I have a nine o'clock appointment with her."

"Okay, I'll let her know you're here." He picked up the phone. "Sorry, I didn't get your name."

"Dr. Logan. I'm from Barron's Staffing." She couldn't make out what the clerk was saying on the phone through the thick glass.

He hung up the phone and leaned forward so she could hear him again. "Dr. McKenna will be right out."

Logan tapped her foot and barely resisted the urge to pace. She didn't want to be standing around waiting to be grilled by some ER chief; she wanted...needed to be working. Her gaze scanned the patients that filled the waiting room. These were the people she should be helping.

The door next to the desk swung open, and a tall, dark-haired woman with striking blue eyes stepped out.

"Dr. Logan?" When Logan nodded, she held out her hand and offered a firm handshake. "I'm Dr. McKenna. If you'll follow me, please."

She trailed after Dr. McKenna as she led the way into the ER proper. The place was busy with nurses and doctors going about their business with very little chitchat. Just the type of place she liked.

CHAPTER 3

DALE HAD A SPRING IN her step as she headed for the ER entrance. Jess had left her a message that the new locum tenens doctor would be starting work this evening. She stopped at the nurses' station and motioned to Paul, the desk clerk.

"Hey, Dr. Parker. What's up?"

"We've got a new doctor coming in tonight to give us a hand. Let me know when Dr. Logan gets here, please." She turned to walk away.

"She's already here."

Dale glanced at her watch. Her shift didn't start for half an hour. She turned back toward the nurses' station. "Where is she?"

He jerked his thumb over his shoulder toward the cubicles along the far wall. "Curtain three, I think."

"She's seeing a patient?"

"Yeah. She checked in and went right to work."

"Thanks for letting me know." Dale scanned the intake board, confirming that Dr. Logan was indeed in curtain three. Since the problems with Gretchen's pregnancy had escalated, Dale had taken over responsibility for the night shift. This was her ER now. No one just waltzed in and started seeing patients without so much as a hello. After taking a moment to shed her jacket, she headed for the curtained cubicles with a determined stride. She paused outside the one containing Dr. Logan and her patient to take a calming breath.

Jess had vetted this doctor, so she must be fine. Dale grinned as she remembered her own time under Jess's eagle eyes just over a year ago. She could laugh about it now. But at the time, it had been more nerve-racking than being under the scrutiny of the captain on her first overseas assignment. She doubted Jess had been any less vigilant about Dr. Logan. Still, she felt an obligation to oversee the new doctor until she was confident in her as well. Working nights was a special responsibility, as backup wasn't as readily available as during the day shift.

Dale pulled back the curtain and peered inside. The woman's back was to her as she spoke quietly with the man on the gurney. She couldn't make out what was being said. There wasn't much she could tell about her physically as a baggy, white lab coat masked her figure. Her straight dark blond hair was pulled back into a ponytail that swept her collar. She guessed that Dr. Logan's height matched her own five foot seven. Before she could make her presence known, the woman turned and spotted her. She frowned and took several quick steps toward Dale.

"Can I help you?" Dr. Logan asked.

She found herself captured by a pair of topaz-brown eyes, made striking by the golden starbursts surrounding the dark irises. It took a moment for Dale to find her voice. She inclined her head toward the hallway. "Why don't we step outside?"

Dr. Logan stepped out of the curtained area and across the hall, out of the patient's earshot. She crossed her arms over her chest. "Is there a problem?"

Taking in Dr. Logan's defensive posture, Dale needed to tread lightly. After all, the woman technically hadn't done anything wrong. And she didn't want them to get off on the wrong foot. Though she still planned on keeping an eye on her. "I just wanted to introduce myself. I'm Dale Parker, the physician in charge of the night shift." She held out her hand.

Dr. Logan took her hand in a firm grip. "Logan. Nice to meet you."

She couldn't help noticing that Logan hadn't offered her own first name. Curious, she glanced at the hospital ID hanging from the collar of her lab coat, only to find it flipped over with the back side showing. *Oh well.*

"Was there something else? I'd like to get back to my patient."

"No. I just wanted to welcome you to the night shift and tell you that if you need anything, just let me know."

"Okay. If you'll excuse me, then."

Dale's gaze remained on Logan until she reentered the cubicle and pulled the curtain shut behind her. She wasn't sure what to think of the new arrival. While she wasn't the most personable, it appeared that she was going to be a hard worker. And that was what was most important. As she walked away, she relived that moment when Logan's vivid gaze had captured her own. *Don't go there,* she sternly berated herself.

"Can I give you a hand?"

Logan jumped. *Damn the woman.* Glancing over her shoulder, she found Dr. Parker leaning against the doorframe of the treatment room. She turned to look at her more fully. Her muscular build was apparent beneath a long-sleeved T-shirt and scrubs. Shaggy brown hair framed Parker's face, softening her otherwise strong features.

From their first meeting, something about Parker had struck her as tantalizing familiar. But that made no sense as they had never met before tonight. Parker's red athletic shoes caught her eyes, and a memory rose unbidden of the woman at the beach yesterday evening. She snorted to herself. Out of all the millions of people in LA, what were the chances that the two of them would end up on the same beach? Even if they had, it didn't lessen Logan's exasperation with the fact that Parker had been dogging her all night.

Logan took a deep breath, making sure her irritation wouldn't show. "I've got it under control." She went back to suturing the patient who'd been on the losing end of a bar fight. Up until now, she'd been perfectly happy with only his snores to keep her company.

"I really don't mind," Dr. Parker said as she came to stand on the opposite side of the gurney. "It's pretty quiet. I'll help you finish up, and then we can grab a cup of coffee." She smiled, tugged a raised stool close to the gurney, then reached for a pair of gloves. "We haven't had a chance to get to know each other."

And if Logan had anything to say about it, that's exactly how it would stay. She didn't want to know anything about her coworkers or vice versa. "It's not necessary. Really, I've—"

The sound of running feet drew their attention. Marco Martinez, one of the residents, grabbed the doorway as he slid to a stop. "Dr. Parker. Ambulance just pulled in. Motorcyclist versus a bus." His eyes were wide. "It's bad."

Dr. Parker rose to her feet. "Marco, finish up here for Dr. Logan." Her calm gaze met Logan's. "Let's go."

Logan was right on Parker's heels as she raced down the hall. They burst through the trauma bay doors together.

"Status," Dr. Parker barked as she slipped into protective gear. "Someone call Dr. Connolly."

Logan glanced at Dr. Parker and froze. Gone was the smiling, placid woman she'd been dodging all night. Her eyes had gone steely gray, her whole demeanor transformed. Here was a warrior poised for battle. *Wow.* She was a mesmerizing sight.

Shaking her head to force away the distracting vision, Logan focused on the scene in the trauma room. The resident hadn't exaggerated; it was bad. The patient looked as if he had been dragged under the bus. She did a quick survey of his most apparent injuries: compound fractures of both tib/fibs, deep abrasions of the chest and abdomen, as well as a possible humerus fracture.

One of the nurses reeled off the patient's stats, even as they worked to finish removing what was left of his clothes, draw blood, and attach him to various monitors.

Logan pulled down her face shield and moved to one side of the gurney. Parker took the other.

The pulse-ox monitor began to shrill.

"Logan, get him intubated."

She moved to the head of the gurney and grabbed a 7.5mm endotracheal tube. Once she had the tube in place, she attached the Ambu bag. Giving the bag several squeezes, she listened on each side to confirm the tube's position. A radiograph would have to wait.

Without being asked, she positioned herself opposite Parker and worked on stabilizing the injuries on her side of the patient. Even in the heat of the moment, Logan was aware of how well they worked together, without getting in each other's way. It was as if they had done so a hundred times before.

The trauma bay door swung open, and a petite redhead blew into the room.

"Glad you could finally join us, Dr. Connolly," Parker said.

What? Why was she ragging on the woman? From what she had seen of Parker tonight, it seemed out of character. It had been less than ten minutes since she had called for the doctor. She shot a look at Parker and caught her grinning behind her face shield. She was joking; it was a common ER coping strategy.

"Had to finish up my checkers game," Dr. Connolly shot back. Her expression turned serious. "What have you got?"

Parker quickly summarized the patient's injuries.

Logan stepped back as the woman, who, was apparently a trauma surgeon, took her place at the patient's side. She felt a strange pang at losing that momentary connection she'd shared with Parker as they worked over the patient. *What's the matter with you?* Angry with herself, she stripped off her bloody gloves and gown, then tossed them in the biohazard bin. All that mattered was work. And there were always more patients to take care of. Yet she couldn't resist one last look over her shoulder at Parker as she headed out of the room.

CHAPTER 4

LOGAN PARKED IN THE SPACE next to her motor home. As she got out of her vehicle, she caught sight of the front privacy curtain that normally covered the inside of the RV's windshield. It had been knocked askew and partially pulled down.

Drake stared out at her from the passenger side window of the cab. When he saw her, he began to whine.

She looked into the side window of the driver's compartment. *What the heck...?* The two captain's chairs were turned to face the cabin of the motor home. Somehow, Drake had managed to wedge himself into the small space between the backs of the chairs and the dash. In all their time on the road, he'd never pulled a stunt like this before. The only way she could see to easily get him out was to open the passenger door.

Logan unlocked the door and swung it open. "What the hell do you think—?" Her words cut off when the stench hit her. She stepped up onto the running board and peered past Drake into the motor home.

He whined and ducked his head.

Ugh! Her aggravation with him instantly vanished. From the look of the mess, he'd had a major accident— probably more than one. He tended to get diarrhea when he got upset. "Oh, buddy. It's okay. I'm not mad at you. It wasn't your fault. Come on out of there."

She opened the main door of the coach just long enough to grab his leash; then they headed for the pet area.

When they returned, Logan tethered Drake to the picnic table at their site. She opened the door and stood on the top step to survey the damage inside. His bed was a mess, as was the front of the couch and several cabinets. *Talk about a shit storm—literally.* An irrational urge to toss a match inside and close the door struck. It was so overwhelming, she didn't know where to start.

"Excuse me."

She turned, surprised that Drake hadn't warned her of someone's approach.

A petite, older woman, who she recognized as the park manager, stood several feet from Drake. They had met briefly when Logan checked in earlier in the week, but she didn't remember her name. Logan never got to know anyone at the many RV parks where they had stayed. She was happy to remain anonymous like all the other transient people passing through.

"I need to speak with you," the woman said, her stern expression making it clear it wasn't a social visit.

Now what? Logan needed to get this mess cleaned up and get some sleep, not deal with more aggravation. She left the motor home door open in hope that it would air out and walked over to the woman. "Is there a problem?"

"Yes. I got several complains about your dog barking last night and this morning."

"I'm sorry. It won't happen again." *I hope.*

"I came by earlier this morning and you weren't here." Frowning, the woman looked her up and down. "One of the other residents said that you were gone all night. You really shouldn't leave him unattended in your coach for such a long time."

This was getting worse by the minute. She'd never had a problem leaving Drake in the motor home while she worked. "I wasn't here because I work nights. Drake normally does fine and is very quiet." Logan moved close to Drake and stroked his big head. "I'm sure he won't cause any more problems."

"Well, I wanted to make you aware of the situation." The woman crossed her arms over her chest. "If I get any more complaints, I'll have to ask you to leave the park."

Damn it. This was the closest park to LA Metro, and it was a twenty-two-mile drive from here to the hospital. She hated the thought of having to find a new park even farther away or face having to board Drake overnight every time she worked. He loved day care but hated staying in a kennel at night.

"I'm sure it was a one-time thing." Logan ran her hand down Drake's back. "Something he ate must have disagreed with him and he had a bad accident. That's why he was barking last night. And to top it off, I got caught in traffic this morning coming back from work and was late getting here."

The woman glanced at the motor home, then back at Logan. "Where do you work?"

Logan stiffened. She never told anyone anything about her life. *Damn it.* Taking a deep breath, she forced herself to make an exception. It might be the only thing that kept her and Drake from getting evicted. "I'm temporarily covering the night shift in the ER at LA Metro for a doctor who is ill."

"You're a doctor?"

Logan made sure her irritation at the surprised tone didn't show. "Yes." When the woman continued to look at her expectantly, she forced herself to continue. "I provide coverage for physicians who need time off or when a hospital has a staff shortage." She could see the woman reassessing her opinion of her.

For the first time since the woman had arrived, she smiled. "My grandson Danny wants to be a doctor." She joined her next to Drake and held out her hand. "I'm Bernice, by the way, in case you don't remember. You're Ashlee—right?"

Logan flinched at the name. Ashlee had ceased to exist two years ago on a cold, snowy night in Boston. "I go by Logan."

Bernice's brow furrowed. "Okay. Logan." She patted Drake. "So this big guy was sick?" Without waiting for an answer, she walked over to the motor home and looked in. "Oh. My!" She came back over and hugged Drake. "You poor thing. Do you have any Pepto-Bismol? I know when my husband and I had dogs, it always took care of their upset stomachs."

"I've got some medication for him." That was a lie, but Logan didn't want to be beholden to anyone. She'd get him something after she took care of the mess.

"Will you be continuing to work nights?" Bernice asked.

"Yes."

"For how long?"

What is this—twenty questions? Logan barely resisted scowling. Damn, this woman was nosy. But she was also the manager of the park, and it wouldn't do to alienate her. Logan had paid for two weeks when she checked in. "Six weeks altogether."

Bernice looked back and forth between her and Drake, then seemed to come to a decision. "If you'd like, I could let Drake out for a bathroom break at night before I go to bed, then again in the morning. I'm up early. That way he wouldn't have to hold it so long."

Drake pressed against her side before she could say no. When she looked down at him, guilt tugged at her. He looked pretty forlorn. And he wasn't a young dog any more. Was it really fair to him to turn down help because she didn't want to be obliged to anyone? *You don't deserve help.* She refused to give in to the dark thoughts. This wasn't about her; she had to do right by Drake.

Logan pushed down all the conflicting emotions and made herself meet Bernice's gaze. "That's very nice of you. If you're sure, Drake and I would really appreciate it."

Bernice smiled. "I'd be happy to." She stroked Drake's neck. "Are you sure you don't want that Pepto-Bismol?"

Drake looked pretty miserable, so maybe his stomach was still bothering him. She'd come this far. "Ah... Yeah. I guess that might be a good idea after all. Thank you."

"Hang in there, big guy." Bernice gave Drake a pat. "I'll be right back."

Logan pulled a blanket from the back of her SUV and spread it on the ground for him. No sense in him having to stand while she was cleaning up, and she didn't want him lying on the cement; it really took a toll on his elbows.

Pushing up her sleeves, she trudged over to the motor home. This was not going to be pleasant. *Talk about the understatement of the year.*

CHAPTER 5

DALE PUSHED OPEN THE DOOR to the staff lounge and was surprised to see Logan sitting on the couch along the back wall with a cup of coffee in her hand. The woman rarely took a break, much less hung out in the staff lounge. Logan was something of a mystery. She was always unfailingly polite and one of the hardest-working physicians Dale had ever worked with, but—other than her first name, Ashlee—she didn't know any more about her than when she'd started work three weeks ago. And she had only found that out by reading it off her ID badge. While Dale respected Logan's privacy, she couldn't help being curious about her. Something she'd seen in Logan's eyes when she thought no one was watching struck a chord with Dale. It was the all-too-familiar haunted look lurking just beneath the surface of so many veterans' gazes. Could Logan be a vet?

Not wanting to miss a chance to spend a few minutes with the enigmatic Logan, outside of working on a case, Dale passed on the cup of coffee she had come in for and went straight to the couch where Logan sat.

"Mind if I sit down?"

"Sure. All yours." Logan popped up from the couch.

Dale shook her head and smiled, keeping her disappointment hidden. *It was worth a try.* She waved Logan back down. "Never mind. Don't let me disturb you." She paused for a moment, hoping Logan would invite her to sit after all.

She didn't.

Not at all surprised, Dale offered a departing nod and headed for the coffee mess in the corner.

The lounge door swung open, and Donna, one of the nurses, stuck her head in. "New arrival. Three-year-old with GI distress. Martinez and Lane are busy with other patients."

Dale set down the coffee pot. "Okay. I'll—"

"I've got it." Logan was out the door before Dale could protest.

She poured herself a cup of coffee and moved over to the couch Logan had abandoned. Knowing many veterans suffered in silence, she needed to break through Logan's overly polite reserve. She was determined to let her know that there were others who understood what she was going through and that she didn't have to suffer alone.

Dale had just taken the last sip of her coffee when the door to the lounge again swung open.

With a scowl, Logan marched into the room, muttering under her breath. A large, multi-colored stain marred the front of her lab coat. When she spotted Dale on the couch, she flung her hands in the air. "What kind of parent feeds their kid with an upset stomach Froot Loops?"

This was the first emotional response of any kind that Dale had seen from Logan. She struggled not to laugh but couldn't tame a grin. "Wouldn't have been my first choice."

Logan stomped over to her locker, popped the lock, and pulled the door open. She tugged off the soiled lab coat.

Dale's gaze swept Logan's back. It was the first time she'd seen her without the coat. The tucked-in knit shirt and belted cotton slacks she wore did nothing to disguise her lush curves. As her gaze dropped lower to Logan's well-rounded backside, she bit her lip. *Nice ass.* When Logan turned, she quickly glanced away.

Logan stared at her for a moment as if she had felt the appraisal.

Dale blushed. She pretended to take a sip from her empty coffee cup to hide her embarrassment at almost getting caught ogling Logan's ass. "Um...if you need it, I have an extra lab coat you could borrow."

"Thanks. I've got one." She turned around and rummaged in the locker. After donning the new lab coat, she emptied the pockets of the soiled jacket, then attached her ID badge to the collar of the clean one. As she turned back around, she grimaced. "Hopefully, his stomach is empty now. This is my last clean one. The campground only has two washers, and it's hard to get an open one most days."

Campground?

Logan's eyes went wide as if she just realized what she had let slip. "I better get back to him." She fled the room.

A myriad of questions whirled through Dale's mind. First and foremost was, why would Logan be living at a campground? The sound of sirens pulled her from her thoughts. The mystery that was Logan would have to wait.

Dale rubbed her aching knee and tried to keep from limping as she headed back to the nurses' station. An influx of teenagers involved in a gang altercation had kept her, Logan, and both residents hopping for the last several hours. She jerked her hand away from her leg when she spotted Logan standing by the counter watching her.

Their gazes met for a moment; then Logan turned and walked away.

When Dale reached the nurses' station, she glanced up at the intake board and let out a big sigh. "Not sorry to see all of them go." The gang members had been uniformly rude, crude, and exceedingly uncooperative.

"Yeah, all the gangbangers are gone." Paul scowled. "But you should see the mess their homies left all over the waiting room. I called housekeeping."

"Good. Thanks for staying on top of things. What have we got waiting?"

Paul glanced at the computer screen. "Five-year-old with lower leg pain after jumping off his bed."

"Okay, I've got it." After the gangbangers, a child would be a welcome change of pace.

Dale raked her hand through her hair. *Damn it!* What was supposed to be a straightforward lower leg injury had turned into something much more serious. The severity of the little boy's injury didn't match with the story the parents were telling. No way had he ended up with a spiral tibial fracture by jumping off a bed. Upon closer examination, the boy also had a number of bruises in various stages of healing. An old healed fibular fracture and old rib fractures, which the parents denied any knowledge of, were present on the skeletal survey.

Farther down the hall, the door to one of the treatment rooms flew open and banged against the wall with a resounding thud.

Mr. Granger, the young boy's father, stormed out of the treatment room. He spun around and gripped the open door. "Get out of here. Right now."

Connie, one of the county social workers, scurried out of the treatment room.

"And stay away from my son," he yelled.

Dale sprinted toward the confrontation. The battering she'd taken earlier in the day was making itself felt with each jarring step. Sliding to a stop next to Connie, she bit back a grimace of pain. "What's going on here?"

Mr. Granger scowled at her. "Keep that," he stabbed his finger at Connie, "woman away from my son." His face took on the shade of a cooked lobster as he turned a furious glare on Connie. "How dare you question my wife and me like that? We would never hurt Nathan."

If Dale was going to have any chance of calming the parents, she needed to get Connie out of the line of fire. She put a gentle hand on her arm. "Connie, why don't you go into the lounge? I'll take it from here."

Connie nodded and walked away without a word.

Dale stepped closer to the door, but was blocked from entering the small treatment room by Mr. Granger. Mrs. Granger was huddled next to the head of the gurney with her arms wrapped around Nathan.

"How could she even suggest we're abusing our son?" Mr. Granger huffed.

"No one said anything about abuse." At least she hoped Connie hadn't. She was new on the job, and Dale didn't know her. "As I told you, Nathan needs to be admitted," she said, making her voice as soothing as possible. Although from the look on Mr. Granger's face, nothing she said would make any difference. "His injury is serious." While Dale knew the boy's injuries didn't require hospitalization, she hoped the parents would not. She was following standard procedure in suspected child abuse cases by admitting Nathan until the family situation could be evaluated. The ER was not the place to evaluate or manage these cases.

"You're not doing anything with my son. I'm taking him out of here. I know how you people work! I've seen the news reports." Mr. Granger stomped back into the treatment room.

"Need some help?" Logan asked.

Dale started; she hadn't heard her walk up. She hesitated to accept the offer. Did Logan think she was incapable of handling the confrontation? Giving herself a mental shake, she thrust down the insecurity. *She doesn't know about you.* None of Dale's coworkers did; she had gone out of her way to make sure of that. She glanced at Logan. If there was one thing the military had taught her, it was that it was always a good idea to have someone watch your back.

"Just stand by for now." If at all possible, Dale wanted to avoid calling in security. In these cases, their arrival often caused the situation to escalate. She glanced into the room, where Mr. Granger had taken up a protective stance next to his wife. She lowered her voice and leaned close to Logan. "But if need be, call security." Dale pointed toward the house phone on the opposite wall. "I'm not letting them leave with the boy."

"Got it," Logan said. "I'll get security if things go south."

After taking a deep breath, Dale stepped just inside the doorway of the treatment room.

Mr. Granger puffed out his chest and moved closer to his wife. He crossed his arms over his chest and glared at Dale as if daring her to come closer.

She held out her hands in a placating gesture. "I'm sure we can all agree that the most important thing here is to get Nathan the care he needs." She shifted position so she could meet Mrs. Granger's gaze over her husband's shoulder.

Mrs. Granger, with tears in her eyes, nodded. She placed her hand on her husband's shoulder. "She's right, Harold."

He shrugged her hand away. "Fine, you treated him." He motioned toward the protective splint on Nathan's lower leg. "Now we're leaving. We'll take him to see his pediatrician tomorrow. He'll take over his care and see that he gets whatever he needs."

While not having much hope that Mr. Granger would be reasonable at this point, Dale tried again. "His injures need to be observed overnight. Sometimes in children, there are complications with a break as severe as Nathan's. He needs to be admitted."

"No! I know what you're trying to do." Mr. Granger turned his back on Dale. "We're leaving."

Logan quickly stepped into the room and stood close to Dale so that their shoulders brushed, effectively blocking the only exit. "Security is on the way."

Dale threw her a grateful look. If they could keep them in the room, it would help contain the situation.

Mr. Granger swept his son from the gurney. As he spun around with Nathan in his arms, the little boy's injured leg banged against the upright rail of the gurney.

Nathan cried out and began to sob. "Daddy, it hurts. It hurts." He buried his face in his father's shirt.

The color drained from Mr. Granger's face. "Oh God." He clutched his son to his chest. Mrs. Granger clung to his arm, tears streaking down her face. "Harold. Please."

The sound of pounding feet announced the arrival of security. "What's the problem here?" the black-clad guard demanded.

Mr. Granger tightened his arms around Nathan and took a step back.

Her eyes wide with fear, Mrs. Granger looked back and forth between Dale and the security guard. She sent Dale a pleading gaze. "Please, don't let him take our son."

"Okay, everyone, calm down." Dale turned and faced the guard. "I've got this under control. Please wait at the nurses' station."

He eyed the Grangers. "You sure?"

"Positive." As soon as the guard walked away, Dale approached Mr. Granger. "Please, let Dr. Logan recheck Nathan's injury." She motioned for Logan.

All his anger gone, he met her gaze. "I swear to you, I would never intentionally hurt my son. Let us take him home."

While Dale knew some abusers were consummate liars, the anguish in his eyes seemed all too real. But at this point, she had no choice; by law she was required to inform child protective services and admit the boy. If she couldn't convince the parents to agree to the admission, then her only other option was to get the police involved.

"Excuse me," Logan spoke up. She focused on Mr. Granger. "I know that you don't know me, but I can assure you, if Dr. Parker says Nathan needs to be admitted, then he really needs to be admitted. She's one of our best doctors."

His wife clutched his arm. "Please listen to her."

Mr. Granger's gaze bounced back and forth between Dale and Logan. "Okay." He nodded, kissed his son's forehead, and then slowly relinquished him to Logan.

"Mrs. Granger, why don't you accompany Dr. Logan? I'll go with your husband to see the clerk and take care of the admission paperwork." Dale mentally breathed a sigh of relief when Logan left the room with Mrs. Granger in tow. She smiled to herself at the thought of what a good team they made.

Dale pushed open the door of the lounge. Logan was once again sitting on the couch with a coffee cup in her hand. Smiling to herself, she headed right for the couch and sat down on the opposite end from Logan without asking her this time.

For a moment, it looked as if Logan was going to leave, but then she sighed and sank back into the cushions.

"Thanks for the help with the Grangers," Dale said. "You did a good job."

"Didn't do anything but stand there."

Dale shook her head. "That's not true. You're the one who spoke up and told them, 'Dr. Parker is one of our best doctors.' That was just the reassurance they needed."

Logan shrugged. "It's the truth."

"Thank you." Dale beamed. For some reason, the praise meant a lot coming from Logan. "I've been impressed with your work as well."

Flushing, Logan looked away. She wrapped both hands around her coffee mug. "Any more problems with Mr. Granger once you got to pediatrics?"

"No." She sighed. "While I'm sure he knows the real reason for the admission, he seemed pretty resigned to it." A yawn caught Dale unaware. She dropped her head back against the couch.

"Well, I better get back out there." Logan started to rise, then frowned. She leaned closer to Dale. Reaching up, she touched her own jawline. "You've got a big bruise here."

Shit. Dale ducked her head to hide the bruise.

Logan's frown deepened. "And on your arm."

She quickly tugged down the sleeve of her T-shirt. "It's nothing."

The lounge door swung open. Molly, one of the first-year residents, leaned into the room. "I've got a dislocated shoulder I can't get back in. Marco is tied up with another patient. I need some help."

Perfect timing. "I'll give you a hand." Dale pushed off the couch and made a quick retreat.

Logan went in search of Dr. Parker. *You need to do this.* She jammed her hands into the pockets of her lab coat. Despite her determination to keep her distance from any coworker, she felt strangely drawn to Parker. And no matter how many times she told herself it was none of her business, after seeing Parker limping earlier, then spotting the bruises on her face and arm, she couldn't let it go. And there was the fact that Parker always wore a long-sleeved T-shirt under her clothes, no matter what she was wearing. Long sleeves were a classic tactic to hide repeated bruises. While it was possible the cause of those injures was something innocent, Logan wouldn't ignore them. She had done that once before, and she wasn't going to make that mistake again.

She pushed open the door to the lounge and let her gaze sweep the room. Parker was the only one inside. With determined steps, she approached the couch. "Mind if I sit down?"

Parker's eyebrows arched. "Sure."

Logan sat down. She fiddled with the edges of her jacket, straightened her ID badge, and then clasped her hands together in her lap.

"Everything okay?"

She jumped at the sound of Parker's voice. It had been so long since she had allowed herself to be concerned about anyone, it was harder than she expected. "Umm... Actually, I wanted to make sure that you were okay."

Brow furrowed, Parker tilted her head. "Why wouldn't I be?"

Logan cleared her throat. "Earlier I happened to notice you limping."

Parker stiffened, a sudden tension emanating from her.

"Then I saw the big bruises on your jaw and arm earlier. You got called away before I could make sure you were really...okay."

Parker rubbed the bruise on her face as if she could make it disappear. "I'm fine. I was playing basketball before work, and the game got a little rough." Her gaze veered away from Logan's. "You know how it goes."

While the explanation was perfectly reasonable, Logan couldn't help feeling that she was leaving something out. Stifling the urge to question her further, she rose from the couch. "Yeah. Okay..." She struggled with what else to say and at that point only wanted to escape. A touch on her sleeve made her start.

"Thank you for your concern."

The warmth in Parker's eyes brought a flush to Logan's face. "You're welcome." She spun on her heel and bolted from the room.

Logan peered into the lounge. Parker was sitting on the couch with her face buried in her hands. *Damn!* So much for hoping she had already left. The strength of her earlier reaction to Parker's brief touch and the warmth in her eyes had spooked her. She'd managed to avoid Parker for the rest of the night. There was no becoming interested in a coworker—ever. Concern for Parker nagged at her, but she forcefully pushed it aside. *Ignore her. Get your stuff and get out of here.*

She pushed the door open, then flinched when it squeaked. Keeping her gaze firmly on her feet, she walked over to the locker and opened it. She pulled her backpack out and slung it over her shoulder, grabbed the plastic bag with her soiled lab coat, quietly shut the locker, then turned, ready to make her escape. Despite her best intentions, her gaze was drawn to Parker, who chose that moment to lift her head.

"Well, I screwed that one up." Blowing out a breath, Parker rubbed her hands over her face. "I shouldn't have missed it."

Don't get involved. Walk away. The command was useless. Logan's feet were already taking her toward Parker. She stopped next to the couch and looked down into Parker's stress-lined face. "Missed what?"

Parker motioned to the empty spot on the couch.

Logan hesitated, then shucked her backpack off and sat as far away from Parker as the couch permitted.

"Remember the Grangers' boy last night?"

"Yeah. The abuse case."

"That's just it." Parker grimaced. "It wasn't abuse. Something just bugged me about the case, but I couldn't put my finger on it. When things quieted down, I went to peds and ran into Doug Pulley." At Logan's puzzled look, she added, "He's a staff pediatrician. Anyway, I discussed the case with him. We went to see the boy, and he examined him." Her shoulders slumped. "I missed the fact that the sclera of Nathan's eyes were tinted blue and that he had a very triangular face. Add to that the bruises, the old fractures we found, and the severity of the injury with the history the parents gave and..." She looked questioningly at Logan.

Logan quickly ran through the differential diagnosis, thinking over several different possibilities. "Osteogenesis imperfecta."

Parker sighed. "You got it. Doug ordered the genetic testing, but he's confident that's what we're dealing with. And I missed it." Parker raked her fingers through her hair. "Because of my screwup, social services got involved, and the parents were made to feel like criminals who were abusing their son."

Not sure when she moved, Logan found herself right next to Parker on the couch. "I only got it because you laid it all out for me. Remember, I examined the boy too. And I didn't notice his eyes either." Usually reluctant to touch, Logan nevertheless laid her hand on Parker's arm. "You did what you had to do." She held Parker's gaze, wanting her to be sure of her sincerity. "I would've done the same."

"Thank you." Parker laid her hand over Logan's where it rested on her arm. "It means a lot that you would say that."

As it had earlier, the warmth in Parker's eyes made Logan's heart pound. *You have to get away from this woman.* She pulled her hand out from under Parker's and bolted from the couch. "Well, I've got to get going." She fled the room without a backward glance.

As she made her way to her car, her thoughts whirled. Over the last two years, she'd had no trouble keeping her distance from coworkers. She didn't know what was different about Parker. But she had no intention of hanging around to find out. Although she had only been here three weeks, it was time to contact Barron's and find a new job.

CHAPTER 6

LOGAN SCANNED THE AREA AS she approached the nurses' station and breathed out a sigh when there was no sign of Dr. Parker. She had worked hard to avoid her whenever possible over the past week. On the occasions they did work together, she kept their interactions strictly professional and quickly made herself scarce afterwards.

"Hi, Dr. Logan," the desk clerk, greeted.

She nodded in acknowledgement, then headed to the staff lounge to put away her backpack. Peeking through the doorway to make sure the coast was clear, she caught sight of a tall black man that she had not met before sitting at the round table in the center of the room.

He looked up and smiled as the door swung fully open. "You must be Logan. Dale had good things to say about you."

An unexpected surge of pride filled Logan. She pushed the unwelcome feeling away.

He rose from his chair. "I'm Harris Franklin. I'm covering for Dale tonight."

Why isn't Parker working? Logan immediately squelched her concern. *Be glad she's not here.* It made things that much easier for Logan. She had other things to worry about tonight—most notably Drake. But also the fact that Barron's Staffing had not found her another locums position. Which in itself was surprising; there were always physicians who needed someone to cover for them while they were on vacation or medical leave.

Forcing her attention back to Franklin, she walked to the table and shook his hand. "Nice to meet you. Well, I better get to it." She pulled off her backpack and turned toward her locker before he could offer any further conversation.

A glance at her watch made Logan frown. She had wanted to check on Drake earlier but had gotten held up waiting for the CT results on a suspected ruptured appendix. She stopped at the counter of the nurses' station and checked the intake board. *Good. Nice and quiet.* Most nights, she preferred being busy, but not tonight. Logan motioned the desk clerk over. "I'm taking my dinner break. I'll be back in half an hour. Call me if anything big comes in."

"Sure thing, Dr. Logan."

The cafeteria was closed at this time of night, but coworkers had gotten used to her leaving the department for her meal break. With an acknowledging wave in the clerk's direction, Logan headed for the main waiting room of the ER. She checked to make sure no one who knew her was around, then slipped out the main doors and headed for the parking lot.

Logan made her way across the ER parking lot to the far corner where she had parked her motor home. While living in the small recreational vehicle had its disadvantages, being able to park it in a regular parking lot was a plus in this situation. She eased open the door and stepped inside.

When no welcoming woof greeted her, she flipped a switch, illuminating the interior of the coach. Drake was stretched out on what was usually the dinette table that folded down and converted into an extra bed when needed. Two steps brought her to his side. Fear spiked when he didn't immediately open his eyes. She sat down next to him.

Drake's eyes blinked open, and he yawned. As he pushed his head into her belly, his tail thumped against the bedding.

Logan's breath whooshed out. "Hey, buddy. How're you doing?" She stroked his big head.

The day care where he stayed while she was sleeping had expressed concern that he had been very lethargic and had refused food and water. Normally, Drake spent the night in the motor home alone, and Bernice let him out for a bathroom break before she went to bed and then again in the morning. But tonight, she hadn't felt comfortable leaving Drake even with Bernice to check on him. If something were to happen to Drake, Logan didn't know what she would do. A huge lump formed in her throat at the very thought, and she blinked back tears. He was her last link to Emily, and she had grown to love the big dog. She shoved away the painful memories.

"Come on, bud. Time for a quick pee, then I'll make you something to eat." *Hopefully before I get called back.* She glanced at her phone, willing it not to ring. She grabbed his leash and snapped it onto his collar. He gave her a pleading look, but she didn't relent. "Drake. Come."

The big dog slowly rose and hopped to the floor. She led him outside to a small area of grass she had scoped out earlier. He quickly took care of business, and they went back into the motor home.

Knowing how much Drake loved warm milk, Logan took a chance and fired up the motor home's generator just long enough to run the microwave for thirty seconds to heat the milk. She poured the warm milk over his dry kibble. If anything would tempt him, this would be it. "You want some cereal?"

Drake's tail thumped against the cabinet, and he began to drool. He knew exactly what those words meant.

Relief washed over Logan as she watched Drake chow down. She wiped his dripping muzzle when he finished.

Without any encouragement from her, he jumped back into the dinette bed and flopped down with a satisfied sigh.

She wagged her finger at him. "Don't get too comfortable up there. As soon as we get back to the campground and set up again with the slider out, your bed is going back on the floor."

Drake woo-wooed as if contradicting her.

"I mean it. As soon as we get back."

He huffed, then lay on his side and put his paw over his eyes.

Logan laughed. She headed back to work with a much lighter heart.

CHAPTER 7

LOGAN ARRIVED IN THE ER just in time to see Dr. Parker come flying backward through the double doors of a trauma room. She slammed against the wall opposite the doors and then crumpled to the floor into an awkward sitting position. Logan tossed her backpack toward the counter of the nurses' station and raced down the hall toward Parker.

She knelt down next to her. "Are you all right?" Parker appeared dazed and didn't respond immediately. Logan's head jerked up when the door to the trauma room banged open and Martinez, a second-year resident, came barreling out.

"Is she okay?" he asked. "We were trying to get the guy restrained, and he kicked her right in the chest."

Logan ignored his question. She was more concerned with accessing Parker. "Get a gurney."

The resident quickly pushed a gurney over.

"I'll stabilize her head and neck. You get her legs." At Dr. Martinez's nod, Logan reached for Parker, intent on easing her down to the floor so she could more easily stabilize her spine. "We're going to put you on a gurney."

Parker weakly shook her head and winced. "No. No gurney. I'm fine." She tried to push herself off the floor and failed. Her left leg was twisted under her at an unnatural angle.

"You are not fine. Let us get you on a gurney."

Adamantly shaking her head, Parker staggered to her feet before Logan could stop her.

Logan grabbed her arm as Parker's knee threatened to fold. *Damn stubborn woman.*

Parker shook her off. "I'm fine. Just got the wind knocked out of me. I can walk." She took several limping steps away from Logan.

"Hey! Where do you think you're going?"

Turning back to face Logan, Parker motioned toward the trauma room, where the patient's loud protests had died out. "Sounds like they've got everything under control. I'm going to take a short break."

"Like hell you are." Logan shocked herself with her vehemence. *It's just concern for an injured coworker.* Even as she thought it, she knew it wasn't the complete truth. Despite her determination otherwise, she was coming to care about Parker. "You're coming with me to an exam room."

Narrowing her eyes, Parker glared at Logan.

Martinez's gaze bounced back and forth between the two women.

She marched over to Parker. "You need to be checked over." Logan moved closer so only Parker could hear her. "Lean on me and let me help you, or I'll strap your ass down on the gurney." She wasn't sure where her anger over Parker's recalcitrance was coming from, but Logan couldn't seem to stifle it. Motioning Martinez back toward the trauma room, she said in a normal voice, "Make sure everything's okay in there."

Martinez hesitated for a moment, then skirted around them and into the trauma room.

Steely gray eyes met Logan's in a brief contest of wills.

Parker blew out a breath. "All right. But it's not necessary."

"Let me be the judge of that." Logan wrapped her arm around Parker's waist. "Put your arm over my shoulders." For a moment, it looked as if Parker would refuse. "Parker," she said, making sure her tone conveyed her seriousness.

"I've told you before. Several times. It's Dale."

What? She chose to make an issue of this now of all times? Logan clamped her jaw shut. This was already more personal than she was comfortable with. Parker looked as if she wasn't going to budge an inch unless Logan complied. "Fine. Dale, will you please put your arm around my damn shoulders so we can get you into an exam room?"

Parker snorted and did as requested.

With her arm around Parker's waist and Parker's arm across her shoulders, Logan couldn't help feeling Parker's heavily muscled back. She had previously noticed the thick muscles of Parker's forearms. But pressed this close to her, she realized Parker was all solid muscle, without an ounce of excess fat. It made Logan uncomfortably aware of her own excess weight. She pushed the feeling away. *This isn't about you.*

They had only taken a few steps when Logan realized Parker was barely allowing her to support any of her weight. Glancing sideways, she could see her trying to hide a grimace. "The whole point here is to actually let me help."

A look of chagrin chased across Parker's face. She gave up and allowed Logan to help her into a small treatment room.

Dale levered herself up onto the gurney, keeping as much weight as she could off her left leg. She barely resisted the urge to rub her knee. The sooner she got this over with, the sooner Logan would leave and Dale could take care of herself.

Logan approached the end of the gurney where Dale sat. "How are you doing?"

"I'm fine. Just got the wind knocked out of me." Dale shifted and unsuccessfully tried to hide a wince.

"Then you won't mind if I check and make sure. An incident report will need to be filed. And I, for one, don't want to explain to Dr. McKenna why you weren't examined."

Dale knew there was no getting around the paperwork. But she couldn't get past the feeling that there was more to it than Logan simply covering her ass. While Logan had made a point over the past week of avoiding her unless it was related to a case, there was no denying the look of real concern in her eyes. It felt personal. *Or maybe it's just your own wishful thinking.* She continued to be intrigued by the enigma that was Logan.

That didn't change the fact that she did not want Logan to examine her. Dale's insides clenched at the thought of the other things Logan would discover that had nothing to do with the bruise developing from the kick she had taken. *Embrace the suck.* The frequent advice of her friend Casey echoed in her head. "All right. Let's get this over with."

"Did you lose consciousness when you hit the wall?"

"No." When Logan pulled a penlight from her pocket, Dale rolled her eyes.

"Humor me." Logan flashed the light into her eyes several times before putting the penlight away.

Dale hated to be poked and prodded, having suffered through more than her fair share of that over the last three years. Struggling to stay still, she reluctantly followed Logan's instructions during the rest of the brief neurological exam.

Logan smiled. "Everything checks out."

"Told you. I'm not hurt." Dale tried to get off the gurney.

Logan stopped her by placing her hands on top of Dale's shoulders. When she squeezed, Dale winced. Arching an eyebrow, she said, "So, you're not hurt, huh?"

"Okay, I'm a little sore right below the clavicle on the left. That's where the kick caught me. I'm sure it's just a bruise."

"Let me grab you a gown so I can take a look." Logan stepped over to the cabinet along the wall and bent to retrieve a patient gown.

Panic held Dale momentarily frozen. "No." The word burst from her, much louder than she intended. There was no way she was baring her chest and shoulder to Logan.

"What?" Logan straightened and glanced at Dale.

"I'm a doctor too. I'd know if I was hurt worse than a bruise." Dale lifted both arms and rotated her shoulders. "See, good range of motion."

Logan stalked back over to the gurney, patient gown in hand. "Great. Then you won't mind me doing a quick exam. After all, I can't very well sign off on the incident report if I didn't actually examine you—now can I?

Damn the woman! Dale scrambled for another excuse.

"Listen." Logan sighed. "If you'd feel more comfortable with someone else doing the exam, just say so."

Dale resigned herself to the inevitable. If a coworker had to find out, it would be better if it was Logan. She at least would be gone in a few weeks. But somehow, that wasn't as consoling a thought as she hoped. In fact, it caused an inexplicable sadness. Dale blew out a breath. "No. You can do it." She removed her lab coat and scrub shirt, leaving her clad in a long-sleeved T-shirt.

Logan handed her the gown, then turned her back.

Dale stared at the gown for a moment before tossing it on the gurney. "I don't need the gown. I've got on a sports bra." No gown would hide what Logan was about to see. Grinding her teeth, she pulled the T-shirt over her head before she lost her courage.

When she turned around, Logan's eyes went wide as her gaze swept Dale's torso.

Dale knew exactly what Logan was seeing. The skin on the left side of her chest and upper arm were pitted with purple shrapnel scars the size of fat raindrops. While time and healing had lessened their severity, nothing would lessen the impact on someone seeing them for the first time. She had grown tolerant of the ugliness. She sighed to herself. It wasn't as if she'd had any choice in the matter. They were never going away.

Logan swallowed heavily. Her eyes brimmed with tears when she met Dale's gaze.

The pity on Logan's face burned in the pit of Dale's stomach. "Could we just get this over with?" she asked, her voice gruff. She glanced down at the damaged side of her chest. A bruise was forming just below her clavicle and extended down to the swell of her breast. "He caught me here." She pointed to the bruise, keeping her eyes firmly on her own chest.

Logan reached toward her with trembling fingers.

She can't even bear to touch you. When Logan's warm fingertips made contact with her damaged skin, she flinched.

"Does that hurt?"

Dale shook her head roughly.

Logan gently palpated Dale's clavicle and upper chest. Her hand slid over Dale's shoulder and carefully checked for any scapular injury.

Forcing herself not to pull away, Dale gripped the edge of the gurney's mattress. She never once looked at Logan.

Continuing her exam, Logan manipulated her shoulder through the full range of motion. "You're right. Looks like just a bruise. You'll probably be sore, but nothing serious. Just to be sure, it would be a good idea to get a chest film."

Dale grabbed her T-shirt from the gurney and pulled it over her head. "I'll think about it," she said, her voice muffled by her shirt.

"Now just let me take a look at your knee—"

"Don't!"

It was too late. Logan had already tugged up her left pant leg.

Logan froze with one hand on Dale's knee, the other hand supporting her calf, and stared at what she had uncovered.

Fuck! Dale's stomach roiled. The one thing she had tried so hard to hide from her coworkers had been discovered. While the cosmetic cover camouflaging the metal parts of her prosthetic leg might fool someone from a distance, there was no way Logan could mistake what she was holding. She shoved Logan's hands away and jerked her pant leg back down. When she finally forced herself to look up, a neutral, professional expression was firmly in place on Logan's face.

Relief washed over her. She couldn't have stood to see the horror some people reacted with when they found out about her amputation. *Please don't ask any questions.*

"I need to examine your knee." Logan's voice was calm but firm.

"No." On this she wouldn't budge. "The prosthetic twisted and got caught under me when I fell. My knee was not injured."

Logan stared at her as if assessing her honesty.

Dale met her gaze head-on.

Logan started to speak, then stopped. Blowing out a breath, she scowled. "I'm trusting you on this." She pointed a finger at her. "Don't make me regret it."

"You won't."

"Do you feel up to finishing your shift?"

I knew it. "Of course." Dale struggled to keep the anger out of her voice. Now that Logan was aware of her deficiencies, everything would change and she would start treating her differently, as if she wasn't capable of doing her job without help.

Another fear nagged at Dale. Knowing Logan already thought less of her, Dale nevertheless swallowed her pride. It took a moment for her to force the words out. "I...ah..." She cleared her throat. "Please don't say anything to anyone else about..." She waved vaguely in the direction of her leg.

Logan stiffened. "Of course not."

When Logan didn't turn to leave, she crossed her arms over her chest. "Could you just give me a couple of minutes—alone?"

Her brow furrowed, Logan glanced down at Dale's leg. "Are you sure you're really okay?"

"Yes. I just want to get myself together." She pulled her discarded scrub shirt and lab coat into her lap. She sure as hell wasn't going to tell Logan that what she needed to do was doff her prosthesis and reseat her damn stump.

"Oh. Okay." Logan walked to the door, then turned back. "I'll see you out there."

Dale waved a dismissive hand, urging her on her way. As soon as the door closed behind Logan, she slumped back against the gurney. *Fuck.*

Struggling to keep her professional persona in place, Logan, avoiding eye contact with anyone, hurried to the first unoccupied room she could find. When the door closed behind her, she slumped against it. *Dear God. Dale.* There was no keeping an emotional barrier by refusing to use her first name now. The sight of Dale with her head bowed as if in shame after baring the horrific scars littering her body was forever seared on Logan's retinas. If that wasn't terrible enough, her horror had been compounded when she discovered Dale's missing limb. It had taken every ounce of her self-control and years of experience to hide her reaction. Tears filled Logan's eyes at the thought of what Dale must have suffered. She roughly brushed them away.

That Dale had come back from such an injury and was able to work in a demanding environment like an emergency room, with no one the wiser, was nothing short of miraculous. While she already respected Dale as an excellent clinician, now she was in awe of her on a personal level. *What an incredible woman.*

Logan staggered when the door she was leaning against was pulled open from the other side. "Sorry. Didn't know the room was in use," Mr. Martian, one of the nurses, said. He had a patient on a gurney in tow.

"It's not. Go ahead." Logan stepped out into the hall and held the door open so he could push the gurney inside. After closing the door behind him, Logan used her sleeve to blot away any possible evidence of her emotions. Giving herself a mental shake, she headed toward the nurses' station.

As Logan passed by the room where she had left Dale, she forced herself to keep walking. *Leave her be.* She had survived much worse than a kick in the chest and probably wouldn't appreciate being hovered over.

The sound of sirens hastened her steps. Logan arrived back at the nurses' station just as the doors of the ambulance entrance to the ER banged open. She sprinted for the incoming patient.

"What have you got?" Logan grabbed the side rail of the stretcher and started to pull.

"OD. Found by his roommate." An EMT rattled off the patient's stats. "We brought as many of the pills and bottles as we could find." He inclined his head toward a plastic bag resting on the patient's legs.

"Get a gastric lavage kit set up," Logan said to Ms. Holland, the nurse who had also arrived to attend the patient.

"On it." She sprinted down the hall and into a treatment room.

Dale loped up to the gurney. She stared at Logan from the other side of the patient, an unmistakable challenge in her gaze.

What the heck? What had she done to garner such a response from Dale?

Returning her attention to the patient, Logan eyed the semiconscious, morbidly obese young man on the stretcher. She was glad Dale was there to help; it was going to take all of them to transfer him to an ER bed.

Logan waited while the EMTs positioned the gurney next to the ER bed with its wheels locked, ready for transfer. The two EMTs took up positions next to their gurney. *Oh yeah. Pick the easy side.* She met the eyes of one of the EMTs, and he grinned. Not that she could really blame him; they had already lifted the patient once. She moved to stand next to Dale. Holland stood by the patient's head. Logan figured the petite nurse wouldn't be able to lift much more than the man's head anyway. As she leaned across the empty ER bed to grab the sheet under the patient, she caught Dale's frown aimed at her. She wondered what was going on with Dale but didn't have the time to worry about it. Wrapping both hands around the rolled bed sheet, she waited for everyone to get ready.

"On three." She braced herself against the side of the bed. "One. Two. Three."

Although she considered herself fairly strong, Logan strained to lift the man high enough to slide him off the EMTs' gurney and onto the ER bed.

Dale had no such issue and took some of Logan's share of the weight.

Once the man was situated, she turned to Dale and smiled. "Thanks."

"No problem." Dale offered a hesitant smile.

The EMTs out of the way, Logan moved to the side of the bed and began her assessment. "Dale, check out the bottles and pills. See what we're dealing with, please."

Dale grabbed the bag and turned away to spread out the pills and bottles on the counter along the wall.

When Logan leaned over the man with her penlight and checked his pupillary responses, he thrashed his head. His belly heaved, and he gagged.

Logan grabbed his shoulder and belt, intent on rolling him onto his side so he wouldn't aspirate if he vomited. Even pulling as hard as she could, she barely got him a few inches off the gurney. Panting with effort, she called out, "Dale. Help. He's retching."

Dale spun around. She dropped the safety rail on her side and wedged her hands under his body, grabbing large handfuls of his clothing. "Now. Pull."

Logan pulled with all her might as Dale pushed from behind. Holland jumped in to help from Logan's side of the bed. When they got him lifted up enough, Dale bent, shoved her shoulder under his back, and straightened. The tendons in Dale's neck stood out in sharp relief with the effort.

Just when Logan thought they were going to have to call for more help, they got him onto his side. The moment that was accomplished, he vomited over the side of the bed.

Every instinct screamed at her to let go of him, but she couldn't. If he rolled even partway onto his back, he would aspirate.

"Patty. Go grab as many blankets as you can," Dale said.

The nurse sprinted from the room.

Dale, her weight pressed against the man's back, managed a grin in Logan's direction. "Hope you got that last lab coat clean."

Logan mock-scowled.

Patty Holland rushed back with an armload of blankets. She locked the safety rail in place on Dale's side of the patient, working around her as she rolled up the blankets and jammed them behind the man. Thankfully, in this case, his size worked to their advantage, as he already almost filled the bed from side to side. After what seemed like forever, she said, "Got it. You guys can let go."

Flexing her hands to get the circulation going again, Logan stepped back and quickly assessed the patient's status. The emesis had stopped, and Holland was suctioning his mouth. Satisfied that things were under control at least for the moment, she looked down at herself and grimaced. The side of her lab coat was heavily splattered with vomit. She peeled off the soiled coat and grabbed a protective gown. *Better late than never.*

She glanced over at Dale, whose face was streaked with sweat. She bit her tongue to keep from asking if she was okay. She knew without being told that Dale would not appreciate the question in front of a coworker. *She's managed just fine up to now without your concern.* "Thank you. I couldn't have done it without you."

"Any time." Unlike Dale's earlier smile, this one reached her eyes, making the gray irises appear streaked with blue.

Beautiful. The unexpected thought caught Logan off guard. *Keep your mind on work,* she sternly ordered herself.

Holland spread some chux pads on the floor to cover the mess.

As a team, Logan and Dale set to work stabilizing the patient.

CHAPTER 8

DALE SAT IN A CHAIR along the back wall, staring unseeingly at her prosthetic leg. The noise of the busy physical therapy department faded around her as her thoughts went back to last night. Logan asking her without hesitation for help with a strenuous task, so soon after discovering her amputation, had been unexpected, to say the least. It had been like a soothing balm over the jangled emotions that having to bare her scars to Logan had caused.

"Earth to Dale."

Dale jumped at the sound of a voice so close. She jerked her head sideways and mock-glared at the offender. "Don't sneak up on me like that."

"Oh right. I'm as quiet as a ghost around here with this damn thing." Casey grabbed the wheels of her chair and spun one in each direction. The rubber squeaked on the linoleum floor. "I can't wait till I can wear my legs again."

"What did Walters say?"

Casey's shoulders slumped. "He wants me to try a different antibiotic. Infection just doesn't want to let go."

"Damn." Dale worked to keep her expression from showing how worried she really was. Casey had been fighting this infection for four weeks. She leaned out of her chair and put her hand on Casey's thigh. "You'll get through this. It's just a temporary setback." She squeezed Casey's leg. "Embrace the suck."

Casey smiled and put her hand on top of Dale's. "Isn't that my line?"

"You taught me well."

"Enough about me. What's up with you? I called your name three times. You were really out in space."

"Sorry. So what's the plan for today? Are we helping here, or are there any new admissions?" While Casey worked here full-time, Dale donated a few hours every day to work with other veterans at the Veterans Administration hospital. Although most of the staff and patients knew she was a physician, she was not here in that capacity. Her volunteer work was the reason she chose to permanently work the night shift at LA Metro. That left her free during the day.

"The plan is for you to tell me what's bothering you."

"Just some stuff at work." She pushed herself off the chair and stood. "Carlo got his temp this morning and has been struggling. I think I'll go see if I can give him some pointers."

Casey grabbed the back of Dale's shorts as she stepped past her wheelchair. "Not so fast."

Dale glared at her over her shoulder, but Casey didn't let go. She blew out a breath.

"What happened at work?" Casey let go of her shorts but looked ready to grab her again if she tried to walk away.

You knew she wouldn't let it go. They had been through too much together for Casey to ever ignore anything that might upset her. And she felt the same about her. Casey had been there for her every step of the way as she struggled to regain her life. She plopped down in the chair next to Casey's wheelchair and quickly conveyed the events at work last night.

Her gaze swept Dale from head to toe. "How bad were you really hurt?"

"I told you. The bruise was it. Why doesn't anyone believe me? Geez."

"Forget who you're talking to?" Casey arched an eyebrow. "Do you remember that time, right after you got your first temp that—"

Dale shoved Casey's shoulder, knocking her sideways in the wheelchair. "Never mind."

Casey laughed. Then her expression turned serious. "So this doctor, she examined you after and..."

She nodded. "Yeah. Insisted on examining my shoulder. And then pulled up my damn pant leg to look at my knee before I could stop her."

"Ah, crap." Casey bumped shoulders with Dale.

"No kidding."

Things were different here than in the civilian world. She looked at her exposed prosthesis. In the VA hospital, she didn't feel the need to wear the cosmetic cover to camouflage the metal parts of the leg. Here, her missing limb was a badge of honor, not a source of pity. Her gaze went to Casey, and she tried to see her as a stranger would. People tended to look past Casey's pretty face, surrounded by thick, wavy blond hair, and her bright hazel eyes and focus on her bilateral above-the-knee amputations. Unlike Dale, Casey refused to hide her missing limbs despite having to strive to be seen in the outside world as something more than her injuries. Hell, Casey even went out in public wearing her stubbies while Dale still struggled with wearing shorts anywhere but in the VA hospital, even with the cosmetic cover over her prosthesis. She wondered how Logan would react to Casey. Dale shook away the strange thought. She couldn't imagine inviting Logan, or anyone else for that matter, to share this part of her life.

"Let me guess, she went all pity-party on you and acted like you were suddenly helpless?" Casey asked.

"No, actually she didn't." Dale was surprised to find herself bristling. After all, she had assumed the same thing about Logan. She filled Casey in on the events that took place after Logan discovered her amputation.

"So she was cool with it. That's good."

"Yeah. It's just..." Dale shrugged. Although Logan had seemed more than okay with it, her knowing still bothered Dale. Then there was the whole incident report thing.

"What?" Casey poked her in the ribs when she didn't respond.

"When I checked my e-mail, there was a copy of the incident report from last night. Logan didn't include anything about my scars or amputation in the report."

"I thought you said you asked her not to say anything." Casey's brow furrowed. "So that's good—right? She respected your privacy."

Dale huffed. "Yeah. I mean, sure. I was worried that she would treat me differently, like I needed help with anything physical involving patients, and start my coworkers wondering about me. Thankfully, she didn't. But I never expected her to leave the information off the official report." She let the familiar sights and sounds of the busy PT department wash over her as she debated whether to tell Casey what was really bothering her. She glanced back at Casey to find her watching her, waiting her out. *Just spit it out.* "Now I feel like I owe her. And it makes me...uncomfortable."

Casey gave Dale's thigh a brief squeeze. "You don't owe her anything. It was her choice to do that. I know I'm just a beat-up helo jockey and not a doctor, but it seems to me that the other stuff she saw had nothing to do with your injury from the patient kicking you, so it's not a big deal leaving it out."

"That's true but..." Pushing up out of the chair, Dale stood. "It doesn't feel that way."

"Then thank her. Maybe bring her a little something as a thank-you."

Dale paced in front of Casey's wheelchair. She didn't know Logan well enough to come up with something she would like—much less accept.

"Stop." Casey leaned out of her chair and grabbed Dale's shorts again. "You're making me dizzy." She tugged at Dale's waistband. "Sit down."

Scowling, Dale looked down at her. "Keep your hands off my shorts, woman."

"You wish some woman had her hands in your shorts."

"Casey!"

Casey threw back her head and laughed at the blush that heated Dale's face.

Dale looked around to see if anyone was paying any attention to their conversation. While the much hated don't-ask-don't-tell policy was no longer in effect, Dale had still not gotten used to not having to hide her sexuality. "You are so bad." She flopped into the chair next to Casey.

"And you love it."

Dale grinned. "Okay, back to Logan. So get her something. Like what?"

"Keep it simple. You're always complaining about the lousy coffee at the hospital. How about a good cup of coffee and maybe a muffin or donut?"

"That could work." But Dale knew the real question was, would Logan accept it? She was all too aware of Logan's almost pathological avoidance of sharing anything personal or becoming friendly with anyone on the staff. *She started calling you Dale,* she reminded herself. It was worth a try; whether she accepted was up to Logan.

"Are you two going to spend all morning jackin' your jaws, or is someone going to give me a hand?" a voice boomed from across the room.

Dale looked over to where Carlo stood between the parallel bars. Even from here, she could see he wasn't standing squarely with the same amount of weight on each leg. It was a common issue with new amputees.

Laughing, Casey flipped him off. "What? Two not enough for you? Hey, Barry, Carlo needs a hand."

Barry picked up his arm that was lying next to him on the table and waved the prosthesis in Carlo's direction.

Carlo returned the one-fingered-salute to Casey.

Casey released the brakes on her chair, pushed away from the wall, then glanced back at Dale. "You good?"

"Yeah." Dale stood next to Casey's chair and squeezed her shoulder. "Thanks."

"Anytime." She motioned with her head toward Carlo. "Come on, you can show him how it's done."

CHAPTER 9

As Dale neared the door to the staff lounge, she glanced at the cardboard tray she was carrying. It held a cup of coffee and a small paper bag with a Del Java logo. Casey's idea had been a good one. Pushing the door open, she let her gaze sweep the room. As expected, Logan was early for her shift and sitting on the couch at the back of the room. Dale knew she needed to be quick before the nursing staff came in for the change-of-shift meeting. She marched up to the couch.

Logan looked up and offered a smile, which quickly disappeared, and her usual placid expression took its place. She nodded in greeting before returning to her journal article.

Holding out the tray, Dale said, "Here. I brought this for you. Just a little thank-you."

When Logan looked up, a frown marred her face. "What for?"

"For yesterday."

Logan eyed the tray as if it held the poison apple that had tempted Snow White. "I can't accept that."

"It's just a cup of coffee and a pumpkin scone. Not a diamond necklace."

Shaking her head, Logan leaned back against the couch as if trying to distance herself from the offering. "I was just doing my job."

Dale blew out a breath. "Logan, I read the incident report."

"I noted everything that was noteworthy." Logan shrugged, apparently trying for casual, but it looked forced.

"Regardless, I appreciate it." She offered the tray to Logan again.

Logan's hands tightened around her journal, and she shook her head.

The door to the lounge swung open, and a group of nurses flooded in.

Dale placed the tray next to Logan's leg. She leaned down so as not to be overheard. "I brought it for you. Toss it if you don't want it." Although she had known it was a possibility, she couldn't help being disappointed by Logan's adamant refusal of her simple gift. After one last glance at Logan, she turned and strode from the room.

Logan glanced over the counter of the nurses' station. Holland was sitting near one of the computer workstations, eating the pumpkin scone. She had left the scone and the coffee in the staff lounge on the table that held the coffee fixings. As it had earlier when she had seen one of the other nurses drinking the coffee Dale had brought, guilt niggled at Logan. The disappointment on Dale's face when she wouldn't accept her gift refused to be banished from her mind. *Forget it. You're making more of it than it was.*

The hair on the back of her neck prickled. Looking up, she spotted Dale standing at the other end of the counter.

Dale met her eyes and smiled.

See. She's not upset.

"Dr. Parker," Holland called.

"What's up?" Dale slipped behind the counter and approached the nurse.

"Labs are back on curtain four." She held up the scone. "Want a piece? It's really good. I can't believe someone just left it with the community coffee stuff."

Dale's head turned in her direction. A look of hurt flashed across her expressive face before she could hide it. Turning away, she presented her back to Logan.

The touch of guilt Logan had felt became a full-fledged sting. *Damn it.* She hadn't meant to hurt her; she just didn't want to feel obligated. *Let it go.* She shook her head, determined to walk away, but she couldn't do it. She waited until Dale finished checking her patient's labs before approaching her. "Could I talk to you for a minute?"

Dale glanced up, her face a neutral mask. "Sure. About which patient?"

Moving closer, Logan lowered her voice. "It's about earlier...the scone and coffee. I—"

"No biggie." Dale's polite demeanor never wavered. "Now, if you'll excuse me, I need to check on my patient." She walked away.

Logan should have been relieved, but as hard as it was to admit—she wasn't. What she couldn't figure out was why. She had spent the last two years keeping people at bay with the same overly polite façade that Dale had just used on her. She had never let it bother her that it might hurt someone's feelings. Why was it different with Dale? Logan wasn't sure she even wanted to know the answer to that question. But the facts were, she had hurt Dale and she felt bad about it. *So what are you going to do about it?* That was the million-dollar question.

CHAPTER 10

LOGAN SHIVERED AND LEANED BACK against the wall of the building as the wind picked up, sending leaves swirling through the staff parking lot. The storm that had been brewing when she went to bed this morning had finally arrived. So far, it had been just a misting rain, but the clouds overhead looked ready to release a deluge at any moment. "So much for it never rains in Southern California," she muttered. She hunched her shoulders inside her jacket and switched hands holding the coffee tray, shoving the now-frozen hand into her pocket.

She shouldn't be doing this. That was what she kept telling herself, but here she was doing it anyway. The slamming of a car door made her head jerk up.

Dale, already dressed in scrubs and sporting a leather bomber jacket, strode toward her.

She marveled again at her confident stride. There wasn't any discernible sign of her missing limb. Logan couldn't help being awed all over again by what Dale had overcome. She had tried hard to convince herself that was why she was making this overture to Dale; she didn't want to have any part in hurting her—even in a small way. But so far she hadn't been very successful at persuading herself of that. *You'll be gone by end of the week.* Somehow, that reminder didn't make her feel any better either and caused a sinking sensation in the pit of her stomach. She'd received notification that the physician she was covering for would be returning to work.

"Good evening." Dale greeted her with the same emotionless demeanor she had maintained during yesterday's shift after Logan had refused her offering.

"Hi."

Dale pulled open the door of the staff entrance and started to step inside.

"Wait!" Logan grimaced. It had come out more forcefully than she intended.

Pausing with her foot propping open the door, Dale met her gaze.

Logan shuffled her feet. *Just give it to her.* She thrust the tray with the two insulated travel mugs and a Del Java bag toward Dale. "Here."

Dale's eyebrows arched, but she made no move to take the tray.

Heat worked its way up Logan's chest. "I'm...I'm sorry about yesterday. That was really nice of you." She ducked her head. "And I was a jerk."

"Thank you," Dale said but still didn't accept the tray from Logan's outstretched hand.

Logan forced her head up and met Dale's gaze. Irises that had been stormy gray just a moment ago were streaked with blue. She struggled not to lose herself in the warmth emanating from Dale's eyes. A gust of ice-cold rain against her back broke the moment.

"Man, that's cold," Dale said. "We usually don't get these types of storms until late December, not early November. Let's get inside."

Logan hurried in and pulled the door closed behind them.

They faced off in the hallway.

"Please take it," Logan said, again offering the coffee to Dale.

Dale glanced at the tray, then at Logan. "Two cups? I know I drink a lot of coffee but—"

Blushing, Logan tugged one of the stainless-steel cups with a Del Java logo out of the holder. "This one's mine. It smelled so good. And you know how lousy the coffee is here."

After finally accepting the offering, Dale opened the bag and peered inside. "Two scones? One would have been enough." She grinned. "Or did the scones smell good too?"

Logan squirmed, and the blush that had just started to fade blossomed once again on her face. "Um..."

"Come on. Let's find an empty conference room and enjoy the coffee and scones before our shift starts."

Relieved to be let off the hook so easily, Logan willingly followed her. The thought that she was making a mistake nagged at her as she walked with Dale. *You'll be gone by the end of the week,* she firmly reminded herself again.

Seated at the head of the conference room table, Dale peered at Logan through half-lidded eyes. Her anger at Logan was gone now, doused by Logan's apology. Maybe she had overreacted to the whole thing. While she had been disappointed last night when Logan refused the coffee and scone, it wasn't completely unexpected. What had bothered her was Logan leaving the stuff on the community table for anyone to take as if it truly meant nothing to her that Dale had put herself out there. It would have bugged her less if Logan had just tossed the offering when she wasn't around.

Logan's gaze remained firmly locked on her half-eaten scone. She had not said anything since a brief 'thank you' when Dale passed her the blueberry scone.

What did you expect? That she was suddenly going to open up and start telling you her life story? Dale snorted to herself at the thought. Despite how it had come about, she couldn't help hoping that this would be the opening she had been looking for to get to know Logan better. Her gaze swept the room as she struggled for something to say. Up to this point, she had resisted asking Logan any personal questions, but now that Logan knew something so private about her, that restraint was waning. *Just do it.*

After pushing her chair back from the head of the table, Dale turned it sideways so she was facing Logan. "I was just wondering...Have you been doing locums work long? Do you like it?"

Logan choked on the mouthful of coffee she had just taken. She waved Dale off as she started to rise from her chair. When her coughing fit subsided, she said, "I'm fine." She picked at her scone. "The work's okay."

Undeterred, Dale tried again. "How long have you worked for Barron's?"

Keeping her gaze on the table, Logan finally said, "A while."

Logan's prevarication made Dale more determined. "Like what? Six months? A year?"

When Logan looked up, her eyes were as guarded as Dale had ever seen them.

Dale stretched out her legs so that her feet were near Logan's chair. She rubbed her left knee, then slid her hands down and slightly adjusted her prosthesis, making no attempt to hide the action from Logan.

Blowing out a breath, Logan met her gaze. It was clear she had gotten the message. "Two years."

"That's a long time." It wasn't uncommon for physicians to work locums at several hospitals, sometimes in multiple states, before making a decision on where they wanted to work permanently. But it was usually over a few months—not years.

Logan shrugged.

"Has it all been in California?"

"No."

"Did you like any other states better?"

She shrugged again.

This was worse than pulling nails. It was more like trying to pry spikes from a railroad tie. And it was starting to feel like an interrogation. While Dale had a lot more questions, this obviously wasn't working as a way to get answers. Still, she couldn't stop herself from asking one last question. She had wondered about this since Logan first arrived at LA Metro. More than once, she had seen the haunted look in Logan's eyes that could come from seeing horrors no one should be exposed to. "Did you serve in the sandbox before you got out and started working locums?"

"Huh? Sandbox?" Logan's brow furrowed.

"You're not a veteran?" Dale couldn't keep the surprise out of her voice.

"No." Logan looked down at herself and snorted self-depreciatively. "I'm no vet." She met Dale's gaze, her earlier guardedness gone. "But I have nothing but the greatest respect for people who are."

Dale ducked her head. "Thanks." Ill at ease with the direction the conversation had taken, she pushed her chair back and stood.

Logan rose and gathered up the remains of their snack. "Well, I guess it's time to get out there."

"Thanks again for the coffee and scone."

"Sure. No problem." Her gaze darted away from Dale.

Sighing, Dale wondered if she would ever get past the barriers Logan had erected to keep people at bay. While she was clearly a caring physician, in the month that they had worked together, Dale had not seen her connect on a personal level with any of the staff. The mystery that was Logan continued to intrigue her. Not to mention her growing attraction to her. *Don't go there,* she fiercely ordered herself. The only thing she had to offer any woman, no matter how appealing, was friendship.

As Dale and Logan rounded the corner, laughter erupted from a group of nurses and residents clustered around the nurses' station. The sound of one voice in particular caught Dale's attention. *Gretchen.* What was she doing here? Gretchen's name wasn't on the weekly schedule, nor had Dale received any notification that she would be returning to work. While she was happy for Gretchen that she was well enough to return, the thought of Logan leaving filled her with a tangible sense of regret.

"Hey, Dale." Gretchen broke away from the group, walked over, and pulled her into a hug.

She glanced over Gretchen's shoulder to find Logan sporting a frown. Maybe Logan didn't want to leave after all. Then she remembered that she would have no idea who Gretchen was. She stepped back from Gretchen and smiled. "How are you feeling?"

"Now that the morning sickness from hell finally stopped, I'm great. Looking forward to getting back to work."

Dale glanced at Logan to see her reaction to the news.

Logan met her gaze, her face a neutral mask. She didn't seem the least bit surprised or distressed.

She already knew. The thought stung. She now saw Logan's peace offering in a whole different light. It wasn't just an apology. Or an opening to a friendship. It was a good-bye. *What did you expect?* she repeated to herself. Shoving down her hurt feelings, she forced a smile and made the introductions.

"Gretchen, this is Logan. She's been helping us out while you were off."

"Great to meet you." Gretchen stepped over and clasped Logan's hand between both of hers. "Thanks for helping out."

While Dale doubted most people would have picked up on it, she caught Logan's unease with Gretchen's overly-tactile personality. She was tempted to rescue her but restrained herself. *She doesn't need or want your help.*

Logan tugged her hand out of Gretchen's grasp and stepped back. "Sure. That's what I was hired for. Now, if you'll excuse me, I better get to it."

Dale sighed as she watched Logan walk away. She glanced at Gretchen, surprised to see her staring with a furrow between her brows. "Not very friendly, is she?"

Bristling at the implied criticism, she struggled not to scowl. "She's a top-notch ER doctor and has been a great help around here."

Gretchen's brow scrunched up and she took a half step back. "I'm glad she worked out." She laid her hand on Dale's arm. "I didn't mean anything by it."

Forcing a lightness to her voice that she didn't actually feel, Dale said, "I know. I didn't see you listed on the schedule this week. Are you starting back tonight?"

"I thought I'd work half shifts for the rest of this week—just to be sure. Then I'll take over from Logan next week."

So Logan would be gone by the end of the week. Dale had known from the start that Logan was here only temporarily. *And you barely know the woman.* That didn't seem to matter— she still felt the impending loss of her departure.

"Why don't we grab a cup of coffee?"

She started, pulled from her thoughts by Gretchen. It took a moment to register what she had said. She glanced at the intake board and shook her head. "I should get busy too. We'll catch up later."

As Dale walked away, one thought dogged her mind. *Logan's leaving.*

CHAPTER 11

DALE STRAIGHT-ARMED THE DOOR AND marched out of the trauma room.

When the door clanged shut behind Dale, Logan glanced at the crestfallen resident, Amber Lane. She felt bad for her, but it wasn't her place to say anything that might undermine Dale's authority. "You need me for anything else?"

Lane looked down at the sedated patient, then back at Logan. "No. I've got it under control," she said with an edge of determination in her voice.

"Then I'll leave you to it." With a departing nod, she left.

As she made her way toward the nurses' station, she couldn't get her mind off Dale. *What's with her tonight?* Dale had been somber all night and on this last case, uncharacteristically critical of the resident. That was very unlike the woman she had come to know over the last five weeks. Several steps past the staff lounge, she stopped and backtracked. She pushed open the door and looked inside. No Dale, so she continued on to the nurses' station.

Checking the intake board, she saw that Dale wasn't with a patient. "What's waiting?" she asked the night clerk.

"Nothing. Dr. Corbett just took the last patient."

Logan glanced at her watch and sighed. There were only three hours left of her final shift at LA Metro. Despite her best intentions, worry about Dale nagged at her as she walked away. *Where is she?*

Lost in thought, she looked up to find herself standing outside the conference room door where they had shared coffee and a scone earlier in the week. The door was ajar, allowing a narrow sliver of light to spill out into the hallway. She peeked inside and saw Dale sitting with her elbows on the table, head propped on her hands, staring off into space. *Don't get involved. Let it go.* The thoughts had barely formed before she found herself pushing open the door to the conference room. *Damn it.*

"You okay? What's going on?"

Dale jumped at the sound of Logan's voice. She had not heard her come in. "I'm fine. It's nothing."

"Doesn't seem that way." Logan blew out a breath. "Look, I know it's probably not my place to say anything..." She ducked her head.

"But?"

"You were pretty hard on Lane."

What? Now she was worried about a resident's feelings? While Logan had been willing to teach the residents, she had kept a strict, professional barrier between them. "Amber's a senior resident. She shouldn't need help putting in a chest tube. Not to mention the fact that she should be able to do a blood gas in her sleep by now."

"I had a hard time getting the tube placed because of the woman's size." Logan put her hand on the back of the chair next to Dale. "I understand what you're saying about the blood gas, but the radial artery was in an atypical location and overlaid by a vein. It's hardly a common occurrence to need to use the dorsal side of the hand and go after the pollicis artery to get a blood gas."

Dale raked her hands through her hair. Logan was right. She had let own problems interfere with her job. "I'll talk to her."

"It's not just that." Logan pulled out the chair and sat down uninvited.

Arching an eyebrow, Dale glanced at her. *Now what?*

Logan flushed. For a moment, it looked as if she was reconsidering. Then her lips pressed into a thin line, and she leaned back in the chair. "I know you said you're fine, but you don't seem fine to me."

What do you care? You're leaving in a couple of hours. As much as Dale wanted to say it out loud, she bit her lip to keep the words inside. *Don't take your troubles out on her—like you did with Amber.* She met Logan's gaze and was warmed by the concern she saw there. She tried unsuccessfully to rekindle her anger with the knowledge that Logan was showing her feelings only because she was leaving and knew it was safe.

Logan reached out and started to touch Dale's arm. She drew back, then shook her head and laid her hand on Dale's forearm. "What's wrong? You've been on edge all night."

Dale looked down at Logan's hand where it rested on her arm. She wanted to pull away, but the warmth seeping from Logan's palm seemed to have welded her arm in place. While she wouldn't speak to her about Casey and the debridement procedure she was facing, Dale couldn't bring herself to totally disregard Logan's honest effort to reach out, no matter how belated. "Just have a lot on my mind. A friend is having some medical problems."

"I'm sorry to hear that. Do you need to leave early? It's quiet. I can handle the rest of the shift." She grimaced slightly. "And Dr. Corbett is here too."

Although troubled, Dale couldn't help smiling at Logan's inability to hide her feelings about Gretchen. It had been clear from Gretchen's first night back that her overly exuberant personality and innocent but frequent invasions of personal space had not endeared her to Logan. She covered Logan's hand where it still rested on her arm. "Thanks, but that's not necessary. Our shift is over in a couple of hours."

"Right." A deep frown marred Logan's face. "Okay, then."

Maybe she doesn't want to leave. That didn't change the fact that Logan was leaving, but the thought still cheered Dale. Becoming aware of her hand still covering Logan's, she withdrew it. When Logan followed suit and removed her hand from Dale's arm, she immediately missed the warmth. She barely resisted the urge to draw Logan's hand back to her arm. *She's leaving,* she reminded herself. Needing some distance, she pushed her chair back. "I guess we should get back to it."

As if on cue, their phones rang simultaneously. Together, they headed back into the fray one last time.

As Logan cleared out her locker, her gaze strayed to the door of the staff lounge—again. Due to the sudden influx of patients, she had not seen Dale, except in passing, in the last hour. She growled under her breath. *Quit waiting for her.* There had been many leave-takings like this over the last two years. Dale was just one of many talented doctors she had worked with. She had never felt the need to say a personal good-bye to any of them. Maybe it was just because she knew how much Dale had suffered and lost. She pushed down her conflicted feelings. *Just get your stuff and go.*

The door to the lounge swung open, making Logan tense in anticipation.

Dr. McKenna stepped into the room.

They had seen each other a few times at shift change, but other than the three days she had worked with Dr. McKenna, Logan had not had any sustained contact with her.

"Oh, good. I'm glad I caught you before you left."

Was she going to ask her to stay? Surprised at how tempted she would be by the offer, Logan immediately quashed the thought. It was definitely time to go.

"I wanted to thank you for the great job you did for us." Dr. McKenna walked over and offered her hand. "Dale has had nothing but glowing praise for your work."

An unexpected flush heated Logan's face. This just proved her point. She was getting too close to the people here—especially Dale. She shook Dr. McKenna's hand, then shoved both her hands into her pants pockets. "Thanks."

"If you ever need a reference, just let me know. I'd be happy to provide one."

"I appreciate that." Logan grabbed her backpack and slung it over her shoulder. "Thanks again." She quickly made her escape.

Walking toward the staff exit, she couldn't stop herself from scanning the halls. There was no sign of Dale. *Stop it. Just leave. What's the matter with you?* Angry with herself, she shoved open the door to the parking lot, taking satisfaction in the loud thump it made against the outside wall.

"Hey, Logan."

The sound of Dale's voice so close-by made her clutch her chest. "You scared me."

"Ditto." Grinning, Dale gestured to the door Logan had sent flying.

Heat crept up Logan's neck. "Sorry."

They stared at each other for several moments, neither seeming to know what to say.

Logan hefted her backpack more securely onto her back. She had wanted the chance to say good-bye to Dale, but now that the time had come, she found herself tongue-tied.

"So...um...where are you going next?" Dale asked.

"I'm not sure. The staff representative I work with at Barron's hasn't found me a new job yet."

"Do you think you'll stay in LA?"

Shrugging, Logan looked down. She had never cared where she worked. *And you shouldn't care now.* "Depends. Barron's only expanded into California this year. They don't have a lot of contract hospitals yet."

"Oh. Well, I guess this is good-bye, then."

Logan glanced up, surprised at the palpable sadness in Dale's voice. Her breath caught as she was captured by stormy gray eyes. She wrenched her gaze away. Mentally stiffening her spine, she forced herself to look at Dale. *Walk away now. This is what you do. No ties.* "It's been good working with you. Good-bye."

Logan marched away. As she reached the edge of the parking lot, her steps faltered. *Don't.* It was useless. As if out of her control, she turned and glanced back at the hospital.

Dale was gone.

So what? She's just like all the other doctors. You never missed any of them. Despite the reminder, an inexplicable regret weighted her steps as she made her way to her SUV.

CHAPTER 12

Ducking her head to combat the blowing sand, Logan trudged toward the RV resort's so-called dog park with Drake. That was about as accurate as advertising the tiny trailer park in the middle of Brawley as a secluded desert oasis. She snorted. *Yeah, right.* The dog park had turned out to be nothing more than a small, barren strip of sand surrounded by a three-foot-tall fence. There wasn't even a bench to sit on. She opened the gate and followed Drake inside. Not daring to take him off leash because of the highway right next to the low fence, she followed him around until he took care of business.

As she stooped down to clean up after him, a gust of wind whipped the smell of rotten eggs into her face. *God, I hate this place.* If the wind wasn't filling the air with sand, the smell from the nearby Salton Sea tainted the air with the odor of decaying fish and sulfur. According to one of the longtime residents of the pitiful RV park, when the Santa Ana winds really kicked up, the smell traveled all the way to Los Angeles, a hundred and fifty miles away.

Drake tugged against his leash, anxious to get out of the blowing sand.

"One more day, buddy, and I promise, we're out of here." She had already declined to extend her employment here. Four weeks had been more than enough. The hospital, while not new by any means, was a decent place to work, but the living conditions in the small desert community left a lot to be desired. The other two trailer parks in town were shoddier than this one. Things were worse for poor Drake. His elbows were still sore from his time in the poor excuse of a day care offered in town. In reality, it wasn't a doggie day care at all but a boarding kennel that allowed Drake to stay during the day. After spending only a few days in a narrow cinderblock kennel, his elbows were abraded and he'd split his tail open. She'd refused to take him back there. Unable to find a better alternative, she unhooked the RV every morning and parked it in the hospital parking lot so that she could check on him during her shift.

Now all she needed was her staff rep at Barron's to find her a new job. But regardless of whether he did or not, they would be leaving tomorrow.

As she walked past the RV park's office, she felt eyes on her. She turned and scowled. Harry Bunch, the manager of the park, was staring out the window at her. The guy gave her the creeps.

A deep growl emanated from Drake.

"Yeah. I hear you." She tugged on his leash, urging him back to her side. It was definitely time to get out of here. Maybe a nice trip to San Diego was in order; she'd never been there. It might be a good place to hang out until the next job offer. A spot on the beach sounded just like the ticket after their stint in the desert.

Her phone rang as they stepped back into the RV. A glance at the caller ID made her smile. It was unlikely the staffing rep she worked with at Barron's would be calling unless he'd found her a job. "Hello, Russell."

"Hi, Dr. Logan. I wanted to call you right away. I found you a new spot."

"Great. Where?" *It better not be in the desert!*

"Mammoth Lakes in Northern California. The hospital is located right in town. The whole area is a year-round tourist destination. Beautiful place up in the mountains. Of course with it being December, skiing and other winter sports are the main attractions."

While Logan wasn't a big fan of the snow, after her time in the desert it sounded pretty good. And if it was a big resort area, chances were good there would be a choice of facilities that could provide adequate care for Drake.

"How long do they want someone?"

"Contract is for three weeks over the Christmas holidays."

Logan grimaced at the mention of Christmas. "Sounds good. I'll—"

Russell cleared his throat. "Before you make up your mind, I wanted to let you know about another much longer offer. It's a little unusual, and I know you said you weren't interested in anything longer than six weeks, but I thought I would mention it."

The six-week limitation was arbitrary. But Logan had found that after much longer, people began to think of her as part of the staff, with the social obligations that went along with that. "I don't know if I'd want to commit to someplace for more than six weeks sight unseen."

"I understand. But you've worked there before. That's not the unusual part. The request from the hospital specifically requested that you fill the position—if you were available."

What? "Where?"

"LA Metro."

Dale. Logan had tried to forget about her. But no matter how hard she tried, the woman continued to slip into her thoughts uninvited. But why would the ER there need someone again so soon? "Did they give a reason for the opening?"

The tapping of a keyboard filtered through the phone line. "Let's see. It says here they recently lost one of their physicians on the night shift because of a medical issue. They estimate six months before they are able to return."

Logan's heart gave a surprising thump of alarm. *Not Dale.* Her mind filled with increasingly distressing scenarios.

"Dr. Logan?"

Angry at herself for the reaction, Logan shoved away the rising emotion. She wasn't sure why she was even considering this. *Dale did just fine before you showed up.* It probably wasn't Dale that was having problems. "So I would have to commit to six months at LA Metro?" she found herself asking despite her reservations.

"Well, that is what they requested, but if you're interested in going back maybe we could work something out? I could tell them you are only available for, say, six weeks. Then you could decide later if you wanted to extend beyond that. Or you can sign on for the whole six months right now."

It was on the tip of Logan's tongue to say no. She never went back to places she had worked at previously. Thoughts of Dale nagged at her. *Say no and go to Mammoth.* She ground her teeth together. The words just wouldn't come. She glanced down at Drake. He was stretched out on his bed, looking worn and tired. The white on his face seemed more prominent than it had just a month ago. And he had never been a big fan of the cold either. *He needs time to recover.* She consoled herself with the thought of how happy Bernice and her grandson would be to see Drake again.

"Six weeks. That's all I'll commit to." As soon as the words left her mouth, an unexpected thrill of anticipation leaped through her veins. *It's just temporary. Just like every other job.*

"Great. How soon can you be there?"

There was certainly nothing holding her here. "Tomorrow night."

"Thanks, Dr. Logan. I'll let the hospital know."

"Thank you, Russell. Bye." She thumbed the disconnect button on her phone. "Well, Drake, how would you like to go see Bernice and Danny?"

The big dog's ears perked, and his tail beat a rapid tattoo against his bed.

With a much lighter spirit than she had felt in weeks, she got ready for her final day at work here.

CHAPTER 13

Dale stifled a yawn and stretched her aching back. She longed to go home and get some sleep, but she had sent Gretchen's husband, Darryl, off to get some breakfast. She had promised to stay with Gretchen while he got something to eat.

The door to the hospital room swung open, and Jess stuck her head in the doorway. She smiled when she spotted Dale and motioned to her.

After a quick check to make sure Gretchen was still sleeping, Dale joined Jess in the hall. She left the door to Gretchen's room partway open so she could still see her.

"How's she doing?" Jess asked. "Donna said she was alert and talking last night."

All the ER staff, doctors and nurses alike, had been checking on Gretchen.

"Her pressure is way down from what it was when she collapsed but still elevated. The visual disturbances have ceased. The proteinuria is still present, but the levels have decreased."

"And the baby?" Jess asked, her voice filled with worry.

Dale felt sick at the thought of Gretchen losing her baby. It had been touch and go over the last few days. "So far, so good." She crossed her fingers in her pocket.

Jess blew out a breath. "This doesn't make any sense. She shouldn't have gotten this bad so fast without any warning. Her blood pressure had to have been rising before this happened. Gretchen's too good a physician to not have known she had pre-eclampsia."

"She knew."

"What? And you didn't say anything?" Jess glared at her.

Dale held up her hands in a placating gesture. "She knew. I didn't until today. I asked Gretchen the same thing. She never said a word, but turns out her husband hasn't worked in almost a year. I don't know what the issue is, and she didn't want to talk about it. She kept working because they needed the money. Anyway, she was keeping things under control when she was working the limited day shifts with the no-trauma restrictions you had her under. But once she came back on nights and had to carry a full workload, things got out of control."

"Why the hell didn't she say something to me?"

"Pride."

Jess jammed her hands into the pockets of her lab coat. "Pride be dammed. I would have made an accommodation for her."

"She wanted to pull her own weight and not have other people take up the slack." While Dale felt bad about what had happened to Gretchen, she would have done the same thing in Gretchen's situation.

"And look where it got her. She could lose the baby." Jess scowled, visibly struggling to gain control of her anger. "Well, she's not going to be working for a while now. I'll get some kind of a fund going for her."

It was a good idea, but Dale wondered if Gretchen would accept. "Count me in." She hesitated to bring up the subject, not wanting to appear callous, but it needed to be addressed. "Um...we're going to need to replace her on the night shift."

"I've already taken care of it. I put through the request for a six-month locums position."

"How soon do they think they can get someone here?"

"I just got the e-mail a little while ago," Jess said. "New doctor will be here tomorrow night."

Relief washed over Dale. After three nights on her own, she was exhausted. While two ER residents at a time also covered the night shift, they were in training and needed supervision. The department required an additional experienced ER physician to cover the patient load. *Someone like Logan.* She mentally berated herself. *Forget her.* But she hadn't; she had thought of her frequently over the last four weeks, wondering where she was and how she was doing.

Gretchen stirred. "Darryl," she called out.

"I better get back in there," Dale said, glad for the distraction.

"I'll go with you. I want to say hello."

Together, they entered Gretchen's room.

CHAPTER 14

LOGAN'S STEPS FALTERED AS SHE crossed the rain-swept parking lot. Now that she was here, she was having second thoughts. Her gaze landed on the bright-red emergency sign mounted above the entrance to the ER. Even through the pouring rain, it shone like a beacon in the night, beckoning to her. That was her reason for being here. Patients needed her.

She pushed through the main doors and headed directly for the patient check-in area. The clerk behind the glass-fronted desk smiled and waved. She nodded in acknowledgement. The door lock buzzed, giving her access to the ER proper.

"Hi, Dr. Logan. Welcome back," Paul said when he spotted her. He picked up a sealed envelope from the counter in front of him and handed it to her.

Logan opened the flap and looked inside. The envelope contained her ID badge and the new security codes for the doors. "Thanks." She headed for the staff lounge to stash her backpack. As she walked, she looked around hoping to catch a glimpse of Dale. The intake board had not listed her name as being with a patient. *The shift hasn't even started yet.* She tried to shrug off her concern. *You're here to work, not worry about a coworker.*

When she went to the locker she had used her last time here, she found it still available. After putting away her jacket and backpack, she noticed the name plate on Dale's locker was missing. Her concern ratcheted up a notch despite her effort to ignore it.

The door to the lounge swung open.

Hope flared. Logan spun around, trying hard to tame her smile.

Dr. Franklin stepped into the room.

The smile fell from her face. Why was he here and not Dale? Was she just not on tonight?

"Hi, Logan. What a nice surprise." He approached and shook her hand. "Welcome back. Glad you were available to give us a hand again."

"Thanks." She hesitated to ask about Dale, but her worry finally got the better of her. "Um...so where is Dr. Parker?"

"She's not here—"

The door banged opened and Martinez rushed in. "I need you right now."

"Excuse me." Franklin sprinted away with the resident.

Logan's stomach sank. Was it Dale she was replacing after all? *It's not your problem.* She knew better than to allow herself to care about anyone. *You don't deserve to care about people.* She slammed the locker closed, then stomped out of the lounge. *Just do your damn job.* That was the only thing she was good at.

Logan leaned against the nurses' station. It was two hours into her shift, and she had not been able to rid her thoughts of Dale. She didn't know what it was about the woman that made her so hard to ignore, even when she wasn't around. She repeatedly told herself it was because of Dale's war injuries, but that excuse didn't hold much water anymore.

Don't get involved. No matter how many times Logan told herself that, it didn't seem to matter. She blew out a breath. Was there anyone she could ask about what had happened to her? Dale was the only person who had ever managed to crack Logan's carefully constructed walls.

All the usual techniques she used to distance herself from people hadn't worked with her.

"Logan?"

Logan jumped and spun around. *Dale!*

"Hey." Dale grinned. "It's great to see you. I was expecting a new doctor, but I had no idea it would be you. Welcome back."

She swept her gaze over Dale from head to toe, unable to tame her smile. Her happiness dimmed at the dark circles under Dale's eyes. She still wondered where Dale had been tonight. "You okay?"

Dale rubbed her face. "Just tired. But I'm great now that you're here." She stepped forward with her arms slightly raised as if she was going to hug her.

Instinctively, Logan stiffened. Avoiding personal contact had become ingrained over the last two years. It helped her to keep her distance from people—literally and figuratively.

Dale's bright smile faltered; her arms dropped, and she stepped back.

Feeling unexpectedly bad, Logan gave Dale's arm a brief squeeze. "It's nice to be back." And as hard as it was to admit, it was true—regardless of her continued reservations.

"Dale, you all set to take over?" Dr. Franklin asked as he approached.

"Yeah. Thanks for filling in. I owe you a couple of hours."

"No problem. I'll remind you in a few weeks when it comes time for my daughter's Christmas pageant."

"It's a deal. At least I'll know you're having a lot more fun than I did tonight."

He laughed. "You've obviously never been to a holiday production featuring four-year-olds."

Dale snorted. "You love every minute of it. Now get out of here. And thanks again."

Logan's teeth clenched as painful memories stirred with this talk of Christmas and families. She despised the approaching holiday and everything associated with it. All it did was remind her of crushing loss and guilt.

When Dr. Franklin walked away, Dale turned to her, humor sparkling in her eyes. Her expression sobered.

Logan cursed herself as she struggled to force a neutral expression. *Maybe I should have stayed in the desert.*

Dale stepped closer and lowered her voice. "What's wrong?"

Logan ruthlessly shoved down the feelings. "Nothing. I need to get back to work." She walked away with a carefully measured stride. Although she could feel Dale's gaze on her, she steadfastly refused to look back.

CHAPTER 15

DALE GRASPED THE STEERING WHEEL and stretched, yawning wide enough to make her TMJs ache. It had been a long shift, and then she had stopped to check on Gretchen before leaving. She backed out of her parking spot. Just before she reached the exit of the lot, she spotted a tow truck driver working in the rain, preparing a small SUV to be towed. *That sucks.* As Dale drove past the truck, she spotted the vehicle's owner and hit the brakes. *Logan.* She pulled into a spot out of the tow truck driver's way, tugged up the hood of her rain jacket, and got out of her Jeep.

"Hey, Logan. What happened?"

Logan scowled. Without a rain jacket or hat, her wet hair was plastered to her scalp. "Damn thing won't start."

"Can I give you a lift?"

The tow truck driver held out a clipboard. "All set, Dr. Logan."

Logan flipped up the plastic protecting the paper and quickly scrawled her name. She turned back toward Dale. "Thanks anyway. I'll ride with him to the dealership. Hopefully, it's something simple, and I can get it back today."

The driver shook his head before Dale could respond. "Actually, the service department at the dealership isn't open on Sunday. All I can do is drop it off. They won't look at it until tomorrow morning. You can come with me, but you'd still need a ride home. I'm not allowed to take you anywhere else."

"Damn it," Logan muttered.

"I'll take you home." While Dale was trying to be helpful, she also realized that this was a chance to spend some time with Logan away from the hospital. She had thought of her often during the last four weeks.

Logan looked back and forth between Dale and the driver. Finally, she turned to him. "Thanks. Go ahead and drop it at the Subaru dealer in Van Nuys we discussed. I'll give them a call tomorrow."

"Sure thing, Dr. Logan." He touched the brim of his baseball cap and walked away.

They watched in silence until he exited the lot with Logan's SUV in tow.

"Come on. My Jeep is right over there."

Logan shook her head. "That's not necessary. I'll call a rental place and have them drop the car off here. I'll need a car until I get mine back."

"It's Sunday. And I don't think they deliver that fast anyway. Last time I used a service like that, they needed a business day's notice. There's no reason to stand around in the rain. I'll take you home. You can deal with it from there."

Shoving her sopping hair off her face, Logan frowned. "You don't have to do that. I can...I can call a cab."

Dale was wet, cold, and more than ready to get out of the rain. The cold always made her left side ache, especially her residual limb, which left her short tempered. Why was Logan being so damn stubborn? The more she thought about it, the more she realized it was most likely Logan's determination to not be obliged to anyone. While Dale could relate, in this case, her patience had worn thin. Logan was being ridiculous. It was just a car ride. "It's a lift home. Period. No obligation. No strings attached." She scowled at Logan. "Now can we get out of the damn rain?"

Logan's flush was visible despite the rain. A look of chagrin chased across her face.

The previously slow, steady rain chose that moment to become a deluge.

They both gasped at the onslaught.

"Come on." When Dale sprinted for her vehicle, Logan followed.

Dale slid into the driver's seat, pushed back her hood, started the Jeep, and turned on the heat, leaving the blower off until the car warmed up.

She glanced over at Logan; she was soaked. The lightweight jacket she wore had been no protection against the rain. Her head was bowed, allowing her hair to drip water into her face and down her neck. Dale turned and reached between the seats. Their shoulders brushed as she rummaged in the storage bin behind Logan's seat. As she straightened up, she found herself eye to eye with Logan. The golden starbursts surrounding her topaz-brown irises captivated Dale, derailing her thought process, and she froze.

Logan jerked her head sideways and sneezed, breaking the moment.

What the heck was that? Dale straightened and handed Logan a towel. "Gesundheit."

"Thanks."

Now that the car had warmed up, Dale cranked the blower of the heater to full, sending a blast of warm air into Logan's face. She smiled when Logan let out a big sigh. "So where in Van Nuys are we heading?"

Logan watched her intently as she gave the location.

So she was still staying at a campground. Careful to keep any indication of curiosity off her face, Dale nodded and pulled out of the lot. The rain continued unabated as she merged onto Interstate 10.

"Where are you going?" Logan asked.

"Huh? Where you told me."

"But this isn't the way. It's off the 101."

"Let me guess. GPS sent you that way?"

"Yeah. Is there a better one?"

That was the downfall of relying on GPS units; the route they used might be the shortest, but it wasn't always the greatest choice—especially in Los Angeles.

"On the best of days, the 101 is a hassle with traffic. On a day like today, it will be a nightmare. We're going to take the 10 to the 405. This way is a little longer distance-wise but will be faster."

True to her word, despite the bad weather, the traffic flowed smoothly. The only sounds in the car were the drumming of the rain on the roof and the slap of the windshield wipers. She glanced at Logan several times, but her gaze remained locked out the front windshield. Dale fished for a topic of conversation aside from work.

As she merged onto the 405, a sea of brake lights lit up in front of them. The traffic quickly slowed to a crawl, then came to a complete stop. Vehicles filled the freeway as far as the eye could see.

Dale cursed under her breath. She glanced over at Logan and gave her a sheepish look. "Okay, usually this is a better way to go." She relaxed when Logan chuckled. "Guess it's just not my day. This is the second time in less than twenty-four hours that I've been stuck in traffic. That's why Harris was covering for me."

"You were stuck in traffic for two hours?" Logan asked, sounding a bit alarmed.

Was she worried they would be forced together for that long? "Actually, it was longer than that. I had already been stuck two hours when I called him. I knew I was never going to make it in time for my shift."

"What happened? An accident?"

Dale shook her head. "No. All this rain caused a mudslide on PCH north of Malibu. I couldn't get through. Had to go up to Sherman Oaks, then make my way back. With all the traffic being diverted, it was a nightmare."

"PCH?"

"Pacific Coast Highway."

"Oh, right. I've been on that, going to the beach."

"While we need the rain because of the drought, I'm getting tired of it. The desert is looking good about now."

Logan snorted. "I'll take the rain any day."

"Not a fan of the desert, huh?" Was that were Logan had been for the last four weeks?

Logan shook her head. For a moment, it appeared as if she wasn't going to elaborate; then she blew out a breath. "The desert sucked. Big-time. When I was first offered the job, I thought it would be a great change of pace. And I'd never been to the desert." She raked her hands through her wet hair. "I mean...Southern California, the desert. I'm thinking a Palm Springs kind of place."

"Um...there are a lot of other less developed desert areas in California."

Logan turned in her seat and mock-glared. "I know that—now."

Dale grinned. "So where did you end up?"

"You probably don't know it."

"Try me."

"Ever heard of Brawley?"

Oh, jeez. Hadn't Logan Googled the place before taking the job? Dale struggled not to laugh. She lost the battle and guffawed.

Logan's glare turned ominous. "I needed the job."

Uh, oh. Dale quickly regained her composure. She didn't want Logan to regret having shared where she'd been. "Sorry. It's just that I've been through Brawley and it's..." She struggled for the right words.

The honking of a horn behind her made her realize traffic had started moving again.

Keeping her gaze on the road, she said, "So that's why you decided to come back to LA Metro when the job opened up?" She couldn't help hoping that Logan had wanted to work with her again. *Or that she missed you,* a small part of her whispered. Dale pushed the thought aside.

Logan was silent for several moments.

Dale feared she had offended her after all. *Damn it.* The first chance she got to spend time with Logan away from work, and she had screwed it up.

Logan spoke up before Dale could apologize again. "My contract was up there anyway. The rep from Barron's told me about the opening here and that the hospital had requested me specifically to fill the spot."

What? Jess never mentioned asking for Logan. Dale looked away from the slow-moving traffic for a moment and gazed at Logan. "I'm glad you came back."

The sound of the rain filled the silence between them.

When Logan finally spoke, her words were so quiet that Dale had to strain to hear her. "So am I."

Hope flared in Dale. Maybe they could have a friendship after all.

Logan's gaze was once more locked outside the windshield. But Dale had heard the words and was content to let things progress at Logan's pace.

Neither spoke for several minutes.

"I was sorry to hear about Gretchen. I hope she'll be okay," Logan finally said.

"I checked on her before I left. She's doing a lot better."

The traffic opened up and started to flow. It didn't take them long to reach Logan's exit.

As they left the freeway, Logan crossed her arms over her chest. The closer they got to the campground, the more Dale could sense the tension radiating from her. She reminded herself what a private person Logan was and how big a deal this must be for her to allow someone to see where she lived.

"That's it. Up on the left," Logan said. "You can just drop me at the front entrance."

The rain continued to come down in a steady downpour.

"You just got halfway dry. No sense getting soaked again. Just direct me to your spot." Dale tried to keep her voice as matter of fact as possible, pretending it was no big deal.

Logan's lips compressed into a thin line. "Okay."

Dale followed Logan's direction and ended up in front of a small RV. She knew a little about recreational vehicles from going on family camping trips as a teenager. The van-style, class C motor home wasn't more than twenty-four feet long. Although it had a slider, for one person, it would be a very small but adequate living space. But she could not imagine living in the cramped space full-time. Why did Logan live in a motor home?

Surprisingly, Logan didn't bolt from the Jeep as soon as Dale parked.

"Thanks for the ride. I appreciate you going out of your way."

"I was glad to help. What time should I pick you up tonight?"

Logan shook her head adamantly. "I'll get a rental."

A yawn caught Dale off guard. She felt her face heat as she covered her mouth. "Sorry."

"Get some rest. And thanks again." Logan reached for the door handle.

"Wait." Dale opened the console between their seats and pulled out a pad of paper. She wrote down her personal cell number, then held it out to Logan. "Here. If there is any problem with the rental, call me and I'll come pick you up." She held up her hand to stop the protest she saw forming on Logan's lips. "Like I said, no obligation. No strings attached."

Logan frowned but took the paper. She tucked it into her pocket, then opened the door. "Thanks again."

"You're welcome." Dale watched her walk toward the small RV.

Logan glanced back as she reached the motor home and hesitated. She turned back and opened the door to the RV partway, stuck her arm inside, then squeezed in through the narrow space.

As Dale left the campground, she puzzled over what she had seen when Logan opened the door. Had there been someone else inside the motor home? And if so, who? Logan had never mentioned anyone else. Once again, she had more questions about Logan than answers.

CHAPTER 16

DALE'S SENSES WENT ON ALERT at the sound of footsteps approaching from behind. She glanced over her shoulder and relaxed. "Hey, Logan."

"Hi." Logan held out a tray with two coffee cups and a small bag.

She narrowed her eyes at Logan, then accepted the items. This was the second night in a row that Logan had shown up with coffee and—Dale peeked in the bag—scones. "You don't need to keep doing this. It was just a ride home."

"And you could just let me give you money for gas," Logan said. She had already offered several times.

Touché. While Dale didn't feel that Logan owed her anything, she wasn't going to protest too adamantly. Logan bringing a treat for both of them gave her a chance to spend some alone time with her. Yesterday, they had retreated to the conference room instead of the more crowded staff lounge to enjoy the coffee and scones before their shift started. Logan's latest offering gave them the chance to do that again. Now, if she could just get Logan to have their evening meal together. Logan always left the department and never offered an explanation as to where she went. *One thing at a time. Don't push her.* "Come on, before my coffee gets cold."

Logan snorted in response but accompanied her.

Dale led the way to the conference room.

As she settled into her seat at the head of the table, Dale asked, "Any update on your car?" The scowl that appeared on Logan's face made Dale immediately regret the question.

"Turns out the computer module they need is on backorder. I'm going to have to see if I can find a different rental place. I don't want to be stuck driving that crappy subcompact for the next two weeks. I called today, and they don't have anything larger available. It was okay when I thought it was just going to be for a day or two, but I hate driving that little thing on the freeway." Logan glanced away. "Makes me nervous."

Dale winced in sympathy. She'd spotted Logan getting out of the dinky car yesterday. She wouldn't want to drive it on the roads here either. "If you can't find something local and want me to take you to one of the national places out at the airport, just let me know."

"That's okay. I'll take care of it. Thanks anyway."

Why am I not surprised? Despite Logan allowing Dale to take her home after her car conked out, she had no illusions that Logan was going to change overnight and give up her solitary ways.

Dale tossed the empty coffee cups and paper bag into the trash before following Logan out of the conference room and toward the staff lounge. She greeted several nurses as they passed.

Logan pushed open the door when she reached the lounge and came to an abrupt halt.

Dale grabbed Logan's hips to keep from plowing into her. Her mind insisted on pointing out the softness of the flesh under her hands before she pulled away. *Nice.* "What is it?" She peered over Logan's shoulder but didn't see anything out of place. Tension radiated from Logan, and she had her jaw clenched tight.

"Nothing." Logan strode over to her locker.

Sure, that's believable. Dale resisted the urge to call her on the obvious lie. They had just had a pleasant interaction while sharing their coffee and scones, and she hesitated to push Logan. She swept her gaze around the room, trying to spot what had upset Logan.

Someone on the day shift had been busy. The lounge was decked out with a plethora of holiday decorations. There was even a small Christmas tree on the table in the corner.

Could that be it? She remembered the look on Logan's face when she and Harris had been talking about Christmas. Did Logan have something against the holiday?

Dale opened her own locker and stowed her jacket. "Looks like someone went all out to get everyone into the holiday spirit."

Logan muttered something under her breath that Dale didn't get, but it didn't sound complimentary.

"Not a fan of the holidays?"

"No." Logan's tone made it clear the subject was off-limits.

Donna stuck her head in the doorway. "Oh, good. Just the people I wanted to see." She fairly bounced across the room.

Dale smiled at the spunky little blonde. "What's up?"

"I'm taking names to participate in our Secret Santa. Everyone else has already signed up." She held out the clipboard she was carrying. "So how about it?"

"No thanks." Logan walked out of the lounge without another word.

Donna frowned as the door swung shut. "What's with her?"

That was a very good question. Dale wished she had an answer. "I guess she doesn't celebrate Christmas." But Dale knew it was more than that; Logan's reaction was far removed from someone who simply chose not to celebrate the holiday. She took the clipboard and looked at the rules. Gift value was limited to twenty dollars, and the giver remained anonymous even after all gifts were opened. While not a big fan of workplace gift giving, she signed her name.

"Thanks, Dr. Parker. If everything is quiet, we're going to draw names at midnight. If you get my name, I have a list."

"I don't think that's allowed."

"I won't tell if you don't." Donna grinned.

"Out." Laughing, Dale motioned toward the door. "We've got patients to see."

Together they left the lounge.

CHAPTER 17

DALE FOUND LOGAN ONCE AGAIN ensconced at the nurses' station with a medical journal. Since the holiday decorations had gone up two weeks ago, Logan had been avoiding the staff lounge as if it were the devil's lair. The rest of the department was devoid of decorations, per hospital policy.

The closer it got to Christmas, the more somber Logan became. And in the last few days, dark circles had appeared under her eyes. She had become more distant than ever.

Worry nagged at Dale. She wished there was some way she could break through Logan's self-imposed isolation.

"Dr. Parker," Donna called out.

Dale stepped behind the counter of the nurses' station.

"Everything is quiet. We're going to open our Secret Santa gifts." Donna glanced at her watch. "Everyone's gathering in the lounge in ten minutes."

Logan shoved back her chair and walked away.

Dale checked the intake board. "Okay. But make sure the patient check-in remains staffed, as well as the nurses' station."

"Sure thing."

After checking to make sure all the patients were stable, Dale headed for the staff lounge. She kept an eye out for Logan but didn't see her. Not that she expected her to step foot in the lounge while the gift giving was going on. Whatever she had against Christmas, it definitely seemed tied to the exchange of gifts.

Donna was already passing out gifts when Dale entered the lounge. She smiled and turned back to rummage under the tree. "Here you go." She wiggled her eyebrows at Dale as she handed her a narrow, brightly wrapped box.

Oh great. How embarrassing was this going to be? It wasn't uncommon to be presented with a gag gift. Dale kept her expression neutral and accepted the package. Conscious of everyone watching, she carefully lifted the tape from one end of the package.

"Don't be a wimp. Tear it off," Brent, one of the senior residents, said.

Laughter erupted.

Dale scowled at him, then ripped the paper, pulling it from the box in one motion. She glanced down at the row of individual boxes of hot chocolate mix and mentally breathed a sigh of relief as she held it up for everyone to see.

"How about a trade?" Molly asked.

"No trades," Donna said before Dale could refuse.

Dale snacked on a cookie and watched her coworkers open gifts. But her mind was only half on what was going on. Logan's increasing melancholy as Christmas drew nearer had her concerned. She had seen too many people suffering from depression during the holiday season and knew what devastating consequences that could have. She would do everything in her power to see that something like that didn't befall Logan. They both had the day, or rather the night, off tomorrow. Maybe she could convince Logan to go out to eat and get her to talk about what was bothering her.

The door to the lounge swung open. "Multiple incoming from a MVA," Nancy, the nurse who had volunteered to cover during the gift giving, said. "Wrong-way driver on the 110 hit another car head-on. First accident caused a major pileup behind it." She shook her head. "It's going to be a mess. I put in a call to Dr. Peterson. He's on his way down."

Dale pushed out of her chair. "Party's over. Let's hit it."

Everyone abandoned their dessert and gifts, quickly exiting the lounge.

"Have you seen Dr. Logan?" Dale asked Nancy as she followed her out of the room.

"She was at the desk when the call came in. She's waiting outside for the first ambulance."

As they neared the nurses' station, the sound of sirens pierced the night. Dale glanced at her watch. It was just after three a.m.

By the time she reached the ambulance bay, the paramedics already had the first patient unloaded. Logan was visually assessing her as they moved toward the door. One of the paramedics reeled off the patient's history and stats. She approached the other side of the gurney and glanced down into the scared blue eyes of a young woman whose head and neck were immobilized. "We're going to take good care of you."

A second ambulance pulled into the bay.

"I've got this," Logan said.

Dale nodded and moved away from the gurney. Another ambulance pulled up, waiting its turn to be unloaded. She motioned Brent, who was in the third year of his residency, toward the ambulance that had just arrived. "Take that one. Molly, you're with me." For now, she wanted to keep the less experienced first-year resident with her until she saw what they were up against.

Together, they approached the second ambulance as the EMTs unloaded the stretcher. The head of the gurney was raised, allowing the patient to sit up. The woman pulled against the strap across her chest. "I don't need to be on a stretcher. I'm fine." She tugged at the strap again. "Where's my sister? Did they bring her here? I need to talk to her. Is she okay?"

"Ma'am, you need to let the doctors take a look at you," the EMT said.

"No. You don't understand. This is all my fault. If I hadn't asked her to get my phone from the backseat because of a stupid text message." She jerked frantically on the straps.

The EMT moved to restrain her.

"They took her away in another ambulance. I have to find my sister." Her voice cracked with rising emotion.

"I'm sure your sister is in good hands." Dale ran a quick visual assessment. The abrasions on her face were most likely the result of an airbag deploying. The woman's shirt kept her from seeing any bruising from the seat belt. Most apparent was the fact that she was not using her left arm. "You're not going to do her any good by hiding your own injuries. Let us take care of you." She motioned toward Molly. "As soon as we finish examining you, Dr. Flaherty will check on your sister's location and get an update on her status."

The young woman adamantly shook her head. "You can't make me stay here. Give me a paper to sign. I have to find my sister."

While Dale understood the woman being upset, she didn't have time to coddle her. It was time to provide a reality check. Dale reached down where the woman had her left arm cradled against her abdomen and lifted it slightly.

The woman yelped and flopped back against the gurney. She glared at Dale.

"Your injuries need to be treated. Dr. Flaherty is going to take care of you." When the woman reluctantly nodded, she lowered her voice for Molly's ears only. "Besides checking her for a head trauma, make sure you check her for a seat belt injury."

Molly met Dale's gaze, then her eyes darted to the patient on the gurney. "What if she decides to leave again and won't let me treat her?"

Dale gave Molly a stern look. "Handle it! We've got a lot more injuries on the way."

As if to punctuate Dale's words, a new ambulance approached, sirens screaming.

"Now go." She motioned for Molly to grab the stretcher.

Pushing away her irritation at the resident, Dale hustled over to the waiting ambulance. She could hear the patient's screams before she reached the back of the ambulance.

The paramedics already had the gurney unloaded.

The first sight of the patient made Dale's stomach roil. She ruthlessly shoved away the reaction. *Do your damn job.* Despite a dressing, one of the patient's lower extremities was a bloody mess. The paramedic had applied a tourniquet just above the knee.

Dale grabbed the gurney. "Move it, people." As a group, the paramedics and Dale raced for the trauma bay. She called for Craig Peterson as soon as they cleared the doors of the ER. She wondered if they would need to call in the backup trauma surgeon.

Dale stretched her aching back as she stepped out of the treatment room. With the arrival of the day shift an hour ago, they had made great progress in clearing out the patients from the multiple-car pileup. The sound of a child's laughter drew her attention.

A dark-haired blur flew around the corner and plowed into her legs.

Dale grabbed the doorframe to keep them both upright.

The little girl wrapped her arms around Dale's leg and giggled. "Hi."

When she recognized the little girl, Dale grinned. *Wonder how she got away?* She had seen Erin only a few times, but she knew that Kim and Jess did not allow her to run amok in the ER. "Hello to you. Where's your mommy?"

Jess came flying around the same corner and skidded to a halt. "Erin Marie McKenna. You know better than to run from Mama." She hoisted Erin into her arms. "Sorry, Dale."

"No problem. I wish I had that much energy."

Erin squirmed in Jess's arms. "No. Run more."

She smiled at the pair. When she saw them together, it still amazed her that Jess was not Erin's birth mother. With her dark hair and blue eyes, Erin looked like a miniature version of Jess.

"No more running, young lady. It's time to go to day care."

"No." Erin tried to buck out of Jess's arms. "See Mommy."

Jess grimaced as she struggled with her daughter. "The terrible twos are not a myth."

Dale bit her lip to keep from laughing. It was certainly unexpected to see the tough ER chief struggle with a recalcitrant two-year-old. Up until now, she would have bet that Jess was the disciplinarian in the family.

"Mommy!" Erin's scream threatened to pierce Dale's eardrums. "Mommy!"

Kim strode up and plucked Erin from Jess's arms. "What's with all the racket?" She arched an eyebrow at Jess. "Took a detour on the way to day care?"

Jess shot Erin a look as if to say, "Now we're in trouble."

Erin laid her head on Kim's shoulder and snuggled against her, the picture of innocence. Her straight black hair contrasted sharply with her mother's blond curls.

"Oh yeah. Leave me to take the blame," Jess muttered. She glanced Dale's way and flushed as if she had just realized she was still standing there. "We've got everything under control here, go ahead and sign out. I know you must be beat. If you see Logan, tell her too, please."

"Thanks." Dale yawned. She was definitely ready to hit the sack, but her empty stomach rumbled in complaint.

"Come on, you two. Mommy and Mama have to work." Jess placed a kiss on Erin's forehead. "And you are going to day care."

Erin started to protest, but at a look from Kim she quieted.

"I bet Charlie is already playing with all the toys upstairs," Kim said.

Erin lifted her head from Kim's shoulder, and her little brow furrowed. "Go up." She bounced in Kim's arms. "Go up."

With a nod in Dale's direction, the threesome headed down the hall.

Watching the family interact had done a lot to lift the stress of the last few hours. She couldn't help the bit of envy that tugged at her. How wonderful it must be to have a family like that.

Dale picked up the pace when she spotted Logan ahead of her in the parking lot. Unable to find her in the department, she had thought she was already gone. "Hey, Logan. Wait up."

Logan slowed and waited for her to catch up.

They walked together to Logan's SUV.

"You did a great job this morning."

Logan shrugged and looked away. "Just doing my job."

It felt as if she were back at square one with Logan lately. Dale pushed down her frustration, determined to keep trying. As Casey often told her, she was nothing if not exceedingly stubborn. "Fine. Then congratulations, you're damn good at your job." It came out a little sharper than she intended.

Logan glanced her way, looking a bit taken aback. "Thanks."

Dale raked her hands through her hair. "Listen, I'm beat, and I know you must be too, but I'm starving. Why don't we—"

"I'm not hun—" Logan's stomach growled loudly. She scowled down at her traitorous belly.

"As I was saying. Why don't we grab a bite to eat? I know this place that makes the best omelets."

Logan hesitated. The voice of Scooby Doo emanated from Logan's backpack. Her eyes widened. "Excuse me. I have to take this." She pulled the phone out and thumbed the screen. "This is Logan."

Dale bit back a grin. Logan was so serious most of the time that she never figured her as the type to have a cartoon character ringtone.

"What! When?"

She sobered at Logan's alarmed tone of voice.

"Where is he now?" Logan listened for a minute, then her knees buckled, and she grabbed for the side mirror of the SUV.

What the hell was going on? Dale rushed to her side and wrapped an arm around her waist. Her worry ratcheted up another notch when Logan didn't immediately step away from the support. She could feel Logan trembling.

"I understand." Logan's voice sounded hollow. "I want everything possible done for him. I don't care what it costs. I'll be there as soon as I can." She disconnected the call. Her hands were shaking so badly, she fumbled with her phone as she tried to put it away.

Dale managed to grab the phone as it slipped from Logan's grasp. Knowing she might be rebuked, she took the chance anyway. She draped an arm across Logan's shoulders and pulled her close.

Logan slumped against her. Tremors rippled through her body. "I can't lose him." Her voice was filled with anguish.

Lose who? Logan had never made mention of anyone else. She wrapped her arms around Logan and stroked her hand soothingly up and down her back. "What happened?"

Logan lifted her head from Dale's shoulder. Her eyes sparkled with tears. "Drake bloated." She pulled out of Dale's embrace. "I have to go."

Dale worked to decipher the cryptic explanation. She assumed Drake was a dog. Was the dog what she had caught a glimpse of in Logan's RV? Although she didn't know a lot about dogs, she had heard of bloat. She wasn't familiar with many details of the condition, other than it could be deadly. When she was in college, a friend's German Shepard had died after bloating.

Logan tugged her key fob from her pocket and promptly dropped it. She scooped the key up and hit a button.

The SUVs alarm blared.

"Damn it." Logan struggled to get it shut off, her shaking hands making her clumsy.

Dale plucked the key from her hand and shut off the alarm. She had never seen Logan like this. She remained calm and rock steady during the most intense traumas. Then again, this was personal. "Let me drive. You're shaking like a leaf." She hid her surprise when Logan nodded. "Come on. My Jeep is right over there."

"We have to hurry," Logan said.

"I promise. I'll get you there as fast as possible."

CHAPTER 18

DALE GLANCED AT LOGAN FOR probably the twentieth time since they had left LA Metro. After giving her the location of the emergency hospital, Logan had not said a word. She had her arms wrapped around her middle and her gaze remained firmly locked outside the windshield, as if by concentration alone she could will them there faster. For rush hour, traffic had been fairly light, but Dale had still cursed every brake light and slow-moving car. The forty-five minutes it had taken them to reach the hospital had seemed interminable.

Her stomach clenched as she pulled into the parking lot of the animal hospital. *Please let him be okay.* Logan had been so down lately, Dale feared what it would do to her if the dog died.

Logan bolted from the Jeep the moment it came to a stop. She didn't even take her backpack with her.

Dale got out, opened the back door, and retrieved the backpack before hurrying after Logan. As she stepped into the lobby, Logan's raised voice drifted over to her.

"What the hell happened, Mark?" Logan, her fists clenched at her side, was right in the face of a heavyset man.

She rushed to her side and wrapped her hand around Logan's clenched fist. "Take it easy."

Logan glared at Dale for a moment. Then the fire in her eyes died, and like a marionette deprived of its strings, she slumped onto a nearby bench. She scrubbed her hands over her face. "I'm sorry, Mark. I know it's not your fault." Her hand rubbed repeatedly over a spot above her breast. "Have you heard anything about how Drake's doing?"

Mark sat down next to her. Dale took up position on her other side. She wondered what the connection between Logan and this man was, but now wasn't the time to ask questions.

"Last I heard, they were going to start an IV and take X-rays to see if there was any torsion. If not, they were going to tube him to decompress his stomach." He knifed his fingers through his hair. "I swear to you. As soon as my staff alerted me that there was a problem with Drake, I checked him over and got him here right away."

Dale was once again left to puzzle out the details for herself. Mark must be the owner of a kennel where Logan kept her dog.

"I know you did. I'm sorry about how I acted. I'm just so—" She roughly shook her head. "I appreciate everything you did for Drake. You must need to get back to work."

Mark stood. "Yeah. I do." He gazed down at Logan, then tentatively patted her shoulder. "Let me know how he's doing when you can."

"Sure. Thanks again."

They watched in silence as Mark left. Dale searched for something—anything—to say.

The door next to the check-in desk opened, and a woman wearing a white lab coat over a set of scrubs stepped out. She glanced around until her gaze settled on them. "Dr. Logan?"

Logan stood. "Yes. I'm Dr. Logan, Drake's owner."

The doctor shook hands with Logan. "I'm Dr. Bader. I've been overseeing Drake's care."

Dale moved to stand next to Logan. She wanted to be close-by, no matter what the news.

"How is he?"

The tremor in her voice made Dale want to reach out to Logan, but she resisted. *Please let him be okay.*

"First off, he's stable. There was no torsion of the stomach."

Logan's breath burst from her as if she had been holding it, and she swayed. Dale put her hand on Logan's lower back to steady her.

"Would you like to come into the back and see him?"

Logan nodded.

"Okay. Then I'll explain everything I've found and where we need to go from here."

Dale was torn. Should she stay here or accompany Logan into the treatment area? Logan glanced her way, and the wounded look in her eyes made Dale's decision easy.

Dr. Bader held open the door for Logan. When Dale made to accompany her, the doctor asked, "And you are?"

"I'm Dr. Parker. I'm..." What was she to Logan?

"We work together in the ER," Logan said. She met Dale's gaze for a moment, then turned back to Dr. Bader. "She's my friend."

Despite the circumstances, warmth suffused Dale at Logan's words.

"Right this way," Dr. Bader said.

Dale smiled at Logan and stepped through the door to join her in the hallway. They followed Dr. Bader into a large area filled with equipment.

Except for the dogs and cats on the exam tables, the area could have easily passed for one of the treatment rooms at LA Metro. Scrub-suited personnel bustled about attending to the animals.

Dr. Bader led them to a back corner of the room away from the main traffic area.

A technician was kneeling on the floor; her body blocked the view of the animal she was attending. An IV bag hung from a hook mounted on the wall near her.

When the technician stood, Dale couldn't hold back a gasp as she got her first look at the huge, dark-gray dog lying on a padded mat. An IV line disappeared beneath the blanket covering him.

Dr. Bader turned, tilting her head to peer at Dale questioningly.

Logan was oblivious to her reaction. She let out a muted cry, dropping to her knees next to Drake. She buried her face against his thick neck, and her shoulders started to shake.

Dale longed to comfort her but held herself back. Her own eyes stung with repressed tears at witnessing Logan's pain. She glanced at Dr. Bader, surprised to find her face impassive as she watched Logan. *She's an ER doctor just like you,* she reminded herself. Neither of them could allow their emotions to get the best of them while at work.

It took several minutes before Logan regained control of herself. Finally, she lifted up onto her knees and swiped at her tear-streaked face.

Dr. Bader pulled a packet of tissues out of her pocket and offered them to Logan without a word.

Logan wiped her face and then, cautious of his IV line, settled down next to Drake's head, propping her back against the wall. The big dog lifted his head and put it into her lap. His tail thumped weakly against the mat. A watery smile lit her face, and she leaned down and kissed his head. "That's my good boy."

Dale leaned against the counter nearby, close enough to be supportive if Logan needed her but otherwise out of the way.

Dr. Bader settled onto the floor in front of Drake and Logan. "Okay. Here's where we stand. As I said before, there was no torsion. However, he did bloat. I was able to tube him without incident and decompress and empty his stomach." She lifted up the blanket to display electrodes attached to Drake's chest and the IV line in one front leg. "He had a couple of short runs of PVCs when he first came in but none since decompressing his stomach. I'm giving him antibiotics and pain medication in his IV."

"So he's going to be okay. He just needs a little time to recover—right?"

Dale's heart went out to Logan. Her tone was equal parts hopeful and pleading for assurance. Dr. Bader's face remained unreadable. She had a bad feeling there was more to come. Otherwise, why hadn't Dr. Bader told Logan all this in the waiting room?

"I wish that were the case," Dr. Bader said.

Logan's hands clutched at Drake as if she was trying to shield him from whatever was coming. "What do you mean?"

"The good news is, we tested his lactic acid level, and it was only elevated by half a point above normal. That means the likelihood that his stomach or other organs suffered any damage is small. The staff at Canine Haven really should be commended. The fact that they got him here so quickly saved his life. It would have been very easy to pass his symptoms off as distress and lethargy caused by an upset stomach. As I'm sure you know, in cases like this, even an hour delay can be the difference between life and death."

Fresh tears sparkling in her eyes, Logan swallowed heavily, then rested her forehead against Drake's. After a moment she took a deep breath, looked up, and visibly squared her shoulders. "So what's the bad news?"

"Once a dog bloats, the possibility that it will happen again rises. Not only that, but the chance of accompanying torsion of the stomach also rises. For that reason, Drake needs a gastropexy performed. That way, with the stomach attached to the abdominal wall, should he bloat again, the stomach would not be able to rotate."

"When do you want to do the surgery?"

"The sooner the better. At this point, I feel he's stable. And, in spite of his age, that he can tolerate the surgery."

Her jaw tightly clenched, Logan repeatedly stroked her hand across Drake's white-peppered face. Dale wondered how old he was. Would he really be able to tolerate the surgery?

"All right." Logan nodded as if convincing herself. "All right. Do the surgery."

Dr. Bader rose from the floor. "I'll have the front desk write up an estimate and get the consent forms ready. They'll bring them to you out front."

Logan reluctantly lifted Drake's head out of her lap. The big dog whimpered. "It's okay, buddy. Dr. Bader is going to take good care of you." She stroked her hands all over his body and kissed his face before standing. "I'll see you soon." Her voice cracked.

Dale pushed off the wall and approached Logan. She wrapped her arm around Logan's shoulders. "He's going to be okay." She hoped she wasn't offering false comfort.

Logan nodded, her eyes brimming with tears. She glanced repeatedly over her shoulder as Dr. Bader led them out of the treatment area.

When they reached the door to the lobby, Dr. Bader said, "After you finish with the paperwork, go home and get some rest. I'll call and update you as soon as I finish the surgery."

"I'm not going anywhere," Logan said, sounding like herself for the first time since this ordeal had started.

Dr. Bader began to protest, but Logan warned her off with a gesture and a shake of her head.

"All right. I'll let you know as soon as the surgery is finished. But be aware, it's going to be a while. Several hours—at least."

"I'll be here." Logan crossed the lobby and plopped down on a padded bench that stretched across the far wall of the lobby.

Logan slumped forward, planting her elbows on her thighs, and buried her face in her hands. *What a*

nightmare. While she had originally taken Drake out of a sense of obligation to her sister, she had grown to love him dearly, and the thought of losing him, especially now, so close to the anniversary of Emily's death, was tearing her up inside.

Dale joined her on the bench. She laid her hand on Logan's back and stroked soothingly up and down, offering silent support.

For the first time since her sister's death, Logan allowed herself to take comfort from another human being. She didn't know what she would have done without Dale's rock-solid presence. Sighing to herself, she finally acknowledged that regardless of all her rationalizations, she had come back to LA Metro because of Dale. Although she was loath to admit it, even prior to today, she had felt a connection to her. Now, Dale's staunch support in this time of need had broken through the protective barriers she had erected around herself after Emily's passing.

She lifted her head and met Dale's gaze. Her gray eyes, darkened to the color of a storm-tossed sky, shone with compassion. Logan's throat closed, and tears threatened to overflow. "Thank you for being here."

"I wish there was more I could do," Dale said. She rhythmically rubbed her own left knee without seeming to be aware of it.

Logan wondered if there was a limit to how long Dale could wear her prosthesis. Was it hurting her? It had been a long, busy shift, and she had mentioned being tired before all this happened. As much as she took comfort from her presence, Dale taking care of herself was more important.

Straightening up, she tried to appear as composed and upbeat as possible. "Thanks again for everything. There's no need for you to stay. I'll call a cab when I'm ready to leave."

"I'm not going anywhere," Dale said, repeating Logan's earlier words. Her tone left no room for argument.

Relief flooded Logan. "Thank you." She gripped Dale's hand.

Dale entwined their fingers as they settled in to wait.

Only a few minutes had passed when Dale's stomach growled loudly. She pressed her free hand to her belly.

Logan let go of Dale's hand, immediately missing the warmth of her palm. "Go get something to eat. I'll be fine here."

"No. I'm all right." Dale's stomach rumbled, giving lie to her words. A blush painted her cheeks.

"Dale."

"Logan," Dale said with the same tone.

Smiling despite her frustration, Logan shook her head. *Damn stubborn woman.* "You need to eat."

"So do you. I'll tell you what. I'll go get us something to eat and bring it back."

Logan didn't think her queasy stomach would tolerate anything, but as long as it got Dale to eat, that was all that mattered. "Sure. Good idea."

Dale eyed her as if suspicious of her sudden agreement. "Go."

Dale pushed off the bench and stood. "Are you sure?"

"Yes. Go."

"I'll be back as quick as I can."

Logan watched her walk across the lobby. Her worry returned when she detected a slight limp in Dale's gait that normally wasn't there. *You should make her go home.* Before she could act on the thought, Dale was already out the door. She shifted on the uncomfortable bench and settled down to wait.

Dale slipped behind the wheel of her Jeep and took a moment to rub her aching leg. As frequently happened after long hours wearing her prosthesis, her residual limb had changed size, making her socket fit uncomfortable.

If she was going to last for however many hours it would be before Drake was out of surgery, she needed to take care of her leg.

Heading down the main street where the animal hospital was located, she spotted a big box store. *Perfect.* She picked the far corner of the giant parking lot, near a stand of trees, as far away from the store as she could get. While she could do what she needed to in a restaurant's handicapped restroom, she preferred the privacy of her vehicle. She got out of her vehicle, opened the driver's side rear door, and climbed into the backseat. She leaned over and grabbed from behind it a small, military-style medical kit. Only this bag didn't hold standard medical supplies but rather everything she needed to take care of her prosthetic and residual limb. Thankfully, she had worn cargo pants today instead of her usual jeans.

She pulled up her pant leg well above her knee. After pressing the button to release the prosthesis, she let out a big sigh as the leg slid off. Anxious to get back to Logan, she didn't waste any time. She stripped off the damp stump sock and rolled down the liner. She didn't dare remove it completely for fear she wouldn't be able to get it back on. After cleaning and drying the exposed stump, then treating any rub spots, she slid the liner back up and put on a dry stump sock over it. It took her two tries to get the thickness of the stump sock right and the fit in the socket as comfortable as possible. With all the stress her leg had taken last night and then the extra hours today without relief, it was a good thing she had tonight off. Otherwise, it would have meant a miserable shift.

Now to get them something to eat and get back to Logan as soon as possible.

Twenty minutes later, Dale pulled open the door to the animal hospital. She had chosen fast food for expediency's sake. Hopefully, Logan's stomach could tolerate an egg breakfast biscuit. As she stepped into the lobby, her gaze went to the back corner, where Logan had been sitting.

She wasn't there.

Her heart rate escalating, Dale scanned the room. No Logan. *Damn it.* She had only been gone forty-five minutes. Had something happened during surgery? She bolted for the front desk. Just as she reached it, a door off to the side opened, and Logan stepped out. Relief weakened her knees when she realized it was a restroom. "Everything okay?"

"He's still in surgery, but one of the techs checked a few minutes ago. So far, so good."

"That's great." She clasped Logan's arm. "Come have a bite to eat."

Logan followed her back to their spot in the far corner. She shook her head when Dale offered her a wrapped biscuit.

"You're not going to be able to help Drake if you make yourself sick by not eating. He needs you to be strong."

Logan scowled but took the breakfast sandwich.

Dale kept an eye on Logan as she ate her own meal. While Logan only nibbled at the biscuit, Dale gave her points for trying.

After they finished, Dale gathered up the remains of their meal and tossed it into a nearby trash can. She returned to Logan and once again joined her on the padded bench. When Logan slipped her hand into Dale's, she sighed and entwined their fingers.

In silent companionship, they waited.

Logan's hand gripping hers painfully tight brought Dale to full awareness. Her eyes popped open. Unsure of how much time had passed, she cursed herself when she realized she must have dozed off. *Some friend you are.*

Dr. Bader, still in her surgical cap and sweat-stained scrubs, strode toward them.

Logan bolted from the bench. Dale hustled after her. They met Dr. Bader halfway.

"He's out of surgery."

Tension radiated from Logan.

Get on with it, Dale silently urged the doctor.

"He came through with flying colors. Vitals were solid as a rock during the whole procedure. I confirmed there was no torsion and no visible damage to his stomach." Dr. Bader smiled.

Logan whirled around and threw herself into Dale's arms.

Dale wrapped her in a tight hug. Suppressed tears stung her eyes.

Logan stepped back, but Dale couldn't bring herself to let her go completely. She kept one arm around her waist.

"When can we see him?"

"Not for another hour—at least," Dr. Bader said.

"We'll be here," Logan said.

Dale smiled at her and squeezed her waist. "Yes. We'll be here."

CHAPTER 19

Yawning, Dale pulled the covers up over her shoulders. Pale moonlight shone through the partially open blinds, throwing a slatted pattern across the bed. She was still tired, but her brain insisted it was time to be up and about. While it was nine in the evening and most people's day was winding down, hers was normally in full swing by now. It didn't matter that it was her day off and that she had only slept five hours. After over a year working nights, she had successfully switched her circadian rhythm.

Knowing she would not be able to go back to sleep, she threw back the covers and sat up. She grabbed her forearm crutches from where they rested against the nightstand and stood, then padded into the bathroom.

The rubber tips of the crutches squeaked on the hardwood floor as she made her way into the kitchen. She peered into the refrigerator; although it was well stocked, nothing appealed to her. Her thoughts strayed to Logan.

Seeing Drake after his surgery, unable to lift his head and barely responsive, had clearly devastated Logan. On the ride back to LA Metro so Logan could pick up her SUV, she had retreated into herself. The pain in Logan's red-rimmed eyes had made Dale want to invite Logan to her apartment instead of leaving her to suffer alone. But her own protective instincts had kicked in before she could make the offer.

Gazing down at the empty space where her lower leg and foot should be, she tightened her grip on her crutches. There was no way she would allow Logan to see her like this.

She flopped down on the couch, unable to shake her worry about Logan. Should she call her? After all the stress of the day, maybe she was sleeping. But the thought of Logan sitting in her motor home alone nagged at her. Grabbing her crutches, she headed back into the bedroom, where she sat on the side of the bed and scrolled through her contact list. When she reached Logan's name, she thumbed the screen to connect the call. The line rang.

The sound echoed from somewhere in her apartment.

Huh? After tucking the phone against her shoulder, she levered herself up and padded into the living room.

Ringing was coming from her jacket, which was draped over the back of a dining room chair.

When she disconnected the call, the ringing from her jacket fell silent. She stuck her hand in the pocket and pulled out Logan's phone. *What the heck?* Then she remembered. When Logan had gotten the call about Drake, she had almost dropped her phone. Dale had grabbed it and must have inadvertently stuck it in her own pocket.

What if the animal hospital had tried to call Logan? She glanced at the lock screen and let out a sigh of relief. There was only one missed call, which had to be the one she had just made. Should she take the phone to Logan now or wait until morning?

A picture of Drake after his surgery flashed through Dale's mind. If something were to happen with Drake and the hospital wasn't able to contact her, Logan would never forgive her. She definitely needed to take the phone to her now.

Dale drove by Logan's site, confirming that her SUV was parked adjacent to the motor home. She circled through the RV park, making her way back to the office and the visitor parking spots.

As she approached the motor home, her nervousness grew. How would Logan react to her showing up? *You're bringing back her phone, not trying to invade her privacy.*

The lights were on inside the RV.

She pulled Logan's phone out of her pocket. Gripping it with one hand, she knocked on the door of the RV with the other.

It took several moments, then the door cracked open and Logan peered out. "Dale?" Dale stepped back out of the way when Logan swung the door open. "What are you doing here?" She sounded more curious than upset.

Dale's thought process derailed when she got a look at what Logan was wearing—or rather, not wearing. With Logan standing backlit in the doorway, the white T-shirt clearly displayed her braless breasts, taut nipples puckering the soft cotton. *No ogling!* But the full breasts so beautifully on display were hard to ignore. Dale forced her gaze up to Logan's face. "Bringing you your phone." She held it up. "I put it in my pocket earlier without realizing it."

Logan leaned out of the RV and snatched the phone from her hand, then quickly tapped in the unlock code.

"There weren't any calls. Except when I tried to call you a little while ago. That's how I found the phone."

Tension leaked from Logan, and she slumped against the door frame. "Thank you for bringing it. I've been so..." She waved her hands in the air. "I didn't even realize it was missing."

"Sorry I didn't realize earlier that I had it."

An awkward silence settled between them.

"Well...I should go."

"Thanks again."

For a moment, Dale thought she might say something more.

But she didn't.

What did you think, that she was going to invite you in? Making sure to keep the disappointment from her voice, she said, "You're welcome. Good night." Dale offered a short wave and walked away.

"Wait."

She had taken only two steps when Logan's voice stopped her in her tracks. She turned back toward the motor home.

Logan fidgeted for a moment, then nodded to herself. "Have you eaten breakfast yet?"

"No. Would you like to go get something?"

"Um... Well, I was getting ready to make breakfast when you knocked. It's nothing fancy, just some microwave stuff. You're welcome to join me. If you want."

Dale struggled to hide her surprise. "That would be great. I'm starving." And suddenly she was.

Logan smiled and waved her in.

Dale climbed the two steps into the motor home, careful to keep from brushing against Logan as she passed in the tight space.

"Have a seat. I'll be right back." Logan stepped into a narrow hallway and pulled a trifold door shut, closing off the back from view.

Dale's gaze swept the interior. A blanket and pillow rested on a two-person couch that filled the space along one wall. On the opposite wall was the kitchen with a sink and microwave. A huge dog bed filled the space between them. There was no way to move about the motor home without stepping on it. A small pedestal table sat in front of the driver and passenger chairs, which had been turned around to face into the coach. While quite small, with the slider out, it was actually a little larger than she expected. Still, she was having a hard time picturing Logan living here full-time with a huge dog like Drake.

Not comfortable invading what was clearly Logan's personal space on the couch, Dale took off her jacket, hung it on the back of the passenger seat, then squeezed behind the pedestal table to sit.

The sound of several cabinets opening and closing sounded from the rear of the RV.

Logan reappeared, dressed in a dark T-shirt and jeans—and wearing a bra.

Dale wasn't sure if she was relieved or disappointed. She shook her head at herself. Maybe a little of both.

"Microwave French toast okay?"

"Sure." Normally, Dale would have offered to help, but with the close quarters, she decided it was best just to stay out of the way.

As Logan went about preparing their breakfast only a few feet away, Dale couldn't help watching her. Now that she was without her customary baggy lab coat, it was hard to resist enjoying the view of her lush curves beneath the form-fitting T-shirt and jeans. Her gaze dropped to the denim hugging Logan's well-rounded ass. *No ogling,* she repeated what was becoming a mantra. Trying to distract herself, she continued her perusal of her surroundings.

A framed photograph hanging near the driver's seat caught her attention.

She leaned over to get a closer look. Mesmerized, she stared at the photo of Logan and Drake as a puppy. The crystal-clear, blue sky and ocean waves in the background provided a beautiful backdrop to the photo. But that wasn't what drew Dale to the image. The candid shot had caught Logan with her head thrown back, her face alight with laughter as she held off a rambunctious Drake. While Logan wasn't a classic beauty, in the photo she was stunning, showing a life and fire inside her that Dale had never seen. She glanced over at Logan. It was hard to believe she was the woman in the picture. Most days, Logan seemed to carry the weight of the world on her shoulders. Dale looked back at the photograph. What had happened to that carefree woman?

Logan approached with a paper plate brimming with French toast strips.

Dale smiled up at her and tipped her chin toward the photograph. "That's a great picture of you and Drake."

Logan's gaze darted toward the photo. The plate dropped from her suddenly nerveless fingers and landed on the table, scattering French toast strips across its surface. She took a sharp breath as pain flashed across her face. Spinning around, she put her back to Dale.

What the heck? Then it hit her. *You idiot.* Dale cursed the tight quarters as she slipped from behind the table. Her toe caught Drake's bed, and she stumbled into Logan's back. *Damn it.* She grabbed onto Logan's shoulders to keep them both upright. "I'm sorry."

Of course drawing her attention to a picture of a much younger Drake would hit Logan hard—especially now. Tension radiated from the muscles under her hands.

Dale quickly withdrew them. "I'm sorry. I should have realized..." Unable to help herself, she gently touched Logan's back, then stepped back as far as she could in the small space—which wasn't far. "He's going to be all right."

Logan took a deep breath, straightening her shoulders, and turned to face Dale. "I know. That's not it. It's just that picture is..." She slapped her hand over her mouth as if to stop the words from escaping. She glanced at the photo again, then quickly looked away, shaking her head roughly. "Forget it. It's nothing." The pain in her eyes gave lie to her words.

The picture is what? Dale longed to ask, but the haunted look in Logan's eyes kept the words at bay. She glanced back and forth between Logan and the photo. What was she missing here?

Logan reached over and tugged back the privacy curtain that covered the windshield so that it hid the photograph. When she looked at Dale, her face had assumed the neutral mask she wore at work. "Have a seat. I'll get the rest of breakfast."

While a million questions raced through Dale's mind, she knew Logan well enough by now to know that when she was like this, there were no answers to be had. She resumed her seat behind the pedestal table and piled the French toast strips back onto the plate.

Logan set out paper plates, forks, syrup, and two glasses of orange juice. "Hope this is okay?"

"It's great. Thanks." Dale hid her surprise when Logan slipped into the driver's seat next to her, which put her so close, their shoulders brushed. She thought after what had just happened that Logan would retreat to the couch to gain some distance.

They shared a quiet breakfast, the tension slowly dissipating.

Dale leaned back and patted her full belly. "Thanks. That hit the spot."

"Good." Logan struggled for a moment to fit through the narrow space between the table and the chair so that she could stand. She glanced in Dale's direction and flushed.

Dale caught her arm before she could turn away. "Thank you for inviting me in for breakfast. You didn't have to do that."

Logan's blush deepened, and she ducked her head. "You're welcome." She set about clearing the table while carefully avoiding looking at Dale.

Again resisting the urge to help, Dale remained seated.

It took Logan only a few minutes to clean up. Once done, she plopped down on the couch. She fiddled with the blanket, then tugged the pillow into her lap and wrapped her arms around it.

Dale racked her brain for something to talk about besides Drake or work as the silence grew uncomfortable. "Well, I guess I should get going." She sighed when

Logan didn't protest. It was clear their time together was at an end.

"Thanks again for bringing my phone."

Dale slid out from behind the pedestal table and snagged her jacket from the back of the chair. "Sorry I took it to start with."

Logan waved off the apology.

Shrugging into her jacket, Dale nodded. She opened the door and stepped down onto the first exterior step of the motor home. She turned back toward Logan. "Have a good day. Or rather, night, in our case."

Smiling, Logan popped off the couch and moved to stand in the entryway.

With Logan standing above her and less than half a foot separating them, Dale found herself with an up-close view of Logan's full breasts. Her normally quiescent libido sprang to life. She quickly stepped backward and lost her footing.

Logan grabbed her arm before she could tumble down the second step.

Serves you right. Dale clutched the handrail on the outside of the motor home and steadied herself.

"You okay?" Logan asked. "Is it your leg?"

"No. I'm fine." *I was just busy getting an eyeful.* Dale ducked her head to keep Logan from seeing her heated face.

Logan laid her hand on Dale's shoulder. "Thanks again for everything you did today."

Dale barely resisted the urge to press her face against Logan's hand. She settled for placing her hand over Logan's. "I'm glad I could help. If you need anything, please call me." She forced herself to remove her hand from Logan's.

"I will."

At one time, Dale would have figured it was just an empty promise, but now she actually believed her. "I'll see you tomorrow at work. Come early. I'm bringing coffee and goodies."

Logan shook her head. "You've already done more than enough."

"I know this great place that makes incredible muffins. They have to be tried to be believed."

"Dale," Logan said, her exasperation clear.

Dale bit back a grin and gave her back the same. "Logan."

Logan mock-scowled. "See you then."

Dale waved and walked away, aware that Logan remained standing in the doorway, watching. She waved again as she reached the end of the row and turned toward the visitor parking.

Although things had not gone as well as Dale had hoped, having Logan invite her into her home felt like a big step in their slowly developing friendship. Now, if she would just get over her unwanted attraction to Logan, things would be good.

CHAPTER 20

DALE ALMOST CHOKED ON THE sip of coffee she had just taken. She set her cup on the conference room table. "He did what?" Logan burst out laughing, and Dale caught her first glimpse of the carefree woman she had seen in the photo yesterday. *Beautiful.*

"He has always been a ladies' man," Logan said. "It wasn't his fault... You stick a big pair of breasts in his face, and he can't help himself."

Dale could relate to that. Grinning, she allowed her gaze to drop to Logan's chest as she flashed back to Logan's breasts only inches from her face last night. She gave herself a mental slap to the back of the head and repeated her new mantra. *No ogling.* "So how did the poor tech react when Drake shoved his huge muzzle between her breasts?"

"Thankfully, after she managed to pry him out of her cleavage, she laughed."

"He's really doing well, huh?"

"He's doing great. Dr. Bader is thrilled with how quickly he's recovering." Logan popped a bite of her muffin into her mouth and hummed. "These are incredible." She looked more relaxed than Dale had seen her in weeks.

"Told you." Dale bit into a cranberry-orange muffin with white icing drizzled over it. The smell and the rich combination of flavors inundated her senses. She washed it down with a sip of her coffee. "So will you be able to bring Drake home soon?"

The smile dropped from Logan's face, and she sighed. "He could be discharged tomorrow, but..." She fiddled with the edge of her coffee cup.

"What's the problem?" Dale reached across the table and laid her hand on Logan's arm.

Rubbing her chest right above her breast, Logan looked away, then met Dale's gaze. "I'm worried about how he is going to do getting in and out of the motor home with a huge abdominal incision."

Dale nodded. The two exterior steps into Logan's RV were surprisingly steep. And there was an additional step inside. "Maybe a ramp would help?"

"Yeah, I thought of that, but it would be a pretty steep incline. When I was at the hospital this morning and they got him up, his rear legs were kind of weak. Plus, I'm not sure Bernice will be able to handle him if he needs help."

"Who's Bernice?"

"She's the on-site manager of the RV park. She looks out for Drake; she lets him out before she goes to bed and again in the morning. But she's this little bitty thing. Drake outweighs her by at least forty or fifty pounds. Her grandson, Danny, helps out too, but he's only ten."

Dale found it hard to believe that Logan accepted anyone's help, but apparently, she made an exception when it came to Drake. "Well, if there's anything I can do to help, just let me know."

Logan blew out a breath. "Thanks. I'll figure something out."

As Dale passed by the nurses' station, she looked for Logan. She had not seen her as she made her rounds. It had been a busy night so far with a constant flow of patients with minor ailments that made it feel more like working in a primary-care clinic than an ER. Logan and her situation with Drake had never been far from her thoughts. As much as she would have liked to take in the big dog while he recovered, her apartment complex didn't allow pets. Even if it did, there was the whole issue of her leeriness of big dogs. Not that she would ever admit that to Logan. Why couldn't she have had a nice, average dog—like a Chihuahua? At least Dale had some limited, if not entirely pleasant, childhood experience with that breed.

She sighed. There had to be something she could do. Drake needed someplace on one level with easy access outside as well as someone capable of looking after him if he had any problems. What other options were there? It wasn't as if Logan had any friends she could ask to care for Drake. Dale stopped in her tracks as inspiration struck. Why hadn't she thought of this before? Logan didn't have any friend in the area to ask—but she did. She knew exactly who loved big dogs and had the perfect setup for Drake. She fished in her pocket for her phone as she headed outside to make her call.

Dale leaned against the wall, just outside the ambulance bay doors, and waited for her friend to pick up.

"This better be good," Casey snarled into the phone.

"Good morning to you too."

"What the hell is so earth-shattering that you had to call at o-dark-thirty?"

"It's not the middle of the night. It's almost six a.m."

"It's not even light out yet! That makes it officially still night." Despite her years in the military, Casey was not a morning person.

"Sorry. I really need your help."

Rustling filtered through the line, and Casey grumbled. "Okay. Okay. I'm up. What do you need?"

"I need you to dogsit for a friend. He just had surgery."

Silence greeted the request.

"Casey?"

"Yeah. I'm still here. I'm just trying to figure out what guy you know well enough that he turns to you to watch his dog while he recovers from surgery."

Huh? She laughed when she realized the problem. "The dog is the one who had surgery. My friend is a woman."

"And that's supposed to be better?" Casey asked. "You want me to take care of a sick dog that belongs to some woman I don't even know?"

Dale frowned. When she put it like that, it didn't sound very reasonable. But damn it, Drake needed help. "Let me explain. Remember the doctor I told you about? The one who found out about my leg?" She went on to give the details of Logan's and Drake's situation.

"So you really care about Logan, huh?"

"She's becoming a good friend." *Who you wish could be more.* She shoved away the unwelcome thought. "And Drake really needs a safe place to recover."

"All right." Casey's sigh reached her ears. "You know I'm a sucker for big dogs. I still miss Zeus. I'll do it."

Dale smiled. Casey might bitch, but she never let her down. "Thank you. I owe you."

"You've got that right. You owe me—big-time."

"Fine." All Dale could think of was how thrilled she was that she'd found a way to help Logan. "Anything you want."

Casey cackled. "I'm holding you to that!"

Oh crap. What had she just gotten herself into? "Casey. Come on."

"Too late. Don't whine now."

"Fine." It didn't matter what Casey came up with to torture her. Logan needed help. "I've got to talk to Logan. I'll call you before we come over later this morning. I know she'll want to meet you first. Thanks again, Casey. I really appreciate this."

"No problem, my friend. I'll see you later."

Dale had a spring in her step as she walked back into the department. She scanned the area around the nurses' station, but Logan was nowhere to be found. *I bet*

I know where she is. She headed for the conference room where they had shared breakfast the last few mornings.

"Thank you, but no." Logan pushed her chair back from the conference table.

"But—"

"I appreciate you trying to help, but I can't turn over Drake's care to some woman I don't even know." Drake was her responsibility, and she couldn't—no wouldn't—abrogate that.

"She's totally trustworthy. And she watches her brothers' dogs, so she's experienced."

Logan shook her head adamantly and started to rise.

Dale put a restraining hand on her arm. "Wait."

Sighing, Logan settled back into her chair. The pleading look on Dale's face was impossible to ignore.

"Casey is an amazing woman. She's military like me." Dale raked her fingers through her shaggy hair, then reached down to rub her injured leg. She was clearly struggling with what she wanted to say.

Logan placed a gentle hand on her forearm. When Dale looked up, Logan was struck by the vulnerable look in her eyes.

Dale swallowed heavily. "She was there for me, without fail, during the lowest time in my life, when I was struggling to regain my independence." She held Logan's gaze. "I promise you Drake will be safe with her."

Logan's heart ached for what Dale had suffered. Casey must be a very special woman, but this wasn't about Dale. Her hand strayed to the spot above her left breast as her thoughts raced. Could she really let someone else care for Drake full-time, as this arrangement would require? What other options were there? Her living conditions were not conducive to Drake's recovery.

"What other viable options are there?" Dale asked, echoing her thoughts. "Isn't this about what's best for Drake?"

Oh, Drake. I've always tried to do what's right for you. But they had never faced anything like this. Blowing out a breath, Logan slumped back in the chair. "It's not that simple. Taking care of a dog Drake's size isn't like caring for an average-sized dog or even a large dog like a lab. You can't just pick him up or even physically make him do something he doesn't want to. Even with a huge abdominal incision, he's strong. Most people have no idea just how strong. Are you sure your friend knows what she's getting into?"

"Yes. Casey loves big dogs. She grew up with a mastiff. They were together for ten years." Dale smiled. "She used to go home on weekends when she was in college to spend time with Zeus. He's been gone fifteen years, and she still talks about how much she misses him."

Logan bit her lip. Was she really going to do this? "I'd have to meet her first and see her place."

"Of course. I told her we would be over later this morning."

She still had reservations but nodded anyway. "Okay."

"Great." Dale glanced at her watch. "Let's take care of the shift changeover, and then we'll head to Casey's."

Logan stopped Dale with a hand on her arm before she could step out of the conference room. "Thank you for once again coming to my and Drake's rescue."

Dale draped an arm around Logan's shoulders and gave her a brief one-armed hug. "Anytime."

She forced herself not to lean into the touch, much too aware of the solid length of Dale's body against hers. *Women are off-limits*, she sternly reminded herself. That didn't stop the part of her that immediately missed the contact when Dale stepped away. Logan followed her out of the conference room.

As they approached the nurses' station, the sound of sirens reached Logan's ears. She checked her watch. *Fifteen minutes and we would've been out of here.* So much for leaving anytime soon.

CHAPTER 21

LOGAN KEPT A CLOSE EYE on Dale's Jeep as she followed her to Casey's. She had input the address into her GPS, but Dale had not taken the route the unit provided. Thankfully, they had not gotten hung up in the ER as she had feared. While she knew that she needed to meet Casey and check out her place, what she really longed to do was go to see Drake. That was her other worry. If she went through with this, how was she going to survive being separated from Drake for two weeks? These last two days were the longest they had been apart in two years.

Dale parked in front of a small ranch house. A bright-red crew cab pickup truck sat in the driveway.

Logan pulled in behind Dale's Jeep. She put her hand over her jittery stomach as they approached the front door. Would the house be decorated for Christmas? She hadn't been inside a home decked out for the holiday since that fateful Christmas. It was hard enough ignoring all the reminders of the holiday strewn throughout the city. *I can do this—for Drake.*

The walkway led through a xeriscaped front yard, straight to the front door with a level entryway. She glanced at Dale, who was shifting from foot to foot. Why was she nervous?

"Um, I should warn you..."

Logan's anxiety spiked. What hadn't Dale told her? Maybe this was a bad idea after all.

Dale's hand on her arm startled her out of her runaway thoughts. "It's nothing bad. It's just that Casey can be, well, kind of brash. She's not the least bit shy about letting people know exactly what she thinks. Please don't take it personally. She may not be the most diplomatic at times, but she's a good person."

Logan barely resisted the urge to pop Dale in the arm for adding to her worries. "Straightforward and honest. I can deal with that."

"Great." Dale rang the doorbell.

A muscular blonde, dressed in jeans and a tight, sleeveless T-shirt, opened the door. She had a pretty face and a physique that Logan could only dream of.

Relief flashed across Dale's face; then she smiled.

Logan's curiosity peaked.

"Hey, Casey."

Casey winked at Dale before greeting Logan. "Hello. You must be Logan." They shook hands. "Come on in."

The entryway opened right into a large living room. There was not a Christmas decoration in sight. The knot in Logan's stomach released, and her knees weakened.

Dale was instantly at her side. She placed her hand on Logan's back. "You okay?"

Her gaze met stormy-gray eyes, and she lost herself in their dark depths.

Casey cleared her throat.

Logan glanced her way just in time to see Casey arch her eyebrows at Dale.

A scowl marred Dale's face.

Logan flushed and stepped away from her. But she couldn't stop herself from touching Dale's arm. "I'm good."

In an attempt to distract herself, she checked out Casey's home. A short half wall with wide openings at either end separated the living room from the dining room. A walkthrough kitchen was adjacent to the dining area. The whole space had an open, airy feeling.

Casey waved her arm encompassing the area. "As you can see, there's lots of room with easy access. There are no steps anywhere in the house." She motioned toward the far wall, which was composed of floor-to-ceiling glass that looked out into the backyard. One section was a sliding glass door. "Let's go out back."

As Casey walked across the room, Logan frowned. There was something peculiar about her gait. Had she been injured like Dale? She glanced over at Dale, but her expression gave nothing away.

They stepped through the sliding glass door to a covered area just outside. The ice plant ground cover cascaded down a bank at the back of the yard and ended at a low retaining wall. It was the only greenery in the yard. The rest of the small area was covered with a light-brown, stamped concrete. A large wrought-iron table with four heavy metal chairs dominated the center of the space.

Damn. The yard was not suitable for Drake. He would have to relieve himself on the concrete, and Logan was positive he wouldn't do that.

"I know what you're thinking," Casey said.

Logan quickly schooled her features, hiding her disappointment.

"She's got—" Dale said.

Casey waved her off. She walked to the side of the house and beckoned Logan over.

There, hidden from sight, a six-by-ten-foot area had been created with scalloped bricks and filled with pea gravel.

"I set this up for my brothers' dogs. It's easy to keep clean and sanitize. Do you think Drake could adapt to using the gravel? I know some dogs can't deal with not having access to grass."

Maybe this would work after all. "He actually prefers gravel. That's what a lot of RV parks use for their dog runs." She smiled, thinking of Drake in better times. "He thinks grass is a gourmet treat because he's exposed to it so rarely."

"Harley, my brother's lab, is the same way. We think he was a cow in a previous life."

Logan threw back her head and laughed. "I swear Drake's part cow the way he moos sometimes."

As Logan and Casey swapped dog stories, Dale wandered over to the patio table. When Casey reached over and touched Logan's arm, a wave of irritation swept through her. She had worked so hard to connect with Logan and break down her barriers, but for Casey, it seemed effortless.

She pulled out one of the chairs from the table and plopped down, feeling totally left out. A hand on her shoulder startled her out of her pitying thoughts.

"Everything okay?" Logan asked, concern shining in her eyes.

Dale nodded. When Logan sent her a warm smile, her bad mood vanished. She glanced up to find Casey smirking at her. She sent her a sharp look, which made Casey laugh outright.

Logan glanced back and forth between them.

Casey smiled at her. "So what do you think, Logan, will you trust me with your boy? I promise I'll take good care of him. And whenever you're free, I want you to come over and spend time with him. What do you say?"

"It's a deal. I'll pay you the same thing I do when I board Drake, forty-two dollars a day." Logan held out her hand.

Casey stared at Logan's outstretched hand, and the smile dropped from her face. "I'm not for hire."

"I can't let you do it for free."

"Yes, you can." Casey's tone was adamant.

Logan crossed her arms across her chest. "No. I have to pay you."

Dale sighed; she should have seen this coming. Logan didn't like being obliged to anyone.

Casey shrugged. "Then I can't do it."

What? "Casey!" Casey shot Dale a quelling look. She clamped her lips together to keep from protesting.

Logan's brow furrowed. "But why would you do it for nothing? I'm nobody to you."

"Sure you are. You're Dale's friend. She thought enough of you to ask me. That makes you special."

Logan, her color high, glanced at Dale, then back at Casey. She shook her head, but it seemed halfhearted. "It doesn't seem fair."

"Tell you what. You can pay me back."

Logan smiled.

"I work at the VA hospital. We always need extra people to help, especially over the holidays. There are a lot of patients that have no one to visit them."

Logan blanched at the mention of the holidays.

No! What the hell are you doing, Casey? Dale tried to warn her off with a look and a quick motion of her hand. Logan couldn't stand to be in the same room with Christmas decorations; what would forcing her to interact with patients over the holidays do to her? Not to mention the fact that the VA was Dale's haven, and she wasn't ready to invite Logan into it.

Casey pointedly ignored her. "Help out at the VA hospital over the holidays. Then we're even."

Logan bit her lip and said nothing for several long moments. Finally, she blew out a long breath. "Okay."

"Great." Casey grinned. "I'll get breakfast started. I make a mean omelet; just ask Dale."

"Thank you, but I can't stay. I need to check on Drake."

"Have you eaten already?" Casey asked.

"No, we came straight from work," Dale answered before Logan could. She smiled to herself. Logan was about to get another dose of Casey's stubborn nature.

"Then you need to eat first."

Logan started to shake her head.

"When was the last time you ate?" Casey's tone would have done a drill instructor proud.

"Um...last night."

Casey snorted. "Right. You mean as in yesterday? You're a doctor. You should know better." She wagged a finger at her. "You need to take better care of yourself."

Logan flushed, then scowled at Casey.

The two of them squared off like two rams about to butt heads.

Dale wasn't going to wait for the crash. "I'm starving," she said. "Would you mind if we ate first? Then I'll help you get Drake's stuff and go pick him up like I promised."

Logan looked away from Casey.

"Please." Dale wasn't above a little wheedling if it got Logan to eat.

Logan narrowed her eyes at her. "All right. But it needs to be quick."

"I've got it covered. Won't take long at all," Casey said. "Have a seat, and I'll get breakfast going."

"I'm helping," Logan said, her tone leaving no room for discussion.

Casey huffed, then, laughing, linked her arm with Logan's. "Right this way." She glanced back at Dale when she started to stand. "We'll bring breakfast out shortly. Take a load off."

As they walked away, Dale was struck by a particularly unpleasant sensation, but she absolutely refused to acknowledge its origin. She sat for a few minutes, repeatedly glancing toward the sliding glass door. *Screw this.* She shoved her chair back and rose to follow them inside. *I just want to help too.*

CHAPTER 22

LOGAN PACED THE LOBBY OF the animal hospital. "What's taking so long?"

They had already met with one of the techs and gone over Drake's discharge instructions as well as getting his medications. If they didn't bring him out soon, Logan was going to wear a hole into the floor.

Dale had tried once to get her to sit down. Just as she was about to try again, the door next to the front desk swung open.

A tech stepped out and held the door open. "Come on, Drake," she said. "That's a good boy." Drake slowly shuffled out. A ridiculously large plastic cone surrounded his head. His head hung down below his shoulders as if the cone was too heavy for him to lift.

Worry tugged at Dale. Was he really ready to be discharged? She glanced over at Logan and saw the same concern on her face. "Hey, buddy," Logan said. She was at his side the moment he cleared the doorway.

Despite Dale's concern for his well-being, she couldn't help being intimidated by his sheer size. Up until now, she had only seen him lying down, and he'd looked huge; now, standing next to Logan, he was enormous.

Drake lifted his head for a moment, then dropped it back down.

Frowning, Logan touched the plastic cone. "Was he licking his incision?"

"No. It's a precaution we take with all of our post-op patients."

Logan shook her head. "Take it off of him."

"His incision needs to be protected."

"I understand. But not with this." Logan knelt down next to Drake and began untying the knot of the gauze that was securing the cone to his collar.

When the cone came off, Drake's head immediately came up, and he made a strange vocalization. Dale had never heard anything like it, but it clearly sounded threatening. Then he lunged at Logan.

Whoa! Her heart pounding in her chest, Dale backpedaled several steps.

Drake smashed his head into Logan's chest, rocking her back on her heels.

Logan laughed.

What the heck?

Logan threw her arms around his neck to keep from being knocked down. He draped his head over her shoulder, and she hugged him close. "Easy, boy, easy. I'm here."

Dale stared at the pair. It was as if he were a different dog. The depressed, ill-looking dog was completely gone. He lavished Logan's face with kisses, his tail wagging so hard, his whole rear end moved.

"You should keep this just in case," the tech said, offering the plastic cone back to Logan when she had regained her feet.

Drake woofed and butted the cone with his head, making both the tech and Dale jump.

"That's a definite no," Logan said. "I don't think he'll bother his incision, but if he does, I'll get one of those blow-up e-collars."

"Good idea. Those are actually much better for a dog Drake's size." The tech put the cone down and then approached Drake. She rubbed his ears. "See you in ten days, big guy. Be a good boy." She smiled and placed a kiss on the top of his head and got a kiss in return for her efforts.

When the door closed behind the tech, Logan turned Dale's way. Her brow furrowed at finding Dale several feet away.

Heat suffused Dale's face. She jammed her hands in her pockets and slowly approached Logan and Drake. *Don't be such a sissy.* He had been friendly with the tech. "Ready to go?" She shot a look at Drake and found him staring at her. His head was higher than her waist. She barely resisted the urge to step back—far back.

Logan frowned and placed a hand on Drake's back. "Is everything all right?"

Dale swallowed nervously. "Sure. Let's get out of here." She hoped she sounded more convincing to Logan than she did to her own ears. She strode to the door and held it open, struggling not to tense when Drake passed her.

Drake didn't so much as glance her way.

Blowing out a breath, she followed the pair to Logan's SUV. This was going to be a lot harder than she had anticipated. A knot was already forming in her stomach at the thought of being in close proximity to Drake for the drive to Casey's.

Logan opened the back hatch of her SUV.

Dale hadn't thought of all the logistics of dealing with a dog Drake's size. Even the simplest thing, such as getting into a vehicle, obviously required planning. How was Logan going to get the huge dog into the vehicle? Dale didn't think he would be able to jump so soon after abdominal surgery. Would Logan want her help? A moment's panic struck at the thought. She forced it down with difficulty. *You want Logan to see what a total wuss you are?* "How can I help?"

"No need. We've got this. You want to go?" Logan asked Drake.

Drake made the same strange woo-woo sound he had earlier.

Dale jumped. The vocalization wasn't a bark, but to Dale's ears, it still sounded intimidating.

Logan seemed to find it completely normal and laughed. "Okay. Foot."

Drake lifted a front paw and placed it in her outstretched hand. She guided his paw up to the floor of the open SUV, then gave the same command again and lifted up his other paw the same way. Once he had both front feet inside, Logan moved behind him. She put her arms around his thighs and her shoulder against his butt, being careful of his incision. "Up." As she strained to straighten her legs and lift him like a weightlifter doing a deadlift, Drake ducked his head and walked forward with his front legs. As soon as he was in, Drake turned around and gave Logan a big slurp in the face.

Blech! Dale grimaced.

Logan didn't bat an eye. She reached into the vehicle, pulled out a small hand towel, and wiped her face, then Drake's. "Love you too." She motioned him back. "Watch your head." She closed the back hatch. Smiling at Dale, she said, "Let's go."

Dale glanced into the window at Drake. Logan had the backseats down, and his dog bed from the RV covered the floor. Even without his food and paraphernalia taking some of the space, he would have easily filled the back of the SUV. Drake positioned himself so that his head was right behind the front seats. Once she got inside, they would be eye to eye. Taking a deep breath, she mentally girded her loins and opened the passenger door.

Logan glanced at Dale, who sat with her hands clenched in her lap and hadn't said a word since they'd left the animal hospital. What was going on with her? She checked on Drake via the rearview mirror. Just the sight of him made her smile. It was so good to have him with her. Logan slid her hand between the seats and patted his chest.

When Logan pulled up in front of Casey's house, Dale let out a relieved sigh and grabbed the door handle the second the SUV stopped.

"Wait." Logan caught hold of Dale's arm, holding her in place.

Dale glanced over her shoulder at Logan.

"What's wrong? You've been acting strange ever since we picked up Drake." There was only one thing Logan could think of that was causing Dale to act so strangely. She held back a disappointed sigh. "Maybe this isn't a good idea after all. I'll take Drake home with me. We'll be fine."

Dale turned in her seat to face Logan. "No. Please don't do that." Her gaze darted into the back of the SUV. "It's just...um... I've never been around a dog Drake's size and..." She ducked her head, but not before Logan saw the bright blush.

She's afraid of Drake. Logan felt like an idiot for not realizing it sooner. She had been so relieved to pick up Drake, and Dale had been so willing to help that she'd assumed Dale would be fine with him. After all Dale had been through, Logan knew how hard it must have been for her to admit her anxiety. "Hey. It's nothing to be embarrassed about. He's huge. It takes some getting used to." She stroked Dale's arm.

Dale looked up.

Captured by the warmth in Dale's gaze, Logan froze.

Drake shoved his big head between them.

Dale yelped and reared back, striking her head on the side window.

"Drake! Back up!" She scowled at him and put her arm across the space between the seats, blocking his access. "Are you okay?"

Dale's smile looked forced as she rubbed the back of her head. "I'm okay."

"I swear he doesn't mean any harm. He has no idea how big he is." Logan leaned over the console. "I'm so sorry. Are you really all right?" She ran her hand up the back of Dale's neck and into her hair, checking for any damage.

Dale's irises changed, becoming streaked with blue, and she licked her lips.

Suddenly acutely aware of her breasts pressed against Dale's arm and the silky feel of her hair between her fingers, unexpected arousal sang through her veins. Logan bit back a groan as her nipples hardened. Her fingers tightened on the back of Dale's head.

Logan wasn't sure who moved, but she found herself inches from Dale's tempting lips. Her gaze bounced between Dale's dilated pupils and slightly parted lips. *Oh God.*

A low rumble issued from Drake.

Dale jerked back. Logan's hand on the back of her head kept her from hitting the window again.

A flush that had nothing to do with arousal burned Logan's cheeks when she realized she had leaned so far over the console that she was almost in Dale's seat with her. She pushed off the side of Dale's seat and slumped back into her own. *Get control of yourself. Remember your promise.* Another second and she would have kissed her.

"He really doesn't like me."

"That's not true." She shot Drake a glare. "He—" Logan caught sight of what, or rather, who had caused Drake to react and barely resisted the urge to bury her face in her hands. "It wasn't you." She pointed out the side window behind Dale.

Dale turned in her seat and did bury her face in her hands when a grinning Casey waved. "Oh, great."

While she knew Drake interrupting them had been for the best, hearing the embarrassment in Dale's voice caused an unpleasant sensation in her chest. She bolted from the car.

Logan hurried to the back of the SUV and opened the hatch, hoping to distract Casey from what she had just witnessed. "Come meet Drake," she called.

Casey came around the back of the vehicle. She met Logan's gaze and waggled her eyebrows.

Heat rushed up Logan's neck and brought a vivid blush to her face.

Never one to be ignored, Drake woo-wooed at Casey.

Logan watched her reaction carefully.

Casey laughed. "Hello to you too." She stepped close to the SUV without a moment's hesitation. Holding out her hand to be sniffed, she said, "Aren't you a handsome boy. I haven't seen a beautiful blue like you in a long time." She glanced at Logan. "How old is he?"

"Almost six and a half."

"Wow. I would have guessed younger. Despite the white on his face, he looks in really good shape." Once Casey was sure Drake had gotten her scent and accepted her, she reached up and stroked the large white spot on his chest, then rubbed his ears.

Drake covered every inch of Casey's face with slobbery kisses.

Dale joined them but kept her distance.

Logan smiled at her and tried hard not to think about what it would have felt like to press her lips to Dale's. *Get your mind off Dale and on Drake.* She turned her back on Dale. "All right, buddy, let's get you out of there." She put her hand on his chest before he could jump out. "Wait." This was going to be the tricky part. While he occasionally had trouble jumping into the vehicle, he never had any problem getting out. But now with his recent surgery and incision, she didn't want him jumping down from the SUV.

"Wait," she repeated and moved to Drake's side. She ran one arm under his chest, just behind his front legs, and the other across his broad chest. If she could just support his weight long enough to ease his front legs to the ground...

Logan started when Casey took up a position on his other side. "Hook your arm under his front leg on your side, and I'll do the same over here," Casey said, seeming to know exactly what she had in mind. "Then use your other arm across his chest and I will too."

"Are you sure? He's heavy."

Casey braced herself. "No problem. You give the word."

"Okay, Drake. We're going to help. One. Two. Three." As they started to lift, she said, "Drake. Out."

Drake stepped forward but otherwise remained passive as they lifted his front half down. "Wait," Logan commanded again. He waited patiently as they repositioned themselves to lift the rest of him down.

"Piece of cake," Casey said with a grin. Drake let out a booming woof. "You're welcome." She leaned over and hugged him.

Logan watched them interact. While she still dreaded having to once again leave Drake, she was confident that he would be in good hands with Casey. She looked over at Dale, who had remained a good six feet away from the action. Logan beckoned her over. "Let me introduce you. He's friendly. See."

Casey, who was busy loving on Drake, glanced up. "Come on. He's a big baby like Harley—just a little bigger." Dale arched an eyebrow. "Okay. A lot bigger."

Dale approached cautiously, while Casey stepped out of the way.

Logan had a hard time reconciling this image of Dale with the one from work. Many times she had seen Dale charge into a trauma like a warrior ready to do battle.

Although Drake hadn't used his specialized training in over two years, she hoped he remembered the commands.

Once Dale reached her side, Logan guided her to stand in front of Drake. She put one hand on Dale's shoulder and the other one on Drake's shoulder. "Drake. Greet. Silent."

Drake lowered his head, then stood perfectly still.

"Offer him your hand. Palm down," Logan said. "He won't hurt you. I promise." Feeling the tension radiating from Dale, she gave her shoulder a firm squeeze.

Dale did as requested. Some of the tension eased from her posture when Drake gently sniffed, then ducked his head under Dale's hand so it came to rest on his neck.

"Stroke his neck. He likes that."

Dale stroked her hand up and down Drake's neck, gaining confidence when he never moved or made a sound.

Logan grinned and resisted the urge to hug Drake. One of the hardest things for Drake to learn was not to vocalize when greeting people while he was working. Many of the traumatic brain injury patients he had worked with were very sound sensitive. From Dale's reactions, she was convinced this wasn't simply a response to Drake's size; Logan was willing to bet she was afraid of dogs. The fact that Dale had stayed with Logan all during Drake's ordeal and found a safe place for him with Casey despite her fear made what she had done that much more special. *You are one wonderful lady.*

Their gazes met and locked.

Casey cleared her throat. "Don't want to tire Drake out too much. Maybe we should get him inside?"

Logan flushed when she realized their hands were intertwined and stroking Drake's back. She pulled away. *Get it together.* "Give me a hand unloading his stuff?"

"Sure." Dale stepped away from Drake.

Drake's head came up, but otherwise he remained motionless.

"Good boy! Release."

Drake came to life with the command. His tail started to wag, and he pressed his head into Logan's belly. She wrapped her arms around his neck and hugged him tight for a moment. "That's my good boy."

Casey came back over and patted Drake. "That was impressive. Where did he learn that?"

A rush of sadness filled Logan. She firmly pushed it away. "He used to be a therapy dog."

"Very interesting." Casey nodded, her gaze going distant.

Logan peered at her. What was that about?

Casey shook herself out of her reverie. "Come on, Drake. Let's get you settled. Your mom still needs to get some sleep before she goes to work tonight." She pointed at Dale. "You too. It's getting late. Both of you need to get some sleep."

"Yes, Mom," Dale said.

Casey flipped her off. "And you're going to eat too before you leave."

Logan smiled. Feeling more lighthearted than she had any right to, she joined Dale in gathering up Drake's stuff.

CHAPTER 23

CASEY SEARCHED THROUGH THE ROWS of gift bags on the conference table. "Ah. Here it is." She pulled out one of the bags and handed it to Dale. "Double-check Ruben's bag, and make sure there's nothing that he can't use and might upset him." She grimaced. "I still remember opening a care package not long after my amputations and finding a pair of shower shoes and some socks. I know it was an honest mistake, but it still packed an emotional punch."

"I know what you mean." Dale rummaged through the bag and made sure there was nothing objectionable, then added it back to the pile on the table. "All set." She glanced at the door to the conference room for the tenth time since she'd arrived. Not that she was counting or anything.

"She'll be here. I even drew her a map to the conference room this morning."

"You saw Logan already today?" The question came out sharper than she intended.

"Yeah. I see her every day. She comes by to have breakfast with Drake." Casey's brow furrowed for a moment before she grinned. "You're jealous."

Dale scowled. "I am not." *At least not much anyway.* "We're just friends."

"Oh, sure." She smirked. "You two looked really friendly all right when I caught you kissing in Logan's SUV."

Heat flooded Dale's face. She had thought often of that moment over the last few days. She still hadn't decided whether she should thank Drake or curse him.

"We were not kissing. Drake startled me, and I smacked my head on the window. Logan was just checking to make sure I was okay."

"Well, damn, I've been going to the wrong doctors, 'cause that sure as hell isn't the way I got checked for a head injury." Casey turned serious. "It was more than that. You can't deny you're interested in her."

"It doesn't matter. You know as well as I do that all Logan and I will ever be is friends." No matter how much a part of her longed for things to be different.

"You could be more. It's clear that she's attracted to you." She walked over to Dale and put a hand on her shoulder. "I know it was hard when you couldn't work things out with Glenda. It doesn't have to be like that with Logan. You've come so far since then. Logan's already seen—"

Dale adamantly shook her head and pulled away from Casey's touch. "No."

"Hello."

Dale spun around at the sound of Logan's voice, wondering how much she had heard. "Hey, Logan."

"Merry Christmas Eve." Casey checked her watch. "Almost."

Logan nodded toward Casey, then tentatively stepped into the room. When she spotted the gifts on the table, she paled, her hands clenching at her sides.

From the start, Dale thought this was a bad idea, and seeing Logan so stressed just confirmed that opinion. She longed to wrap her in a comforting hug and tell her she didn't have to do this but held herself back. She had to trust Logan to make her own decisions.

"You feeling okay?" Casey asked.

Logan shoved her hands into the front pockets of her jeans, and her face assumed the carefully neutral expression she wore at work. "Fine. What do I need to do?"

Casey looked ready to question Logan further, but Dale put a hand on her arm and shook her head. "We'll be going to the orthopedic ward on 5 West. I work with amputees, coordinating their care with the various departments. I know the ins and outs of the system pretty well since I'm..."

Dale tensed at the mention of amputees and glanced at Logan. She'd be seeing a number of people today with amputations who had not yet received their prosthetics. Would it remind her that Dale wasn't whole anymore either?

Casey's brow furrowed, and she sent Dale an unreadable look before turning her attention back to Logan. "Anyway, today we'll be passing out care packages to every patient on the ward." She motioned toward the bags. "Let me show you how this works. The bags are broken up into groups of ten. Each bag is labeled with a patient's name and room number. So all you have to do is take a group of bags, deliver them to the correct patient, and visit with each person for a few minutes. That's all there is to it."

Tension radiated from Logan in palpable waves. Her posture was so rigid, it looked as if she would shatter at the slightest movement.

Casey tilted her head and peered at Logan, then shot Dale a worried look. "Uh... Dale or I can go with you into the first few patients' rooms just to get you started."

Jaw clenched, Logan nodded. When she reached for the first set of bags, her breathing accelerated. She picked up the bags with trembling hands, then immediately dropped them back onto the table. "I can't. I'm sorry. I can't." She ran from the room.

"What the hell?" Casey asked as she made to follow her.

Dale grabbed her arm. "Stay here."

"But—"

"Casey, stay here, please. I'll make sure she's okay."
She sprinted after Logan.

When Dale reached the end of the hall, she slid to
a stop. The corridor ended in a T-junction. She glanced
down each hallway. Logan was nowhere in sight. *Damn
it!* Where could she have disappeared to so quickly? She
walked partway along one hallway lined with locked
office doors, then turned around and made her way
down the other side of the junction to the elevators.
She couldn't picture Logan getting on an elevator in her
agitated state.

Dale ground her teeth. She'd had her share of panic
attacks early in her recovery. *Think! Where would you
go?* She glanced around. The door to the stairway caught
her eye. She rushed to the door but caught herself before
she shoved it open. The last thing she wanted was to
startle Logan. Dale eased the door open and peered into
the landing. When she didn't see Logan, she stepped
forward and let the door shut behind her. Loud, fast
breathing alerted her to Logan's presence.

Logan was in the back corner, under the open
stairway, bent over at the waist with her hands on her
thighs. Her breath sawed in and out at a rapid pace.

She approached her slowly. "Logan. It's Dale."

There was no response.

Dale needed to stop Logan's hyperventilation before
she passed out. "Logan. Listen to me. I'm here now.
You're safe." She kept her voice calm and soothing. "You
need to slow down your breathing. Can you do that for
me?" Carefully, so as not to make things worse, Dale
lightly touched Logan's back. When she didn't flinch,
Dale gently stroked her hand up and down. "Everything's
going to be okay."

Logan looked up; her face was pale and beaded with
sweat. She struggled to get her breathing under control.
She brought her hands up and cupped them over her
mouth for several breaths.

"That's it. Nice and easy." Dale let out a relieved sigh when Logan's pulse began to slow and her respiratory rate dropped. "Good. Now take some slow, deep breaths."

As soon as Logan had herself under control, she stepped away from Dale. "I'm sorry you had to see that."

"You've got nothing to be sorry for." Although she normally wouldn't admit this to a coworker, if it helped Logan, she would. "Believe me, I've had my share of panic attacks."

Logan's eyes went wide. She hesitated for a moment. Finally she said, "I haven't had one in a long time. I thought I'd gotten past them."

"They can sneak up on you with the right trigger. It was the gifts, wasn't it?"

Logan gulped and nodded.

Dale moved closer until their shoulders almost touched. She knew it was helpful to talk about the trigger event. Now, with Logan's defenses down, might be the only chance she had to reach her. "Will you tell me about it?"

Logan stiffened and shook her head. A single step put her back against the wall.

Dale understood her reluctance, but she wanted so badly to be able to help Logan. Shoving her hands into her pockets, she stepped out from under the stairway. "Well, umm...I guess I should get back. Are you sure you're okay to drive home?"

"I'm fine." Logan dabbed the sweat from her face with her sleeve and then, acting as if nothing had happened, joined her on the stairway landing. "Would you tell Casey that I'll come pick up Drake and get his stuff as soon as she gets home from work?"

"What? Why would you do that?"

"I made a deal that I'd help, but I just...I can't. Especially today, so—"

"No. Casey wouldn't want you to do something that hurts you. I don't want you to either. You don't need to pay Casey back for taking care of Drake. I know it's only been a few days, but she's completely taken with him. She has really missed having a dog around. And Drake still needs time to heal."

"I didn't keep my commitment." She crossed her arms over her chest. "He can't stay with her."

The determination in Logan's voice made it clear that Dale was fighting a losing battle trying to convince her. "If you're bound and determined to help, we'll come up with something else." She racked her brain for an alternative. "How about New Year's Eve? You're off too, right?" Logan nodded. "We always have a party in the patients' lounge in orthopedics. You can come help with that."

While Dale wasn't completely comfortable with involving Logan in the party, after her reaction today, she didn't want to expose her to any more Christmas activities.

Clearly indecisive, Logan shuffled her feet.

"It's still the holidays. You're keeping your word."

"All right. I can do that."

"Great. I'll let Casey know." Although Dale knew she needed to get back and help Casey, she didn't want to leave Logan. "Are you sure you don't want to talk about what happened?"

"No." Logan's voice took on the overly polite tone she'd used when they had first started working together. "There's nothing to talk about. I'm over it now."

That was clearly a lie, but Dale let it go. Logan had to choose to confide in her. It wasn't something that could be forced.

Logan pulled open the stairwell door and motioned for Dale to precede her.

They walked together to the elevators.

"I'll see you tonight, then." Dale hoped for a quiet Christmas Eve. After the panic attack Logan had suffered, she didn't need any more stress.

"Okay. I'll see you at work." Logan boarded the elevator.

Dale glanced at her watch. So far, Logan was a no-show. It had become a nightly custom to share coffee and a pastry in the conference room before the start of their shift. After the events at the VA that morning, concern for Logan had been at the forefront of her mind all day. Something Logan had said about her reaction to the gift giving nagged at her. "Especially today." Dale knew all too well how anniversaries of traumatic events could be a powerful trigger.

Had Logan suffered another panic attack after leaving the VA? The thought of her suffering through another episode like that made Dale's stomach burn. She pushed away her uneaten scone.

She glanced at her watch again and sighed. Only twenty minutes to the start of the shift. Logan wasn't coming.

The door to the conference room banged open, startling her. Molly stuck her head in the doorway. "Sorry, I know you're not technically on-shift yet but—"

Dale shoved her chair back. "What have we got?"

"High-rise apartment fire. A mass-casualty alert has been issued. First victims just rolled up, and more are on the way."

"Have you seen Dr. Logan?"

"She's already in the ambulance bay."

So now Logan was avoiding her. Dale pushed away the hurt and focused on her job. "Let's go."

Fatigue weighted Dale's step as she made her way to the couch in the staff lounge. This had been the worst Christmas Eve—ever. "Hey, Kim," she greeted before flopping onto the opposite end of the couch. "How're you holding up?"

Kim McKenna straightened from her slumped position and offered a halfhearted smile. "I think that's my line."

Dale scrubbed her hands over her face. "That was hellacious." She eyed Kim, whose curly blond hair was tousled as if she had run her hands through it numerous times. Stress lines etched her face. "And you're avoiding the question, Doctor."

Kim dipped her head. "It's always hard when a child..." Her voice caught.

"I know." The victims of the fast-moving high-rise apartment fire had flooded a number of local ERs. At LA Metro alone, there had been three deaths—one of them a child. "Thanks for coming in, especially with it being Christmas Eve. I know you weren't on call tonight." Even if she had been, she wouldn't have been called in. As a psychiatrist, Kim didn't have a direct part in treating patients in this type of situation, but her help in consoling survivors and the families of the victims and dealing with the chaos had been invaluable.

"You know I'm always glad to help."

"Where's your little one tonight?" Jess was also in the ER working because of the mass casualty alert. Dale couldn't imagine how hard it must have been to leave Erin on such a special night.

A smile blossomed at the mention of her daughter, wiping away some of the stress from Kim's face. "She's with Jess's sister, Sam. When Jess got the call, I decided to come with her and see if I could help out. Erin was asleep, so Sam volunteered for babysitting duty." Kim laughed. "Although knowing Sam, I'll probably find her and Erin sharing milk and cookies while they wait for Santa when we get home."

"They better not be."

Both women started at the sound of Jess's voice. She strode across the room, leaned down, brushed back Kim's hair, and cupped her cheek in her hand. "You doing okay?" Her voice was filled with tender concern.

Kim smiled up at her. "Better now."

Dale sighed to herself. A fierce longing to have someone in her life to soothe her at times like this filled her.

Jess straightened, her face assuming the usual professional mask she wore. She turned to Dale. "The last serious burn victim was transferred." Her jaw muscles clenched, and she looked away for a moment.

A sick feeling filled Dale's stomach as she thought about the horrific burns on the little boy. He was one of the reasons she had needed to escape into the lounge.

"We're waiting on the admission paperwork and beds for the last half a dozen victims," Jess said.

"Thanks for all the help." She glanced at her watch; it was just before five a.m. "Logan and I can handle the rest of the shift on our own. Go home and spend Christmas morning with your little girl."

"Thanks." Jess offered her hand to Kim and tugged her off the couch. "Let's get out of here."

"I need to check on Riley before we go so I can update Sam."

Dale wondered why, then remembered. Riley was married to Jess's sister, Sam. She envied the two sisters' closeness. While not outright hostile, her brother had adopted his own don't-ask-don't-tell policy regarding her sexuality. As a result, they no longer shared the close involvement in each other's lives they once had.

When they exited, she sank back against the couch. Her gaze lit on the Christmas tree in the corner. The festive decorations looked totally out of place in face of the suffering that had taken place tonight. Many of the families affected by the fire would never view Christmastime the same way again. Her thoughts turned to Logan. Dale looked again at all the decorations. For once, she agreed with Logan; she couldn't stand the sight of them. She pushed off the couch and fled the room.

As Dale tugged her jacket on, she approached the nurses' station. "Have you seen Dr. Logan?"

"She already signed out," Paul said.

"Okay. Thanks." Dale held back a sigh. She hadn't gotten much more than an occasional glimpse of Logan during the whole shift. Worry nagged at Dale. After witnessing Logan's panic attack, she had no doubt that something very traumatic had happened on Christmas to Logan or someone she loved. How would dealing with the death and terrible injuries over the last ten hours affect her?

Dale stopped next to the staff exit and pulled her phone out of her pocket. Placing a call to Logan, she waited impatiently for her to answer. *Damn it.* The call went straight to voice mail.

She shoved open the door and stepped out into the bright morning sunshine. Although she had changed out of her scrubs, the smell of smoke permeated her skin and the cloying stench of burned flesh clogged her nose and throat.

She needed to clear her mind and body of the horrors of last night, and she knew just the place to do that.

CHAPTER 24

AFTER A QUICK STOP AT her apartment to shower, Dale headed for Point Dume. She hoped that the early hour and it being Christmas morning would keep the tourists at bay. The one factor on her side was that the area she favored, Pirate's Cove, was small and difficult to reach. Most people opted for the larger and much easier to access state beach on the other side of the promontory.

Dale breathed a sigh of relief as she pulled into the parking area. There were only two vehicles in the tiny lot. Her heart picked up speed at the sight of a blue Subaru Forester like the one Logan drove. Was Logan here? She cursed herself for not paying attention to Logan's license plate previously. Shaking her head, she pushed away the longing to be with Logan. Even if Logan had gone to the beach, what was the likelihood that she would have picked this beach, almost an hour away from the RV park, instead of one of the much closer ones?

Standing at the top of the stairway that led down to the secluded cove, she gazed down at the steep descent. The stairs were always a challenge, even when she wasn't tired, as she was now. Taking a firm grip on the railing, she started down.

Dale scanned the cove as she worked her way down the stairway. There was no one in sight on the small sheltered patch of sand. When she reached the bottom of the stairs, she opened her leather jacket and drew in a breath, letting the crisp ocean air fill her lungs and wash away the lingering stench of last night's suffering and death. She stopped to massage her cramped thigh before rounding the outcropping and moving onto the beach.

That was when she spotted the person sitting against the cliff wall where she had planned to spend the morning, in a natural alcove protected from the wind.

Damn! So much for solitude. As she started to walk away, her thoughts went back to the vehicle in the parking lot. Could it be Logan's? She tried to convince herself it was just wishful thinking. She peered at the person, who faced away from her, preventing her from making out if it was a man or a woman. A long-forgotten memory arose of another encounter on this very beach with a woman and her huge dog. *I'll be dammed. Logan and Drake.*

It seemed fate had thrown them together from the very start. The significance was too much for Dale to ignore. While she was loath to intrude on someone's privacy, she couldn't make herself walk away; she had to know.

Striding forward until she was a few feet from the person, she stopped. "Logan?"

The person's head jerked up.

Seeing Logan's tear-streaked face broke her heart. She closed the distance between them in a flash and squatted down next to Logan, cursing her prosthetic that kept her from kneeling easily.

Haunted, red-rimmed eyes filled with the pain of her secrets met Dale's gaze.

She dropped onto the sand next to Logan. Cupping Logan's face in her hand, she stroked her thumb across her cheek.

Logan leaned into the touch. "How did you find me?"

"I didn't. This is the place I come when I need to clear my head. I've always been drawn to the sight and sound of the ocean."

"Me too. I just had to get away. Last night was..." She swallowed heavily. "Those families will never think of Christmas the same way again. Especially the teenager that started the fire; she'll never forgive herself for her brother's death."

"It was an accident; she didn't do it intentionally."

Logan stiffened and pulled back. "It doesn't matter. She'll never be free of the guilt."

That's when it dawned on her that Logan might be speaking from personal experience. "Tell me about that Christmas."

Logan didn't even pretend to not know what Dale was asking about. Fresh tears welled in her eyes, and a tremor shook her body. "My sister died on Christmas Eve."

Oh, Logan. Repressed tears stung Dale's eyes. "I'm so sorry."

Logan shook her head roughly. "No. That's not right. She was murdered on Christmas Eve." She spat the words out as if they were too bitter to keep inside anymore. "Emily was unloading Christmas packages from her trunk when some bastard stabbed her to death—over some fucking gifts." Logan's voice caught, but she forged on. "When they found her, torn-open boxes were scattered all around her, covered in her blood."

Logan's pain and anguish struck Dale like a physical blow. "I'm sorry." It was so inadequate, but she didn't know what else to say. She wrapped her arms around Logan and pulled her close.

Logan resisted for a moment, then gut-wrenching sobs shook her frame and she collapsed against Dale.

Holding her close, Dale pressed her cheek to the top of Logan's head and murmured soothingly until the storm had passed. When Logan started to pull away, Dale tightened her arms around her. "No. Don't. Please." After hearing what Logan had suffered, she needed the comfort as much as Logan did.

Logan relaxed against her and wrapped her arms around Dale's waist.

Dale wasn't sure how long she'd sat holding her. When Logan shifted uncomfortably, she reluctantly released her. Only then did she become aware of her own tears.

Logan gently brushed Dale's tears away.

Dale draped her arm across Logan's shoulders and leaned back against the cliff wall.

Logan settled against her.

In companionable silence, they watched the waves, two wounded souls drawn together by their shared pain.

Over the last hour, dark clouds had moved in, and the temperature had dropped, but Dale was loath to disturb Logan where she rested against her side. And despite the cold seeping through her jeans and making her leg ache, she wasn't eager to let go of Logan.

A sudden change in the wind blew an icy gust into their little alcove. They both gasped. A misty rain followed on the heels of the wind.

Dale gave Logan's shoulders a brief squeeze. "I guess we should go." She climbed awkwardly to her feet. Brushing sand from her clothes, she tried to surreptitiously rub some circulation back into her leg.

Logan dusted the sand from her own clothes.

Aware of Logan's watchful gaze, Dale struggled not to limp as they made their way back to the steps. Challenging to start with, the ascent was going to be treacherous in the rain.

"You go first," Logan said, motioning toward the narrow stairs. Only one of them could go up at a time.

"No." No way in hell was she going to go up first. If something should happen, she wasn't going to be the cause of Logan getting hurt. "You go first. I'll be right behind you."

Logan crossed her arms over her chest. "No. You first. I'll be right behind you."

Dale squared off with Logan, mirroring her position. "No. Go on."

Logan's brow lowered, and she shook her head.

Dale stared at her for several long moments. "So we're just going to stand here in the rain?"

"Apparently." Logan motioned toward the steps. "Unless you decide to move your ass up the stairs—first."

Dale growled. "Damn stubborn woman," she muttered.

Logan snorted. "Pot calling the kettle black."

Dale couldn't believe this was happening. She thought Casey was relentless. She threw her fiercest glare at Logan, who still didn't budge an inch. "Fine. Have it your way."

Logan's expression instantly softened. She put her hand on Dale's arm. "Thank you."

Dale gazed into Logan's eyes and took a step closer, drawn in by the emotion swirling in the topaz-brown depths. A cramp in her thigh brought her up short. *Damn.*

"What's wrong?"

"Nothing."

Logan's eyes narrowed.

Dale needed to get up the stairs—while she still could. "Come on." She grabbed the rails and headed up the steps before Logan could question her further.

By the time they approached the top of the stairs, Logan had a death grip on the railing. Dale had faltered several times, but caught herself and recovered. As hard as it was to watch her struggle, Logan knew Dale would resent her intervening. She had to do this for herself if she could. At least she had given in and allowed Logan to follow her up the steps.

When they reached solid ground, relief washed over Logan, and she barely restrained herself from pulling Dale into her arms, well aware that she wouldn't appreciate the emotional display. She blew out a breath. "The cove is great, but those stairs are a bitch. My calves are burning."

Dale turned around, surprise evident on her face. "Yeah. They do give you a workout."

Logan stepped close to her. "I'm glad we both ended up here today."

"Me too."

The world around them receded as Logan lost herself in Dale's stormy gray eyes.

Dale closed the distance between them until their bodies lightly brushed. Her irises changed, becoming streaked with blue.

Logan's heart rate tripped double time. She knew they were about to kiss and what a bad idea it was but couldn't seem to make herself move.

An ice-cold gust of rain doused them, cooling her rapidly rising libido. She gasped and stepped back.

"Son of a bitch," Dale muttered.

Logan was torn between thankfulness at the interruption and shaking her fist at the sky. At the moment, her body was all for the latter. "Come on." She grabbed Dale's hand and headed for the parking lot.

By the time they reached the lot, the storm had struck full force.

Reluctantly releasing Dale's hand, Logan said, "See you tonight." She ducked her head against the pounding rain and headed for her SUV.

Dale grabbed her arm before she could walk away. "Come home with me."

After what almost happened a few minutes ago, that didn't seem like a very bright idea. And then there was the whole issue of the Christmas decorations that she was sure were at Dale's place. She couldn't face that today. Logan started to shake her head.

As if she had guessed her thoughts, Dale said, "There aren't any decorations."

Logan hesitated as dark thoughts stirred. *You deserve to be alone. What would she think of you if you told her everything?* Would Dale even want to be around her if she knew of Logan's part in Emily's death? Guilt swamped her, and she struggled to push the feeling down.

Dale wrapped her arm around her shoulders and tugged her close as if she sensed her rising emotions.

Logan burrowed her face against Dale's rain-soaked leather jacket.

"Please," Dale whispered close to her ear.

Logan couldn't bring herself to deny Dale. She straightened and met her warm gaze. "Okay."

Dale lightly touched Logan's cheek with her free hand before letting her arm drop. "Great. Call me from your car, and I'll give you the address. That way, if we get separated you'll be able to find my place." She turned away and headed for her Jeep before Logan could change her mind.

Logan trudged toward her SUV. Once inside, she pushed her sopping hair off her face. She shouldn't have agreed to go with Dale. While that was undoubtedly true, she clung to one thought: with the myriad of beaches along this stretch of the coast, they had ended up on the same one, Dale once again showing up just when she needed her most—that had to mean something. Her phone rang, pulling her from her thoughts. She retrieved it from her pocket. A smile tugged at her lips as she pressed the connect button. "Hey, Dale."

CHAPTER 25

DALE HAD BEEN UNCHARACTERISTICALLY QUIET since meeting in the parking garage. Logan peered at her through half-lidded eyes as they rode the elevator to Dale's apartment. Did she regret inviting Logan to her home? Logan was certainly having second thoughts.

When the elevator dinged, announcing their arrival on the third floor, Dale started. She shook her head, then hesitantly met Logan's gaze. "I'm at the end of the hall."

Worry tugged at Logan as they walked down the hall. Dale was unsuccessfully trying to hide a limp. Had she injured herself on the stairs at the beach? Or was it from wearing her prosthesis too long? She longed to ask the questions but resisted since Dale seemed uncomfortable with any mention of her injuries.

Dale unlocked the door to her apartment, pushed it open, and motioned Logan inside.

Logan stepped just inside the door and hesitated, very aware of her shoes that were leaving sand and drops of water on Dale's hardwood floor.

Dale had no such concerns. She pulled off her soaked leather jacket and hung it on a nearby hall tree. "Give me your jacket, and I'll hang it here to dry." Her athletic shoes squished as she made her way into the living room. She glanced over her shoulder and seemed surprised to see Logan still standing by the door. "Come into my bedroom, and I'll get you some dry clothes. Don't worry about the floor. I'll take care of it once we get dry. Then I'll make us something to eat."

A rush of unexpectedly strong arousal short-circuited Logan's brain at the "come into my bedroom."

The pulsing at her core was just as quickly doused when the rest of Dale's words sunk in. No way was she going to try to squeeze into Dale's too-small clothes. Dale was superbly muscled and not the least bit skinny, and while they were the same height, that didn't change the fact that Logan had twenty-five pounds on her—if not more. "That's okay. I'll just take off my socks and shoes." She quickly shucked the aforementioned items and tucked her wet socks into her shoes. "My pants dried out in the car." She walked into the living room, her toes curling at the feel of the cold wood beneath her bare feet. "You go ahead and get changed. I'm fine."

Dale glanced down at Logan's pants, then back up, a scowl marring her face. "You're not very good at telling an...untruth."

"I'm not—" Logan grimaced when Dale arched an eyebrow. Okay, so she was lying, but for a good reason. She didn't want to be forced into admitting Dale's clothes were going to be too small for her. "They'll be dry soon. I'm good."

"You're being ridiculous. We're both soaked." She tugged Logan by the hand. "Come on. I've got sweats that will fit you." She met her gaze and clearly read her real concern. "No worries."

Logan ducked her head, a flush heating her cheeks at being so transparent. She allowed Dale to lead her to her bedroom. A queen bed was centered on the far wall with a leather chair and ottoman tucked in the corner next to it. A short, double-sided oak bookcase filled the wall opposite the bed and had a large TV perched on top. She caught a glimpse of what looked like forearm crutches before Dale shoved them under the bed.

Dale rummaged in the chest of drawers and pulled out a pair of sweatpants, a long-sleeved T-shirt, and a pair of thick athletic socks. "Here you go. The shirt might be a little tight," she stammered, a bright blush lighting her face.

What did she have to be embarrassed about? Logan was the one who was going to look like a fat blimp.

Dale cleared her throat. "But the pants will fit fine."

Logan doubted that very much. Clenching her teeth, she forced herself to accept the clothes, at the same time cursing herself for not thinking this through before agreeing to come home with Dale. But she had few options other than leaving. And if she was honest with herself, she didn't want to do that. She was freezing and needed to get out of her wet clothes, as did Dale. "Thanks."

Dale returned to the dresser and pulled out a second set of clothes.

She darted her gaze around the room. "Um...where should I change?" No way was she going to strip in front of Dale. She couldn't imagine Dale would be comfortable with that either.

"The shower is right through there." She pointed toward an open doorway. "Towels and washcloths are on the rack above the commode. Shampoo and body wash are in the shower."

No way! Logan hugged the clothes to her chest. Changing into dry clothing was one thing, but she had no intention of getting naked and showering. That was way too far out of her comfort zone. "Ah...no thanks. I'll just change into the dry stuff, and I'll be fine."

"You'll never get warm unless you get a hot shower. Go on. Just leave your wet clothes on the counter, and I'll get them after I take my shower."

Logan shook her head.

Dale stepped closer. Her brow lowered, and her eyes turned steely gray.

Uh. Oh. Logan was coming to know that look.

"I only have the one full bathroom, and I'm not taking a shower until after you do. So the longer you delay, the longer I have to stand here and be miserable and cold."

Logan had no doubt that Dale would do exactly as she said. "That's dirty pool."

"You're right." Dale motioned toward the streaks of sand and water they had left on the floor. "We've got dirty water and sand. Get your ass in the shower so I can clean up this mess and get out of these wet clothes."

Logan growled at Dale's twisting of her words. "I can help clean up."

Crossing her arms over her chest, Dale met her glare. "Just get in the shower."

And she calls me stubborn. She huffed out a breath. "Okay. But you have to let me fix us something to eat. I can make whatever you had planned. I'm a good cook."

Dale started to protest, then grinned. "Deal. You shower and I'll set everything out for you in the kitchen." She turned and walked away before Logan could change her mind.

As much as it made her uncomfortable using Dale's shower, the thought of getting out of her wet clothes and warming her chilled body quickened Logan's steps.

As soon as the bathroom door clicked shut, Dale slumped against the wall outside the bedroom with a pained groan. Although she was going to pay a steep price, she didn't regret inviting Logan home. She couldn't bear the thought of Logan spending the day alone. And truth be told, regardless of the fact that Logan had a stubborn streak a mile wide, Dale took comfort in her nearness.

Pushing off the wall, she gritted her teeth against the stabbing pain that shot up her leg. She just hoped like hell that she would be able to get the prosthetic back on after her shower, because right now, it felt as if a nail were being driven into the base of her stump. She glanced down the hall at the water and sand on the floor, then glared down at her soaking wet shoes covered in sand. She was going to have to at least take off the shoes. But that meant exposing her prosthetic foot. *Damn.* What was the point of cleaning up if she was just going to continue to track sand everywhere? *Screw it.* She limped back to the front door and removed her shoes and socks before cuffing the bottom of her jeans.

She was tempted to put on a pot of coffee or make some hot chocolate, but either would keep her awake. And at some point, she would need to sleep before work tonight and so would Logan.

First things, first. Knowing she didn't have a lot of time, she set about cleaning up the floor.

Dale kept an ear tuned for the shower shutting off. Thoughts of Logan, naked with hot, soapy water cascading down her lush curves, brought a warm flush to her chilled body and was a welcome distraction from the pain of wearing her prosthesis far too long.

When the shower cut off, Dale quickly finished with the floor and headed for the kitchen. She regretfully pushed aside her fantasies. That was all they would ever be—unfulfilled fantasies.

Surveying the items on the kitchen counter, Dale made sure she hadn't missed anything Logan would need.

"What am I making?"

Dale glanced up.

Logan stood at the entrance of the small kitchen. Her T-shirt hugged Logan's every curve and stretched tight over her ample chest.

Good lord. Her mouth suddenly desert dry, she had to clear her throat twice before she found her voice. "I was going to make pecan pancakes."

Logan crossed her arms over her chest and eyed the ingredients spread across the counter. "So you like to cook too?"

"Honestly, not really, but I make an exception for today. It's a family tradition to have them for breakfast..." Dale caught herself before she could say Christmas morning.

Logan's expression dimmed, and Dale felt like kicking herself.

Dale picked up the box of pancake mix. Her enthusiasm for the Christmas treat had fled with Logan's smile. "Actually, I wasn't thinking. I don't have a written recipe. How about you make something else, eggs maybe?"

Logan took the box from her hand. "I can make the pancakes." A smile touched her lips. "I don't need a recipe."

"You don't?"

Logan elbowed her. "Don't sound so surprised. I told you. I'm a good cook. I'd like to make them."

Dale grinned. "That's good, 'cause mine usually aren't that great. I always tell myself it's more the thought that counts."

"I've got this under control. Get out of those wet clothes and shower." Logan shooed her out the room.

"Yes, ma'am." Dale threw her a mock salute.

As Dale padded into her bedroom, the squeak made by her forearm crutches on the hardwood floor sounded louder than usual. She dropped down onto the side of the bed and shoved the crutches underneath it. While a quick massage during her shower had helped ease some of the pain of her residual limb, she knew it was going to be a bitch donning the prosthetic. Eyeing the damn thing with more distaste than usual, she forced herself to pick it up. She had already put a dry sock and shoe on the prosthesis. She did the same with her real leg.

After having worn the prosthetic for over sixteen hours, what she really needed to do was leave it off until she left for work tonight. She blew out a breath. That wasn't going to happen. Not with Logan here. She retrieved all her supplies from the bedside table.

After pulling up her sweatpant leg above her knee, she inspected her residual limb. She had developed a silver-dollar-size rub spot directly over the distal end of the stump. *Damn it!* Without proper care, the skin could easily break down and become infected.

She took care of the stump, then carefully rolled a clean liner over it. She hesitated, then prepared to don the prosthesis. "Embrace the suck," she muttered, repeating Casey's favorite phrase as she pushed the limb into the socket. Tears sprang into her eyes. *Fuck, that hurts*. She took slow, deep breaths until the worst of the pain had subsided.

Once she was sure she could stand, she got to her feet. She hissed as she pushed the stump all the way into the bottom of the socket until she heard the lock click. Clenching her jaw, she took several steps. It hurt like a son of a bitch, but she managed not to limp too blatantly. She hoped it would be enough to convince Logan that she was fine.

She gathered up their wet clothes and wrapped them in a dry towel. When she opened her bedroom door, an enticing aroma caught her attention. She took a deep breath, and her mouth started to water.

Dale headed down the hall as fast as her leg would allow.

The dining room table was already set with plates and silverware. Logan stepped around the corner with two glasses of orange juice. She stopped in her tracks when she caught sight of Dale.

Logan's gaze swept down Dale's body. She looked up with a scowl. "Why are you still wearing that?"

She wasn't wearing anything from earlier. "What?" Dale tried to figure out what had garnered Logan's disapproval.

"Your prosthetic. You've had it on a really long time."

Dale's jaw dropped open. She couldn't believe Logan had even mentioned her prosthesis, much less questioned her about wearing it. Shame at her infirmity swept her. She ducked her head. "It's fine."

Logan set the juice glasses on the table with an audible thump. "Apparently, you're not very good at telling...untruths either. You're not fine, or you wouldn't be limping."

Dale jerked her head up and scowled at Logan. "I'm just a little tired." She hefted the bundle in her arms. "I'm going to go throw these in the washer."

Logan caught Dale's arm before she could walk away. "Look me in the eyes, and tell me you're not in any pain."

Damn the woman! "I know when I need to take it off. I'll do it later."

Logan stared into Dale's eyes for several moments, then shook her head. She reached for the wet clothes Dale still held.

"What are you doing?" Dale tightened her arms around the bundle.

"Getting my clothes. I'm leaving."

"What? Why?"

"If you won't take care of yourself while I'm here, then I have to leave so you will."

Dale stared at her in openmouthed shock. Logan was so matter of fact, as if it were no big deal for Dale to remove her leg and allow Logan to see her at her weakest. Thoughts of seeing pity in Logan's eyes made Dale's stomach churn. She hung her head. "I can't."

Logan put a gentle hand on Dale's arm. "I understand."

Dale looked up and met Logan's gaze, which was filled with warmth and caring.

Tugging the clothes from Dale, Logan said, "I'll bring your sweats to work once I get them laundered." She sorted out her stuff and then turned toward the door.

Longing warred with shame inside Dale.

"Wait!" she said before Logan could open the front door. For weeks, she had longed for the chance to spend time alone with Logan, and now that she had it within her grasp, she was screwing it up. Her gaze darted to the dining table set for breakfast. The scent of pancakes lingered in the air. "Please stay."

Logan turned to face her. "Will you take care of yourself? If not, I can't stay." Her tone was calm, but resolute.

Dale clenched her fists at her sides. "Yes."

Logan quickly returned to her. She cupped Dale's face in her palm. "Thank you."

Leaning into the touch, Dale allowed it to ground her and soothe her anxiety. She reluctantly pulled back. "Let me throw this stuff in the washer, then we'll have breakfast."

Logan caught her arm. "And you'll do what you need to?"

Dale blew out a breath. Logan was the most infuriating—and intriguing—woman that she had ever met. "Yes. That too."

Logan briefly squeezed her arm before turning toward the kitchen. "Good. Hurry up. If I leave the pancakes warming too long, they'll get soggy and won't be any good."

After tossing the clothes in the washer, Dale made her way to the bedroom. She closed the door behind her, leaned against it, and let out a shaky breath. It wasn't as if no one had ever seen her without her leg; plenty of people had at the VA. But this was Logan, who was not only a coworker, but also the woman she was strongly attracted to, despite her best attempts to ignore it.

Knowing that Logan was waiting, Dale moved to the side of the bed and plopped down. She pulled up her pant leg and released her prosthetic, unable to hold back a sigh of relief as the pressure on the stump eased. She removed the stump sock and liner, then shoved her pant leg back down. As she stared at the empty pant leg, her breathing began to accelerate at the thought of facing Logan like this. A mental picture of Logan, her eyes brimming with warmth and understanding, filled Dale's mind. She latched onto the image and fought the rising panic attack.

After several long moments, Dale took a shuddering breath, then some deeper ones. That had been the closest she had come to a panic attack in almost two years. She didn't miss the irony of the fact that the same person who caused her to have the attack was the same one who had stopped it. *Enough of this.* She needed to either do this or let Logan leave.

Dale reached under the bed and pulled out her forearm crutches. Mentally squaring her shoulders, she padded out of the room.

The open architecture of the apartment allowed her to see Logan standing next to the dining room table. She looked up as Dale approached.

"Have a seat, and I'll grab the pancakes from the oven," Logan said. But instead of going into the kitchen, Logan headed her way.

Dale stood straight and tall, waiting for Logan's reaction. When Logan put her hand on Dale's arm, just below the cuff of her crutch, she forced herself not to recoil.

"Thank you for letting me make breakfast. I really love to cook, and I haven't gotten a chance to do that in over two years. I've only got a microwave in my motor home."

That's it? I'm standing here with no leg, and she's talking about cooking. Logan never ceased to amaze her. The tight knot in her stomach released its grip. "Bring them on. I'm starving."

Logan smiled. "You got it."

Logan leaned against the kitchen counter and blew out a breath hard enough to ruffle her hair. That had gone better than she expected. After seeing the shame and vulnerability on Dale's face, she had almost backed off on her insistence that she remove her prosthetic. She knew it was asking a lot, but there was no way that she could stay otherwise. Her admiration of Dale continued to grow. *And your attraction.*

Shoving away the unwelcome reminder, she grabbed a hot pad off the counter and pulled the pancakes from the oven. The nutty, sweet scent rising from the platter made her stomach growl. She snagged the bottle of syrup she had warming in a bowl of hot water from the sink.

"Ta-da." Logan set the pancakes and warm maple syrup on the table with a flourish.

"They look great. Mine always fall apart." Dale took a deep breath. "They smell even better." She forked two of the pancakes onto her plate and smothered them in syrup.

At the first bite, her eyes closed, and she let out a moan that sent a flush through Logan's body. "These are incredible. What did you do? My mom's are really good, but they never tasted this fantastic." She took another bite.

"Family secret." Logan smiled at the memories of her grandmother. It was the first time since Emily's death that she had allowed herself to remember any of the good times with her family.

Dale polished off the first pancake before replying. "Well, if these are the only ones I'm going to get..." She tugged the plate of pancakes over to her side of the table. "Mine!"

Logan laughed, something she never thought she would do again on Christmas. "Give me one of those." She mock-threatened Dale with her fork before stabbing one of the pancakes and flipping it onto her plate.

Dale grinned as she quickly forked a third pancake onto her own plate.

A short while later, Logan put her fork on her empty plate. While there had been no conversation during the meal beyond "pass the syrup, please," it had been a comfortable silence. Now that she was warm and pleasantly full, she was getting sleepy.

"You want the last one?"

Logan glanced up. Dale already had the last pancake halfway onto her plate. "Go ahead." She smiled when Dale didn't offer even a token resistance. *Guess she really does like them.*

Dale downed the last pancake with the same enthusiasm she had the previous five. She pushed her chair back and patted her stomach. "Those really were excellent. Thank you."

"You're welcome." Logan stood and began to gather up the dishes. Her fatigue was beginning to weigh her down. She still had at minimum a half-hour drive home, probably more with the continuing rain.

Using the table, Dale pushed herself into a standing position. "You cooked. I'll clean up."

It was on the tip of Logan's tongue to protest. The stubborn jut of Dale's chin made her stifle the words. She had already pushed her as far as she dared today. After all, Dale had her pride, and Logan respected that. "Okay."

Dale's eyebrow arched, then her eyes narrowed. "But?"

Logan smothered a smile. "But nothing. Seems fair to me." She picked up the plates and silverware and took them into the kitchen. She'd tried to keep the mess to a minimum while cooking, but there were still utensils, bowls, and the griddle that needed cleaning. While it bothered her, she forced herself to leave it to Dale.

The tap of Dale's crutches announced her arrival. She set their glasses onto the kitchen counter.

A huge yawn caught Logan unaware. She scrubbed her hands over her face, trying to push away the encroaching grogginess. "I've got to get going. I'm beat."

Dale glanced out the storm-drenched kitchen window. "The storm has really gotten bad. Are you okay to drive?"

"I'll be fine."

"You could stay."

Logan met Dale's gaze. The warmth in her blue-streaked gray eyes drew her in. It surprised her just how much she wanted to say yes. But she couldn't. It was too outside her comfort zone. "Thank you, but no." She smothered another yawn.

Dale sighed. "Okay."

They walked together to the front door. The tap of Dale's crutches on the hardwood floor filled the silence between them.

Logan grimaced as she slipped into her wet shoes.

"Dang. I forgot to put the clothes in the dryer."

"No problem. You can bring them to me tonight."

They stood together for several moments, neither seemingly eager to part.

This time it was Dale who yawned.

Logan shook herself. "I'm out of here. I'll see you tonight." She opened the front door. Before she gave herself a chance to really think about it, she turned back to Dale and placed a kiss on her cheek. Her lips tingled at the brief contact. She forced herself to step back. "Thank you for today."

When Dale reached out to touch Logan's cheek, her crutch clanked against the doorframe. Her face flushed. "See you tonight. Bye."

Logan found herself staring at the closed door. She touched her still-tingling lips. With a sigh that was part sadness and part relief, she headed for her SUV.

CHAPTER 26

As she approached the counter, Dale scanned the nurses' station for Logan. When she realized she was stroking the cheek that Logan had kissed, heat flooded her face, and she jerked her hand away. The kiss had been totally chaste, but that hadn't stopped arousal from coursing through her veins. Then, of course, her damn crutch had hit the doorframe and doused her ardor like a bucket of cold water. Worry had nagged at her after Logan left, but finally, exhaustion had won out, and she'd gotten some much-needed rest. She hoped Logan had done the same.

"Merry Christmas, Dr. Parker," Molly said from her spot at the computer workstation in the otherwise deserted nurses' station.

"Merry Christmas." It was technically still Christmas Day for several more hours. Usually, she enjoyed the holiday, but this year, she would be glad when it was over. As she pulled off her jacket, she glanced at the intake board. There were currently only four patients in the department. "Has it been this quiet all evening?"

"I've only been here since six, but it's been dead the whole time."

"Good. Keep your fingers crossed it stays that way." After yesterday's disaster, everyone could use a break.

Molly nodded. "I'm with you on that. Last night was..." She roughly shook her head. Something behind Dale caught her attention. "Hey, Dr. Logan."

"Good evening," Logan said.

Dale wasn't surprised that Molly didn't wish Logan a Merry Christmas. While Logan was usually careful about keeping her emotions to herself, her complete disregard for the holiday had been unmistakable. With what Dale now knew, she was amazed that Logan coped as well as she had during the holiday season.

Dale turned to face Logan, an automatic smile tugging at her lips. "Hi."

Logan returned the smile and held up a plastic grocery bag. "Come on." She motioned down the hall toward the conference room.

Dale glanced at her watch. With only four patients, changeover wouldn't take long, so they still had plenty of time before the official start of their shift. She couldn't see what was in the bag and didn't much care as long as it allowed her to spend time with Logan.

The ambulance bay double doors swung open with a whoosh before Dale got half a dozen steps from the nurses' station.

Sighing, she turned back. Logan did too.

A pair of EMTs pushed a gurney through the open doors. "Forty-four-year-old white male. Facial trauma. Heart rate one-thirty-five, BP ninety over sixty-two, diaphoretic, and complaining of chest pain. Second ambulance is right behind us with the girlfriend."

Another EMT pushed a second gurney into the ER. When the woman strapped to the stretcher spotted her boyfriend, she spewed a string of curses and struggled against the restraints. "Twenty-three-year-old white female. Multiple BB pellets in the neck. Possible fractured hand." He reeled off the rest of her stats, ignoring her continued ranting.

Dale exchanged a look with Logan and then headed for the woman, while Logan took the man.

Karen Armstrong, a former resident and now an attending, came trotting down the hall. "What have we got?"

Logan waved her off. "I'm taking this one." She grabbed the side of the gurney. "Let's go," she said to the EMT.

"You just wait, you bastard," the woman yelled as her boyfriend was taken away.

Molly joined Dale next to the woman's gurney.

"Get her into an exam room, and I'll be right there."

When Molly grabbed the gurney, the woman bucked hard against the straps. "What the fuck are you...ten? I want a real doctor."

Molly started and took a step back.

Dale glared at the woman. "Knock it off." She motioned for Molly. "Go on, get her in a room."

Molly reached for the railing and flinched back when the young woman began to curse in earnest.

"Let's go." One of the EMTs took a firm hold of the stretcher and shoved it down the hall. Molly docilely followed him.

Dale shook her head. So far, Molly wasn't impressing her. She was almost six months into her residency and still way too tentative with patients.

"Give her a chance. She'll toughen up," Karen said.

Dale nodded. She hoped Karen was right. "Go ahead and sign out. Logan and I have this covered." She loped after the gurney.

Dale walked up to the nurses' station with Molly in tow. "You can't let a patient get to you like that. It's not personal. Especially as an ER doctor, you're going to see people at their absolute worst."

The woman with the fractured hand and BB pellets lodged in her neck had continued to harangue Molly during the exam and removal of the BBs. Molly had tried to turn over the procedure to Dale several times.

Molly sniffed back tears. "I know. But—"

"No buts. Learning to deal with all types of people is part of our job. You have to do your best to ignore bad behavior while remaining calm and professional. We have a legal obligation to provide emergency care regardless of how unlikable or disruptive a patient is. You need to toughen up." It didn't help the situation that Molly did look extremely young or that her demeanor was meek at the best of times.

"Okay. I'll try."

Dale forced a stern expression onto her face. Several times she had seen other residents cover for Molly when she couldn't cope. That had to stop. They weren't doing her any favors. "I understand that it's hard, but you need to do more than try. Stop asking other people to take on the difficult patients for you. Not everyone is cut out to work in the ER. If that's the case, you need to find that out now—not later in your residency."

Molly's shoulders slumped, and her eyes filled with fresh tears. "Okay."

Dale blew out a breath. She hated being so hard on the resident, but Molly's behavior was becoming a pattern. As she turned away from Molly, Dale spotted Logan bent over, looking at one of the computer monitors. She took a moment to lament the fact that Logan was wearing a baggy lab coat that hid her ass. She mentally slapped herself on the back of the head.

As if sensing the regard, Logan looked up.

A blush heated her cheeks. Dale glanced away, hoping Logan wouldn't notice.

"Got a question for you," Logan said.

"Sure." Dale stepped over to the monitor. X-rays of a facial series were displayed on the screen. "That the chest pain guy?"

"Yeah. Mr. Arron's cardiac enzymes came back normal, and his EKG was unchanged. I think the chest pain was brought on by stress. I guess getting repeatedly punched in the face could do that to you." Logan shook her head. "What's the procedure here for reporting domestic violence?"

"You need to call in a report to the local authorities. Unless it's an imminent threat type of situation, it's best to wait until the end of shift. Police rarely come out at night. Then you have two days to file a written report. I'll show you the forms. Is he going to press charges?"

"I tried to convince him to, but no luck. He swears this is the first time it happened."

Dale arched an eyebrow. After dealing with the girlfriend, she found that hard to believe.

"I didn't believe him either," Logan said. "Is she going to file against him for shooting her with the BB gun?"

"He said he shot her? That's not the story she told. According to Ms. Bishop, her boyfriend's twelve-year-old son shot her accidentally while trying to break up the— in her words— 'disagreement' between them."

"What do you suggest, then? The shooting has to be reported. But do we additionally file domestic violence reports on both of them?"

Dale nodded. "I think it's the best way to go. Let the police and social services sort it out."

"Okay." Logan motioned toward the grocery bag she had abandoned on the counter earlier. "Things have quieted back down. How about we head for the conference room and have our snack?"

"Sounds good." As they headed down the hall, Dale asked, "What did you bring?"

"Well, most places were closed because of—" She clearly couldn't bring herself to say the word.

Dale reached out and squeezed Logan's shoulder in silent understanding.

"Anyway, wasn't much open, but I found a grocery store, and it had a surprisingly big bakery inside. So I picked up an assortment of rugelach and some bowls of cut-up fruit that looked really fresh. And I have a thermos with hazelnut coffee."

Dale's stomach rumbled.

Logan laughed. "And here I thought you might still be full from all those pancakes."

Elbowing her, Dale said, "It wasn't that many." She turned serious as she met Logan's gaze. "Did you get some rest?" Of course, she was really asking about a lot more than that but wasn't sure Logan would respond now that they were at work.

"Yes, I did. The time we spent together this morning... it helped a lot."

Dale's heart fluttered at the openness and vulnerability in Logan's gaze. She longed to pull her into her arms as she had on the beach and shield her from anything ever hurting her again. Even as she thought it, she acknowledged the impossibility. She settled for placing her hand on the small of Logan's back, enjoying the warmth that permeated her palm.

Logan hustled into the staff lounge at the end of the shift to pick up her jacket and backpack. She was eager to get to Casey's, as she had not gotten to see Drake yesterday. By the time she had left Dale's, Casey had already taken Drake to her parents' home, where she would be spending the day. She'd had some reservations about that, but Casey had reassured her that she would keep a close eye on him, and it was much better than leaving him alone all day.

The lounge door swung open, admitting Dale.

"Hey, Logan. Could I interest you in going out to breakfast? I still want to introduce you to the omelets at Gina's Café."

While tempted, Logan needed to be with Drake. "Sorry. I already have plans for breakfast with Drake and Casey."

A scowl flashed across Dale's face before she abruptly turned away. "Yeah. Okay. Some other time."

She jerked open the door of her locker with more force than necessary.

Taken aback by Dale's sudden change in mood, Logan frowned. Did Dale think she was trying to co-opt her friendship with Casey? Logan shook her head. That didn't seem like Dale at all. Unwilling to ignore the possibility, she approached Dale. "I'd like to have breakfast together. Why don't you come with me to Casey's?"

Dale turned, her smile once again in place. "Really?"

"Of course. Get your stuff and let's go."

As she turned back to her locker, Dale felt like kicking herself for overreacting. Casey had told her that Logan had breakfast every morning with Drake. While she knew her jealousy of the time they spent together was ridiculous, she hadn't managed to squash it.

The ringing of Logan's phone pulled Dale from her thoughts.

Logan pulled the phone out of her pocket and glanced at the screen. "Speak of the devil." She hit the connect button. "Hi, Casey. We were just getting ready to head your way. Dale's joining us."

When the smile dropped from Logan's face, Dale tensed. Had something happened to Drake?

"I understand. Maybe tomorrow." The disappointment in Logan's voice was palpable.

She moved closer to Logan. "What's wrong?"

Logan pulled the phone away from her ear. "Casey's too tired for company."

Dale frowned. That didn't sound like Casey. Something wasn't right here. "Let me talk to her."

Logan handed over her phone.

"Hey, Case. You okay?"

"No biggie. Just tired after a day with the family."

Now Dale knew something was wrong. Casey loved the time she spent with family and always claimed it energized her. Aware of Logan standing close to her elbow, she held up one finger, and walked several feet away and turned her back on Logan. "Okay." She lowered her voice. "Logan's out of earshot. What's wrong?"

"Nothing—"

"Don't give me that crap." Worry for her friend harshened her tone.

"You are such a pain in the ass."

Dale let out a growl. "Casey."

Casey's sigh filtered through the line. "Fine. Look, I developed a good-sized rub spot. I don't want to take the chance of another infection; that last one was bad. I've already talked to Bob. He's going to check my socket tomorrow and make an adjustment. In the meantime, I'm not wearing my legs."

Relief swept through Dale. This was something they both dealt with. "So why did you lie to Logan? She'd understand."

The silence dragged on for several long moments.

"Casey?"

"Logan doesn't know."

Know what? Then it hit her. The question was—why? Casey never had a problem with anyone knowing about her amputations. Dale had been out in public with her plenty of times when she used her wheelchair or wore her stubbies instead of her full-length legs. She had always seen Casey as an inspiration and role model and hoped to one day be as comfortable with her own amputation.

More confused than ever, Dale mentally shook her head. "Why not?"

She was met with continued silence.

"Why not, Casey?" There was more here than met the eye.

"Remember the first day you brought Logan here to meet me?"

Dale's brow furrowed. "Of course."

"I looked out the peephole before I opened the door. You looked so nervous. Then, when I opened the door and you saw I was wearing my full-length legs and jeans, you seemed so relieved."

"Okay. So I was a little worried that Logan might not feel comfortable leaving Drake with you at first if she knew. But I figured by now—"

"It wasn't just that. At the VA, as soon as I talked about my work with amputees, you started looking stressed before I even got a chance to mention my own amputations."

Had she? Dale thought back to that morning. It hadn't been about Casey, but about her own discomfort with having Logan there. While of course Logan knew the truth, she had still wanted Logan to think of her as whole. Having her see other amputees without their prosthetics and think of Dale that way had bothered her. Her stomach sank with the realization that Casey had done something she never did—hid her amputations—because of her. "I'm so sorry, Casey. I never meant for you to do that."

"It's okay."

"No it's not!" Dale realized her voice must have gotten loud when Logan laid a hand on her shoulder.

"Everything okay?" Logan asked, low-voiced.

"Everything's fine. We're going to Casey's."

Logan raised an eyebrow.

"Are you sure about this?" Casey asked.

"We'll be there in about forty-five minutes. Don't do anything. I'll make us breakfast."

"Ah. That's okay. I can manage."

Dale grinned. Casey was well aware of her cooking skills or, rather, lack of them. "Better yet, we'll let Logan make breakfast. She's a much better cook than I am."

"You're sure?" Casey asked again.

"That she's a better cook? Positive," Dale said, knowing full well that wasn't what Casey meant.

"Dale." Casey's voice held a warning tone.

"I'm positive. I'll take care of everything."

"Okay. Let yourself in when you get here."

Dale said goodbye, disconnected the call and handed Logan her phone back.

"What's going on? I thought Casey didn't want any company?"

Dale needed to make this right. "There's something I have to tell you before we go to Casey's."

The lounge door swung open, and several nurses filed in.

"Come on. We'll talk outside in the parking lot."

Logan's brow furrowed, but she followed Dale without comment.

When they reached Logan's SUV, Dale leaned back against it. "Looks like it's going to be a beautiful day." The storm clouds had cleared, leaving the sky a brilliant blue usually only seen on a picture postcard. She took a moment and closed her eyes before lifting her face toward the sun, soaking it in.

"What's going on with Casey, Dale?"

Straightening, Dale jammed her hands into the pockets of her jacket. She wasn't sure how to start this conversation. "It wasn't because she was tired that Casey didn't want you to come over."

Logan's eyes narrowed. "She lied to me?"

"Not maliciously. She has...I mean she is..."

"Is she having problems with Drake?" Logan took a step closer. "Is he too much for her? Why didn't she just tell me that?"

"No. That's not it." Dale raked her hands through her shaggy hair. This was harder than she thought. Maybe she should have let Casey be the one to tell Logan. She shook her head roughly. She had caused this, and now she needed to fix it.

"Whatever it is, just spit it out."

Oh great, now she was pissed. Dale was really screwing this up. *Stop being a coward and tell her the truth.* "She lied because of me." She ducked her head as guilt washed over her.

"Why would you want her to lie to me?"

"I didn't mean for her to." Looking up, she blew out a breath, then blurted it out. "Casey's like me. Only in her case, she's a bilateral trans-femoral amputee."

Logan blinked rapidly several times, then took a big step back as if wanting to distance herself from Dale. "You didn't trust me."

The hurt in her voice pierced Dale's heart as painfully as an arrow. "At first, I was worried you wouldn't think she was capable of taking care of Drake. I figured once you got to know her and realized she could, you'd be fine with it. But then she thought I still didn't want you to know, so when she wasn't up to wearing her prosthetics today..." It all sounded pretty lame now.

Logan crossed her arms over her chest. "Right. Like I said. You didn't trust me."

Regret weighted her shoulders. "I wanted to help you with Drake so much that I made a mistake." Not to mention letting her own insecurities rule her. Yesterday had drawn them so much closer, and now she had probably ruined their friendship. And let Casey down to boot. "I should have been honest with you. I'm sorry." She dropped her gaze and pushed away from Logan's SUV. "I'll see you tonight at work."

Logan caught her arm. "I thought we were going to Casey's?"

Hope flared. "You still want me to go with you?"

Logan leveled a stern look at her. "On two conditions."

"Anything." Maybe she hadn't completely messed things up between them.

"Give me the benefit of the doubt next time." Logan poked her in the chest. "And don't lie—even by omission."

Dale put her hand over her heart as she gazed deeply into Logan's eyes. "I promise."

Her tense posture relaxing, Logan smiled. She laid her hand for a moment on top of the one Dale had over her heart. "Good. Thank you." She pulled open the driver's side door. "I'll meet you at Casey's." She shooed Dale away. "Get your butt in gear. I'm hungry."

Laughing, Dale trotted toward her Jeep. The day was looking up after all.

CHAPTER 27

LOGAN PULLED UP IN FRONT of Casey's house. She glanced in her rearview mirror, but there was no sign of Dale. She'd lost her two streets back when Dale had gotten caught by a stoplight. Her mind was still reeling from Dale's revelation. After noticing Casey's gait and the way she seemed to purposely set herself before doing anything physical, she had been convinced that she had suffered some type of injury. Never in her wildest imagination had she suspected that Casey was a double amputee. She had grown to like Casey at lot in the short time they'd known each other. And of course, she was grateful to her for looking after Drake. But now, she also respected and admired her for how she had reclaimed her life after a devastating injury.

While she was ticked at Casey for lying to her, she understood why she'd done it. It didn't have anything to do with Casey herself but with protecting Dale. Logan could understand the impulse. The fact that Dale hadn't trusted her was what had really hurt. Especially after all they had shared yesterday. But the fact that Dale had come clean and her heartfelt apology had gone a long way in assuaging Logan's hurt.

A rap on her side window startled her out of her thoughts.

Dale stood next to the SUV.

Logan opened the door and got out.

"So what are you making us for breakfast?" Dale asked as they walked toward the house.

It had felt great to have Dale praise her cooking to Casey, but that wasn't going to stop her from giving Dale a hard time. "Now I get it. You only want me for my cooking skills." Logan flushed. That had not come out the way she meant.

Dale's eyes darkened, and she looked as if she was about to comment, then thought better of it. "I'll cook if you want." She grinned "But don't say I didn't warn you."

Logan elbowed her. "Never mind. I'm happy to cook for you anytime." As soon as the words left her mouth, she silently berated herself. *What do you think you're doing? This isn't a long-term deal.* She had already become more attached to Dale—and Casey—than she should.

Dale rubbed her hands together. "All right."

When they reached the front of the house, Dale motioned Logan to follow her. She walked over to the side of the house, blindly reached over the five-foot wooden gate to unlatch it, and headed into the back yard. As Dale tugged the sliding glass door open, she called out, "Good morning."

Logan followed her into the living room.

Casey was sitting at the far end of the sofa, wearing sweatpants that had been shortened so that they just covered her residual limbs. Drake was stretched out next to her, hogging the rest of the couch. His big head was resting on her thigh. A wheelchair, with two padded rests extending from the narrow seat, stood next to the couch. She puzzled it out after a moment. They must be for Casey's residual limbs so they didn't hang down and swell.

"Hey," Casey said by way of greeting.

Drake raised his head. His tail thumped against the arm of the couch, but he made no move to get down.

Logan scowled. He knew he wasn't allowed on the furniture. Her gaze landed on his shaved abdomen and long incision, and she relented. But she couldn't let it go completely. She shook her finger at him. "Don't get used to that. Once you're healed, it's back to the floor for you."

Drake woo-wooed as if contradicting her.

Casey laughed and patted him. "You tell her, boy."

Logan turned her scowl on Casey.

The smile dropped from Casey's face. She pressed her palms against the cushion of the couch and straightened her posture.

Logan marched over and stood directly in front of her. She glanced down at her legs, then back up. "I don't appreciate being lied to." She looked back at Dale for a second before allowing her expression to soften. "Don't do it again."

Casey met her gaze unflinchingly and an unspoken understanding passed between them. She stuck out her hand. "Deal."

"Deal." Logan affirmed and took her hand.

Dale watched them shake hands. Once again, she marveled at Logan's easy acceptance. There Casey was, sitting with two missing legs, and Logan hadn't even batted an eye. Her only reaction had been being pissed at Casey for lying to her. At the reminder of Casey hiding her amputations because of her, guilt washed over Dale again. Logan wasn't the only one she owed an apology.

Her steps lagged as she moved toward the couch.

Casey looked up at her.

The look of understanding on her face was Dale's undoing. "I'm sorry." Unexpected tears stung her eyes.

Casey opened her arms.

Dale started to lean down, then stopped. Her gaze darted back and forth between Casey and Drake. Although she knew the dog was friendly, she still had some trepidation with getting so close to him.

Logan moved away from the couch. "Drake. Come here."

For a moment, it looked as if the big dog wouldn't obey.

Logan loudly cleared her throat.

Drake got off the couch with surprising alacrity. As he approached Logan, he looked back over his shoulder and gave Dale a look as if he knew she was to blame for him losing his comfortable spot.

Logan loved on him as soon as he reached her.

Momentarily distracted by Logan, Dale turned back toward Casey. She slumped down onto the couch and into Casey's arms. "I'm sorry," she whispered again.

"We're fine." Casey tightened her arms around her for a moment, then released her. "Everything is out in the open now." She shoved Dale's shoulder hard enough to knock her over. "So you're throwing me over for a better cook, huh?"

Dale laughed, grateful for the break in the tension. She sat back up next to Casey. "Wait 'til you taste her cooking. You'll be the one begging her to cook for you."

"We'll see about that." Casey grinned at Logan. "Okay, Chef. What culinary creation are you going to make for us?"

"Great. No pressure or anything," Logan muttered.

"Don't listen to her. You don't have to cook if you don't want to," Dale said.

When she started to get up from the couch, Logan waved her back down. "It's okay. I'm happy to cook, but I need to feed Drake first." He looked up at the mention of his name and leaned into her.

"Sorry. I already fed him," Casey said.

"No problem." She eyed Casey and Dale. "What do you want for breakfast?"

Casey waved her hand in the direction of the kitchen. "Have at it. Whatever you want to cook. Unlike Dale, I have a fully stocked kitchen and a refrigerator filled with real food."

"Hey." Dale elbowed Casey.

Logan nodded as if accepting a challenge. "All right, then. Breakfast...coming right up." She patted Drake's shoulder. "Come on. You can watch and make sure I get it right."

Dale smiled when Logan marched toward the kitchen like a warrior going into battle. She couldn't help but admire her ass as she walked away.

Casey nudged her. "She's something, isn't she?"

The admiration in Casey's voice made Dale turn to find her staring after Logan with a glowing smile on her face. An unpleasant sensation lodged behind her breast bone. She shoved the feeling down. "Yes, she is."

Casey pushed her wheelchair back from the table and let out a satisfied groan. "That was incredible. I didn't even know I had the makings for eggs Benedict in my kitchen."

"Told you she was a great cook," Dale said. She smiled at Logan before popping the last bite of her breakfast into her mouth.

Heat crept up Logan's face. "I'm glad you liked it. But no need to go overboard. I didn't go all out with a traditional hollandaise sauce. I made the less complicated blender version." Although, she had to admit the eggs Benedict were good. It had been years since she'd made them, and was pretty proud of the way they had turned out.

"No matter how you made it, it tasted fantastic. Now I get the whole begging thing Dale was talking about earlier." Casey waggled her eyebrows. "I could be good at begging." She threw back her head and laughed at Dale's and Logan's matching blushes.

Logan scrubbed her hands over her face, wishing she could wash away her blush. She scowled at Casey, which only made her laugh harder.

Once Casey had regained her composure, she wheeled her chair away from the table. "Come on, Dale. Logan cooked, so we're cleaning up." She turned to face Logan and arched an eyebrow as if expecting her to protest.

Logan forced herself to lounge back in her chair. "Don't look at me like that. I've got no problem with it." She sensed that she needed to be exceptionally careful not to treat Casey any differently than she had previously. Not that she would normally be tempted to, but after seeing her in the wheelchair, trying to help was an automatic response. But she had no doubt that Casey, like Dale, would not appreciate the special treatment.

"Good. Why don't you and Drake go outside and enjoy the sun while Dale and I clean up?"

Logan stood and reached for her empty plate. The least she could do was help clear the table. A scowl from Casey stopped her in mid-reach. She held up her hands. "Fine. Drake and I will be outside." She patted her leg and called to Drake.

When she heard the sliding glass door open, Logan wasn't sure how much time had passed. She might have dozed off in the warm sunshine. Opening her eyes, she spotted Dale smiling down at her. "Hey. All done?"

Yawning, Dale nodded. She put her hand on the back of Logan's chair. "Thanks again for making such a great breakfast."

"You're very welcome." Logan allowed herself to get lost in the warmth of Dale's gaze.

The noise of Casey's chair going over the threshold broke the moment.

Logan stood as she approached. "I should get going."

"Wait. I want to talk to you about something before you go."

"Okay." Logan sat back down.

Dale slipped into the chair next to her.

"What's up?" Logan asked.

"It's about Drake."

Logan shot a worried glance at him where he lay stretched out on a blanket, soaking up the sun.

"It's nothing bad," Casey said quickly. "I've just been thinking about it since you said he had been a therapy dog. Do you have his paperwork and vest?" At Logan's nod, Casey continued, "Would you be willing to let me take him to the VA? He would really brighten the day of a lot of people there."

Logan looked over at Drake. At six years old, he was still in good health. Despite his incision and being only eight days post op, he was getting around without a problem and was back to his old self. Therapy work wasn't strenuous, and he would be on a leash. Still, Logan hesitated to have Drake out and about when she wasn't there. "Would it be possible for me to bring him to the VA?"

Casey frowned. "Yeah. But not until all your paperwork and background check get taken care of. That usually takes several weeks—at least. I could take him now because I already work there and am cleared." She sighed. "But I guess it can wait."

Logan owed Casey a lot and couldn't bring herself to disappoint her. And it was a win-win situation. Drake had loved working as a therapy dog, and by going with Casey, he'd get a chance to do that again. "Well, I think we need to wait until his stitches come out. That's only three days away. After that, what if I were to accompany you to the VA but you were the one who handled Drake?"

Casey reached over and laid a hand on Logan's arm. "That would be great. Do you have time to walk me through his commands this morning? That way I can practice with him before we go."

"Sure. I can do that."

Dale's chair scraped across the cement when she suddenly stood. "Well, I guess I'll be going."

Logan looked up at her, concerned by her strange tone of voice. "Are you too tired to stay?"

"No. I just figured..." She shot a look at Casey. "... that you didn't need me hanging around."

Logan frowned. What was going on with Dale? "I'd like you to stay. Unless you're too tired."

Dale shook her head and smiled. "No. I'm fine."

Taking a moment, Logan clasped Dale's arm before turning back to Casey. "Ready to get to work?"

Casey stared at Dale for a moment. "Are we good?"

Dale moved over to her friend and tousled her hair. "We're good."

Logan's gaze darted back and forth between them. She felt as if she was missing part of the conversation. She shook her head. Maybe she was just imagining things. She hoped this would be a chance for Dale to get more comfortable around Drake. "Come on, Drake. Time to work."

CHAPTER 28

LOGAN KNELT NEXT TO DRAKE and wiped him down with a damp rag, making sure his slate-gray coat was spotless.

Casey slid open the glass patio door and stepped outside. "You guys ready to go?" Drake woo-wooed in answer. "That's one vote."

Standing, Logan did her best to hide her trepidation. The last trip to the VA hospital had been stressful and embarrassing due to her panic attack. "Sure. Let's go."

Casey put her hand on Logan's arm when she reached her. "Most of the Christmas decorations at the hospital have already come down. But if it gets to be too much while we're there, just say the word, and we'll leave."

Logan flushed and looked away. She was clearly spending too much time around Casey; she had learned to read her too well. They had never talked about what happened that day. Now Logan wondered what Dale had told Casey.

As if she had read her thoughts, Casey said, "All Dale said was you'd had a very traumatic experience at Christmastime. Anything else wasn't her story to tell." She gently tugged on Logan's arm until she met her gaze. "The people you're going to meet today have suffered their own traumatic events or live with someone who has. Believe me, we all understand about triggers. There is nothing to be embarrassed about."

"Thanks." Uncomfortable with the turn of conversation, she eased her arm out of Casey's grasp and patted Drake. "Time to go, Drake."

The big dog woofed and charged into the house, making them laugh.

Logan and Drake followed Casey out of the house and waited while she locked up. "Where's the best place to meet you? I won't be able to take Drake inside without you—right?"

"Right. Instead of taking two vehicles, why don't you and Drake come with me? Visitor parking is a pain because that lot is always packed. I've got a staff parking sticker which makes things easier."

It had been difficult to find a spot the last time she was at the VA. She glanced over at Casey's crew cab pickup. The truck was much higher off the ground than her SUV. "I know Drake's incision is healed, but he's got a lot more healing to do inside. I'm hesitant to have him try to jump into your truck."

"He doesn't have to jump—"

"No. I don't want you trying to lift him up." After learning the reason why Casey had been unable to don her prosthetics, Logan had been relieved when she'd arrived today to see Casey once again wearing her prosthetic legs. She did not want her doing anything that might cause a problem.

"I promise. I won't lift him."

Frowning, Logan glanced down at Drake, then back at Casey's truck. Then how did Casey propose to get him into her pickup?

"Come on. Drake and I will show you." She took Drake's leash from Logan and led the way over to the passenger side of her truck.

After opening the front passenger door, Casey reached in and did something inside, then opened the rear passenger door. Only it didn't work the way a standard door would, but opened rear-facing so that when open, the two doors were like the back doors of a van. She reached in again and held up what looked like a wired remote control. "Check this out." She pushed a button on the remote.

Logan's jaw dropped when the front bucket seat rotated until it was facing sideways, extended out from the truck, and lowered itself down so that it was no higher off the ground than the seat of a couch was. She had never seen anything like that.

"It's called a valet seat." Casey grinned. "Now watch." She reached into her pocket, pulled out a small plastic bag full of dog treats, and laid one on the seat.

Drake, his tail wagging, grabbed the treat.

"Good boy." She patted the seat. "Drake. Seat."

It took a bit of maneuvering on his part because of his size, but within short order, Drake was sitting on the seat.

Casey rewarded him with another treat. "Good job." She took a moment to tuck his tail in so that it wasn't hanging down, then said, "Stay. Going up." With a press of a button, the seat began to rise. "Duck," she said as the seat started to turn. Drake obediently ducked his head and in moments, was inside the truck in the now front-facing seat. "Drake. Back." The rear seat had already been folded down and had a blanket covering it for padding.

Drake's tongue lolled out of his mouth, and he gave a doggie grin but didn't budge.

Casey stared at the big dog for several moments, then glanced at Logan.

While impressed with what Casey had accomplished with Drake in just a few days, she struggled not to laugh at Casey's flummoxed expression. Drake was a wonderful dog, but he could be a stubborn brat usually right around the time you wanted to show someone how well trained he was.

Casey mock-scowled at Drake. "Quit making me look bad in front of your mom. You know you can't stay up front." She took another treat from the bag and waved it under Drake's nose, then put it on the back bench. "Drake. Back."

Drake glanced back, looking unimpressed.

Casey growled. She put a second, then with a quick look at Drake, a third treat on the seat.

Satisfied with the offering, Drake used the empty space where the console between the seats normally was to move into the backseat. After taking his time eating his treats, he lay down with a sigh.

Muttering under her breath, Casey closed the rear passenger door and motioned for Logan to get into the front.

Logan tossed her backpack into the back with Drake before climbing into the truck.

Casey opened both driver's side doors the same way that the passenger side doors had opened. The driver's seat was also a valet seat. Once Casey was settled behind the wheel, she met Logan's gaze.

Logan's curiosity must have shown on her face.

"I can climb into the truck with my prosthetics, but it's much easier with the seat. It was put in when I was still using a wheelchair full-time. Usually, vehicles have a valet seat only on one side, but I transport a lot of vets to different events, and it's not uncommon for one or more of them to be in a wheelchair."

"You do a lot for the veteran community—don't you?"

Casey shrugged. "I owe the vet community a lot." She took a moment to pull out her cell phone and accessed some type of app. Tucking the phone back in her pocket, she said, "Let's get going."

When Casey put the truck in gear but didn't make any use of the hand controls, an unexpected spark of concern intruded at the thought of her driving using two prosthetic legs. Logan chided herself for the reaction. Clearly, Casey drove all the time.

"I only use the hand controls when I'm not wearing my legs," Casey said, as if she had once again divined Logan's thoughts. "That's what I was doing with my phone. I have an app that switches the microprocessors in my prosthetics to driving mode, which allows me to drive safely—just like anyone else." Casey laid her hand on Logan's shoulder for a moment. "If there is something you want to know, just ask me."

Logan flushed at being so obvious. At the same time, she couldn't help noticing how much more comfortable Casey was talking about her amputations than Dale. "Thanks for saying that."

"No problem." Casey pulled out of the driveway and headed down the street. "Now let me tell you about what to expect today."

Logan tensed at the reminder of where they were going. She took a deep breath and tried to relax as Casey began to fill her in on what they would be doing during Drake's first visit as a therapy dog.

"My office is just down the hall. You can leave your backpack there while we make the rounds," Casey said as they turned the corner.

An automatic smile blossomed on Logan's face when she spotted Dale standing a short ways down the hallway.

"I thought you were working in PT today. What's up?" Casey asked when they reached her. She glanced at Logan, then back at Dale with a grin.

Dale flushed. She hefted the duffle bag she was carrying. "I am. I just thought I'd stop by and ask Drake how his first day at work was going."

Casey snorted. "Sure you were." She patted the big dog by her side.

Logan shot her a quelling look, then put a hand on Dale's arm. She was well aware of Dale's continuing unease around Drake. She had gotten somewhat better, though. "Thanks for checking on us." She quickly got lost in the warmth of Dale's gaze.

The loud clearing of Casey's throat made them both start.

Heat crept up Logan's neck. She knelt next to Drake and adjusted his vest to give herself something to do. Her fingers skimmed underneath the strap that went under his chest, and she frowned. "Damn."

"What's wrong?" Dale asked.

"I thought it would be high enough up, but this strap is rubbing the edge of his incision and the bare area of his chest and belly where they shaved his hair." Logan tugged on the offending strap. She sighed as she glanced up at Casey. "I'm sorry. I should have made sure about his vest in advance. I guess we aren't going to be able to do this today. He's required to wear the vest, but I can't take a chance of it creating a rub spot."

"Is there some way we can wrap his incision?" Casey asked.

"I'm not sure that would work. It might bunch up under his vest and cause more problems." Logan sank back on her heels next to Drake. She hated to disappoint Casey.

"What about a T-shirt?" Dale asked.

She eyed Drake and his vest, then grinned up at Dale. "That could work." *Damn.* Her happiness was short-lived. "But I don't have one with me."

"No problem," Casey said. "We won't have any trouble finding someone who would be happy to lend Drake their shirt."

Logan shook her head. "It's not a matter of lending. For this to work, we'd have to cut the sleeves out of the shirt. I've put T-shirts on him before, and that's the only way they fit and don't rub under his armpits. I wouldn't feel comfortable accepting a stranger's shirt and doing that."

"I'm sure one of the guys wouldn't—"

"I've got a shirt he can have," Dale said, already opening her duffle bag. She pulled a dark-blue T-shirt out of her bag and handed it to Logan. "Casey, have you got a pair of scissors in your office?"

"Sure." Casey traded Logan the T-shirt for Drake's leash before opening her office door and flipping on the lights. She propped the door open. After rummaging in a drawer for a moment, she pulled out a pair a scissors and spread the T-shirt out on her desk. Eyes wide, she turned back toward the door. "Dale, this is—"

"It's fine. Go ahead." Dale made a sharp motion with her hand.

Logan's gaze darted back and forth between them. Was there something special about Dale's shirt? "Wait."

But it was too late; Casey had already cut into the T-shirt. She quickly finished removing the sleeves and brought the shirt to Logan. As she handed it over, she threw a look at Dale that Logan couldn't interpret.

Dale shrugged.

Logan knelt next to Drake and removed his vest. She spread the shirt out across her knees. Emblazoned in white across the front was *USNS Mercy* with a silhouette of a large ship that had a red medical cross on its side. She knew nothing about the Navy but recognized it as a hospital ship. Had Dale served on it? A darker thought intruded. Or had Dale been treated on the ship when she was wounded? Pushing aside the questions for another time, she put the altered shirt on Drake and then fitted his vest back in place. The shirt not only covered his chest and protected him from the strap rubbing but also covered the full length of his incision and all the areas where his hair had been shaved off.

She rose to her feet with a smile. After handing Drake's leash to Casey, she turned to Dale and leaned in close to place a kiss on her cheek. The feel of Dale's soft skin against her lips caused her to linger longer than she intended. "Thank you for doing that for Drake."

"You're very welcome."

The warmth in Dale's voice and in her eyes was almost Logan's undoing. Her gaze dropped to Dale's lips.

Casey cleared her throat, once again reminding them of her presence. "So are we good to go?"

A blush heating her cheeks, Logan took a hasty step back. She busied herself with Drake, hoping the color would rapidly fade from her face. "Um... Yeah. Let's get to work."

"Come on. I'll walk with you to the elevator," Dale said.

When they reached the elevator, Dale gently patted Drake's shoulder, surprising Logan. "Good luck, big guy. Go make lots of people happy." Drake pressed his head against Dale's hip, eliciting a smile from her. "See you guys later."

Logan watched her walk away, once again marveling at what an incredible woman Dale was. If only things could be different. Refusing to give in to the depressing thought, she forced herself to smile. "You heard the woman. We have work to do."

Logan followed Casey and Drake as they moved to exit the patient's room. So far, their visits had gone very well. Even with a two-year hiatus, Drake had easily stepped back into his role as a therapy dog. And Casey was a natural at handling him.

"Please bring him back again for another visit," the patient called before they could step out of the room.

"I will. If you behave and don't give the nurses a hard time." Casey wagged an admonishing finger at the man. "I will hear about it if you do."

He grinned and put his hand over his heart. "I promise. Take care of that big boy."

"Good man." Casey gave him a thumbs-up.

"Bye, Drake. See you soon."

Casey smiled as they headed down the hall. "Drake is going to be a popular guy around here, not only with the patients but the nurses. Bill spends a lot of time hospitalized, and while he may only be thirty-two, he can be a real curmudgeon at times. If the prospect of seeing Drake again puts him on his best behavior, the nurses will be forever in your debt."

Logan laughed and patted Drake's side. "We're happy to help." And surprisingly, that was the truth. After all the anxiety she'd had prior to arriving, it felt good to see the smiles on patients' faces. And she couldn't help being moved by their heartfelt gratitude.

Casey stopped at the end of the hall. "I want to talk to you about seeing one last patient before we give Drake a rest. This one will be very different than any we've seen so far."

"How so?" All the patients they had visited up until now had been on the orthopedic ward.

"I'd like to take him onto the general medical ward. The patient I want him to visit suffered a head injury in a helicopter crash last year and is wheelchair bound. He's here being treated for pneumonia." Casey ran a hand through her hair. "I'm not sure he'll even react to Drake; he's been so depressed lately. If he does respond, he has very poor motor control, so he might be a little rough trying to pet Drake. And the other thing is, he doesn't speak. Do you think Drake will be okay with all that?"

Logan's thoughts immediately went to Emily and the work she did with Drake and her TBI patients. "He's worked with that type of patient before. He'll be fine with everything."

Casey glanced down at Drake. "He has?"

Of course Casey would be curious. Logan struggled with her reluctance to talk about her sister. But this was different. If not for Casey, Drake wouldn't be getting the chance to continue the work her sister had trained him to do. She had seen today how happily he had greeted each patient, his head high and his tail wagging enthusiastically. He clearly loved the work.

Logan's hand went to her chest and pressed against a spot just above her breast. She swallowed past the lump in her throat that thoughts of Emily always brought. Blowing out a breath, she stepped close to Drake and hugged him, drawing strength from his presence. It still took two tries to get her voice to work. "My sister was a neurologist. She trained Drake specifically to work with people who had suffered a traumatic brain injury. She always believed that those patients would react positively to an animal when they wouldn't to anyone else." This was the most she had spoken of her sister to anyone outside of Dale in over two years. Keeping her gaze locked on Drake, she braced herself for all the questions that were sure to come.

"That's great. I can't wait to introduce Drake to Ben and his wife, Amy. Let's go."

Surprise rippled through Logan. Her head came up, and she stared at Casey for a moment before looking away when her emotions threatened to overwhelm her. It was clear from the compassion on Casey's face that she hadn't missed the significance of Logan referring to her sister in the past tense. Clearly, Casey understood a lot more than just emotional triggers for panic attacks. Her silent support allowed Logan to push past the sadness and focus on helping the patient. With an acknowledging nod in Casey's direction, she followed her to the elevators.

Logan stood next to Amy as Casey and Drake approached Ben's wheelchair.

"Hey, Ben. Look who I brought to see you. This big boy is Drake."

Ben's gaze flickered to Casey for a moment, but otherwise he didn't react.

Casey released the Velcro strap that kept Ben's arm secured against the armrest of the wheelchair. "He sure would like it if you petted him. Wouldn't you, Drake?"

Drake moved closer and with no prompting from Casey, slowly and carefully laid his big head in Ben's lap.

Ben's gaze remained distant, and he made no acknowledgement of Drake or anyone else in the room.

A disappointed sigh escaped from Amy. Logan's heart went out to her. She'd been ecstatic when she met Drake. It turned out that Ben's family had a Great Dane when he was a child. She had hoped the sight of the dog would draw him out of his deepening depression.

Drake lifted his head from Ben's lap, bringing himself eye-level with Ben. He woo-wooed, making everyone jump.

"Drake. No." Casey quickly tugged him back.

Damn it, Drake. What are you doing? Logan sent Casey an apologetic look. She had told her Drake would be fine, and now he pulled a stunt like this.

Ben's attention locked on Drake. "Da..." He flailed his arm as if trying to reach for Drake.

Casey froze in place. She shared a stunned look with Amy.

Drake pulled away from her and put his head back in Ben's lap.

Logan winced when his arm landed heavily on Drake's neck, but Drake never moved.

"That's right," Casey said. "This is Drake."

"Da...ka...da...ka."

"Oh my God. He spoke." Tears flowing down her face, Amy rushed to her husband's side. Drake lifted his head. She guided Ben's hand so that he could stroke Drake's neck and chest. "Isn't he beautiful?" She hugged Drake and then pressed Casey's hand. "Thank you. Thank you so much."

Logan choked up at the emotional scene. She glanced at Casey, whose eyes were just as watery, and they both grinned. She was so proud of Drake. She sent a thought to Emily. *You did a great job with him, Sis.* It was the first time in over two years that thoughts of her sister brought pleasure, not pain.

"That was amazing," Casey said for the third time.

Logan laughed. "Yeah. It was." She glanced down to where Drake lay stretched out on a blanket in Casey's office. "Although I have to admit that at first, I was ready to strangle him."

"Me too." Casey leaned down and patted Drake's side. His tail thumped against the blanket. "My bad, boy. Obviously Drake knew what he was doing. People don't give dogs enough credit. They are masters at reading body language and emotions."

"You did great handling him today. We'll need to set up a schedule so I can drop Drake off here one morning a week." After seeing how well Drake had done today, Logan realized that he was more than ready to come home.

"What do you mean?"

Logan sighed; she couldn't miss the trepidation in Casey's voice. While she was happy at the prospect of having Drake with her again, she also knew how attached Casey had grown to him and how hard this would be on her. "I really appreciate everything you've done for Drake...and me. He's doing great. Thank you for that." She met Casey's gaze. "It's time for him to come home."

For a moment it looked as if Casey was going to protest, then her shoulders slumped and she said, "I understand." She turned away, but not before Logan saw the tears in her eyes.

Damn it. Drake was her dog, and she wasn't about to give him up, but that didn't make her feel any less bad for Casey. She stared at Casey's back, torn between reaching out to comfort her and letting her have some space.

Drake took the decision from her when he stood and stepped between Casey's legs and laid his big head over her shoulder. Casey wrapped her arms around him and buried her face against his neck.

"Um... I think I'll go see if Dale's almost done in PT. Why don't you and Drake join me after he's rested a little while longer?"

"Okay. We'll meet you there," Casey said without turning around.

Knowing that Drake was doing a better job comforting Casey than she could, Logan made her retreat.

It wasn't until she was halfway down the hall from Casey's office that it dawned on Logan: she didn't know where the PT department was located. She couldn't bring herself to go back and ask. After wandering around for a several minutes, she gave in and asked a passing staff person.

Logan hesitated at the entrance to the PT department. Should she just go in? Or ask someone where to find Dale?

"Can I help you?"

Logan started at the voice coming from behind her. She turned to face a heavyset, middle-aged woman who regarded her over the silver frames of her half glasses.

"Is Dr. Parker here?" When the woman frowned, Logan realized her mistake. "I'm Logan. A friend of Dale's."

The woman continued to regard her skeptically.

"I'm here with Casey and my therapy dog," she added. As they had made their rounds with Drake, everyone seemed to know Casey.

A smile softened the woman's features, and she reached out to touch Logan's arm. "That's your big boy? Drake?"

How did she know Drake's name? Logan didn't remember meeting her earlier. "Yes."

"Where is he?" She looked around as if he might be hiding just out of sight.

"He's with Casey. They're going to meet me here in a little while."

"Well, in that case, follow me. Dale's in the back, working with one of the boys, but you can watch until she's done."

Logan trailed after the woman as she led her deeper into the huge PT department.

"Dale's in there." She pointed toward a room off to the right.

"Jayne," someone called out.

"Be right there," Jayne said. She made a shooing motion. "Go on in. I'll let Casey know where you are when she gets here. I can't wait to meet Drake," she called back over her shoulder as she walked away.

Left to her own devices, Logan approached the door and peered inside. The far side of the room held a rack filled with various free weights, several large exercise balls, and other miscellaneous equipment. The area closest to the door sported two low, wide, padded platforms. One was freestanding; the other was against the wall. The platform alongside the wall was where Dale was located.

Logan couldn't help but stare. Dale wasn't wearing her prosthesis, but that wasn't what grabbed Logan's attention. It was the first time she had seen Dale in shorts. The form-fitting garment hugged her muscular thighs and ass. She wrenched her gaze away and focused on the man next to Dale.

Although *man* hardly seemed appropriate. He was just a kid, looking barely out of his teens. He was also missing one leg below the knee. Unexpected anger at the grave harm the men and women she had seen today had suffered gripped Logan. She forced away the unproductive emotion. Her anger wouldn't help anyone.

She moved just inside the room and leaned against the wall. Dale and the young man were the only ones in the room. While she could clearly see what was going on, she could hear only an occasional word of their conversation. Her gaze was drawn back to Dale, who was on her hands and knees demonstrating an exercise. She arched her back as she tucked her chin toward her chest. After a few moments, she lifted her head, letting her back relax and bow inward slightly in the reverse of the previous position. She repeated the moves once more, rose up on her knees, and motioned for the man to try.

Once he finished, Dale got back down on her hands and knees. Logan watched with avid interest. Dale lifted her bent leg, like a dog peeing on a fire hydrant, and repeated the action several times.

Drawn as if by its own accord, Logan's gaze latched on to Dale's flexing glutes. She swallowed heavily, barely resisting the urge to fan herself. The room seemed to have gotten uncomfortably warm all of a sudden. She frowned when Dale returned to a seated position and the man took up the exercise.

He only did two repetitions before rising up onto his knees and pointing to his groin.

Dale moved closer and put her hand against his hip on the side of his body with the missing limb, then ran it down to the junction where his leg met his body. He nodded at something she said before moving to the edge of the platform, out of the way.

While facing the wall, Dale lay down on her back, extended her legs, and propped them on the wall. Once in position, she scooted closer to the wall.

What the heck was she doing?

Dale slowly let her legs spread wide open and held them there for several moments, closed her legs, then spread them again.

Heat rushed through Logan and pooled low in her belly. She bit back a groan.

When Dale moved aside to let the man try the exercise, she breathed a sigh of relief. Maybe she should just wait out front for Casey?

But she remained in place as if her feet were glued to the floor.

After a brief attempt at the exercise, the man once again shook his head. He gestured at his leg. His sharp hand movements conveyed his growing agitation.

Dale calmed him with a hand on his shoulder. She spoke to him for several moments, too quietly for Logan to hear anything.

He repeatedly shook his head, then laughed. "A frog?" he asked.

Frog? Logan tipped her head, wondering if she had heard right.

Dale clapped him on the back and grinned. She turned slightly so that her back was fully toward Logan. Moving back to the center of the platform, she returned to her hands and knees. This time, she lowered herself so that her weight rested on her bent forearms and knees. She spread her knees wide as she flowed into the stretch that did resemble a frog.

The sight of Dale in that position shot Logan's pulse into overdrive. *It's just an innocent exercise.* But her brain refused to cooperate. All she could picture was herself kneeling behind Dale's spread thighs and... Searing arousal set Logan's blood on fire. A whimper escaped before she could stifle it. She ruthlessly slammed the door shut on those images. It could never happen.

Unable to take any more, she bolted from the room and ran right into someone just outside the doorway. Strong hands latched onto her biceps.

"Whoa. Where's the fire?" Casey's gaze swept Logan. She glanced past Logan into the room where Dale was and smirked. "Never mind. I see it."

The heat of her blush matched the fire raging through Logan's veins. Drake pushed forward to greet her. She sidestepped him and Casey. "Be right back. Need the restroom."

Casey's laughter filled her ears as she fled.

Dale looked up at the sound of raucous laughter. Casey stood in the doorway with Drake. She thought she'd caught a glimpse of Logan for a moment too, but then she was gone. She quickly sat up and tucked her residual limb underneath her.

Jeff whistled. "Wow. That's one big-ass dog."

Distressed by the thought that Logan might reappear at any moment, she ignored his interest in Drake. "We're done here. Work on the exercises over the holiday, and we'll start again next week."

Appearing crestfallen at the abrupt dismissal, Jeff reached under the platform and retrieved his forearm crutches. "Okay."

Dale cursed herself for letting her own anxiety spill over onto Jeff. She stood next to him and clasped his shoulder for a moment. "You did fine today. Don't let a setback get you down. It's happened to all of us. Just remember how far you've come. You'll get back to where you were before." She motioned toward the door. "Get going. I'll see you at the New Year's Eve party."

His smile reappeared. "Thanks. See you tomorrow night."

As soon as he reached the door, Dale scrambled for her prosthetic that she had left propped against the wall next to the platform. With her back to the door, she grabbed the liner from the socket of the prosthetic and began to put it on.

"Hey. All done for the morning?"

She spared Casey barely a glance and returned to applying the liner. She cursed under her breath when she had to roll the liner down and reapply it because she'd wrinkled it in her haste. Blowing out a breath, she finally stood and pressed the now-covered stump into the socket of the prosthetic until it locked.

Casey put Drake at a down/stay before walking over. "What's wrong?"

"Was that Logan with you?"

"Yeah. She needed to..." Casey smirked. "Take a break. She'll be back."

Dale scowled. "Damn it, Casey. How much did she see?"

"Huh?" Casey's brow furrowed. "See of what?"

"I had my damn leg off. You should've warned me you were bringing her down." The thought of Logan seeing her uncovered stump made her feel sick to her stomach.

Casey put her hand on Dale's arm. "I thought we agreed earlier to meet. Logan came down ahead of me." She glanced at her watch. "About half an hour ago. I just got here. Why are you so upset? She's seen you without your leg."

Dale slumped onto the platform. She dropped her head down toward her chest and cursed. It was even worse than she'd thought. "My stump was completely bare, not even a sock. And she was here—watching? Damn it!"

Casey threw back her head and laughed.

Dale jerked her head up and glared at her. How could she think this was even remotely funny?

"Oh. She was watching you all right. But she sure as hell wasn't looking at your stump."

"How do you know that?"

"She nearly ran me down when she hotfooted it out of the room. Believe me, she didn't look the least bit upset." Casey grinned. "Although, she did look like she could have used a nice bucket of ice water." She waggled her eyebrows. "To sit in."

Dale's thoughts raced. The idea that Logan had been aroused despite the fact that her bare stump had been in plain sight sent arousal skittering down Dale's spine.

A brief image of her and Logan entwined brought reality crashing home. There was a big difference between Logan seeing her like that from a distance and being intimate, where Logan would be forced into close proximity to her stump—not to mention exposed to all her scars. Dale wouldn't subject her to that.

Casey's hand coming to rest on her shoulder pulled her from her thoughts.

"Hey, why so glum? She thinks you're hot. That's a good thing—right?"

"It doesn't matter. You know I can't get involved with her."

"But—"

"Drop it, Casey. Please." As Dale rose to her feet, she frowned at the exposed metal parts of her prosthesis unencumbered by the cosmetic cover she wore at work. She sighed. Hardly mattered now; Logan had seen a lot more than that. "Come on. I'm done here. Let's find Logan."

CHAPTER 29

DALE STOPPED IN THE DOORWAY of the visitors' lounge on the orthopedic ward and surveyed the room. Colorful streamers dangled from the ceiling with helium balloons floating among them. A large glitter-covered *Happy New Year* sign hung on the back wall where a refreshment table had been set up. Casey and Sharon had done a great job with the decorations.

"Hey, Dale," Jeff called as he padded toward her. "What do you think?"

"Looks great. Did Casey put you to work?"

"Yeah. Told me it was time I got off my lazy butt." He grinned.

"She's right. About time." It was good to see him engaged with the party preparation. She'd been concerned he might be slipping into depression over his recent setback.

"I saw Dr. Walters today." From the look on his face, it couldn't be bad.

"And what did he say?"

"I can start back using my prosthesis next week. I already talked to Bob about doing a socket check."

"That's good news." Dale clapped him on the back. "You better be ready for PT. I'm not going to cut you any slack like I did this week."

His hands tightened on the handles of his forearm crutches, and he stood straighter. "I'll be ready."

The sound of laughter and excited voices drew their attention to the door. Patients were starting to arrive. Some were ambulatory with the assistance of crutches or walkers, but most were in wheelchairs. For a few lucky ones, their families were here to celebrate the coming new year. But for most, the staff and volunteers stood in for missing family members.

Dale waved when she spotted Casey, who was pushing a patient in a wheelchair into the room. "I need to get the refreshments set up. Why don't you go help Casey get everyone situated by the TV?"

The large television mounted on the wall was already tuned to the New Year's Eve coverage in New York's Times Square. The administration was willing to bend the rules only so far for the party. It would end at nine p.m. for them when the ball dropped in Times Square at midnight.

"Sure. Glad to help." Jeff padded away.

As she filled plastic cups with nonalcoholic punch and set them out on a table, Dale's thoughts strayed to Logan. Her gaze was drawn to the doorway with each new arrival. After what had happened in the PT department yesterday, Logan had seemed a little distant at work last night. Maybe Casey had misinterpreted what she'd seen? She couldn't help wondering if Logan would even show up tonight. It would probably be for the best if she didn't. Her attraction to Logan had become a problem that was impossible to ignore. There was no sense in torturing herself with something that could never be. Her shoulders slumped.

"Don't look so glum. She'll be here."

At the sound of Casey's voice so close-by, she almost dropped the cup of punch she had just poured. "Damn it, Case. Quit sneaking up on me like that."

"I called to you—twice." Casey snorted. "A whole platoon of marines could have marched up, and you wouldn't have noticed."

Scowling, Dale elbowed her. "I was busy setting up."

"Sure. Whatever you say." Casey's gaze swept her. "You look really nice. New outfit?"

Dale's cheeks heated, and she nodded. "Thanks." After spending almost an hour trying to decide what to wear, she had given up on finding anything suitable in her closet and done something she hated—shopping for clothes. She had just wanted to look nice for the party; it had nothing to do with Logan. *Yeah, right!* Great, now even her own subconscious wasn't buying her excuses.

"You look very nice too." In total disregard of her prosthetics, Casey was wearing a knee-length dress.

"Thank you."

The sound of new arrivals drew her attention back to the door. It wasn't Logan. A sigh escaped before she could stifle it.

"She'll be here," Casey repeated.

As if summoned, Logan appeared in the doorway. She had forgone her usual ponytail, leaving her hair down so that it just brushed her shoulders. She wore a long-sleeved, V-neck print top over dark-blue slacks.

Dale knew she was staring, yet couldn't seem to stop herself. Logan looked great.

"She looks nice—doesn't she?" Casey asked.

Even from across the room, Dale's gaze was drawn to the enticing bit of cleavage Logan was showing. "Oh, yeah." She blushed at the unexpectedly husky timbre of her own voice. She cleared her throat. "I should go... um...let her know where we are."

Casey laughed. "Good idea. I'll go with you."

The prickling of her senses made Logan scan the room.

Dale strode toward her.

Her vision narrowed; all she could see was Dale. She moved with the grace of a sleek, superbly muscled jungle cat. A forest-green long-sleeved blouse that hugged her body and tailored black pants clinging to her strong thighs accentuated the impression.

The closer Dale got, the faster Logan's heart beat.

"Hey, Logan. Glad you made it," Casey said.

She was vaguely aware of Casey but couldn't take her eyes off Dale. "Hi." Logan flushed when it came out much breathier than she'd intended.

Casey laughed and waved a hand in her direction. "I'm over here."

Logan wrenched her gaze from Dale. Barely resisting the urge to scrub her hands over her burning cheeks, she turned her attention to Casey. "Good evening."

"Ready to make the rounds and spread some New Year's cheer? We've got punch and some snack mix to pass around."

"Sure." Logan glanced at Dale. When she realized where Dale's attention was focused, the arousal she was trying so hard to squash roared back to life.

"Earth to Dale," Casey said with a laugh.

Dale started and looked away from Logan's chest. Her color high, she said, "Right. Pass out the snacks. I'd better finish up with the punch."

When Dale walked away, Logan's gaze dropped to her ass.

"Great pants, huh?" Casey asked.

As if red were destined to be her normal color tonight, Logan's face flamed. "I should go help Dale."

"She could use your help all right," Casey muttered.

"What?"

Casey linked her arm with Logan's. "Never mind. Come on, let's get this party going."

Leaning against the wall behind the refreshment table, Casey snorted to herself as she watched Dale and Logan. *Sure, they're not the least bit interested in each other.* They had only spent the whole evening watching each other when they thought no one was looking. It had been clear for some time that they were attracted to each other, but neither had the courage to act on it. But Casey knew it was much more than just physical attraction. While she didn't agree with her, she knew what was holding Dale back. She wasn't as sure about Logan. Obviously, she had her secrets. What she couldn't understand was why two intelligent, accomplished, strong women who cared for each other were giving up a chance at happiness without even trying. Casey shook her head at the pair.

"Hey, Casey. Almost time," Sharon said. "Need a hand filling the cups for the toast?"

"Sure."

Sharon joined her behind the table and set to work. "So what's the deal with Dale and Logan? Are they involved or not? I've been getting mixed signals all night."

Of course Sharon, with her training in psychology and years as a social worker, would have picked up on the interplay between them. "They're friends."

"Nothing else?" Sharon's interest was clear.

"No. Just friends," she forced herself to say.

"Good to know."

A group of patients filed up to the table and picked up cups of punch.

Sharon quickly grabbed two of the plastic cups and slipped from behind the table.

"Where are you going?"

Sharon grinned. "Logan's new here. Just want to make sure she doesn't feel left out of the celebration."

Casey didn't believe that for a second. As much as she wanted to, it wasn't her place to warn her off. Besides, knowing Logan, she wouldn't be receptive anyway. Casey lost sight of Sharon as the table was swamped with people getting cups of punch for the rapidly approaching toast. Where the hell was Dale?

"Ten minutes!" someone called.

The small crowd dispersed from around the table as quickly as they had appeared.

Casey scanned the room for Logan. When she spotted her, she cursed under her breath. Not only was Sharon at Logan's side, but two male patients were standing close-by, looking overly eager.

Dale came striding up. "Sorry. Benson was bending my ear, and I couldn't get away."

"No problem. Here." Casey pushed two cups toward Dale. "Take that to Logan and stake your claim before midnight strikes."

"It's not actually midnight, you know." Ignoring the cups, Dale joined her behind the table.

"Smart-ass." She nudged Dale and motioned across the room. "Midnight or not, the vultures are just waiting for their chance to be the one who shares a kiss with Logan when that ball drops."

When Dale looked in the direction Casey indicated, a fierce scowl took up residence on her face. She shook her head roughly. "Knock it off, Casey."

"Suit yourself. Maybe I'll try my luck with her."

Dale whirled around with fire in her eyes. "What!"

Casey smirked. "I thought you weren't interested?"

"Casey." Dale's voice came out as a low growl. She crossed her arms over her chest.

"Five minutes," someone called out.

Why was she being so stubborn? No matter what Dale said, it was clear that she wanted to kiss Logan. Hell, Casey had seen them almost kiss already. Maybe all Dale needed was an excuse? "Remember when I agreed to look after Drake, and you said you owed me big-time?"

Dale's eyes narrowed and she nodded.

"You said name it, anything. I'm naming it. Kiss Logan at midnight. And I don't mean a peck on the cheek. A real kiss on the lips."

"Casey." This time, it sounded distinctly like a whine.

"Go on, hurry up."

Dale squared her shoulders. "Okay." She turned and marched away.

Dale made her way through the crowd as quickly as she could. Her insides were shaking with the thought of kissing Logan. She wasn't sure if she should thank Casey or curse her. Brushing past one of Logan's admirers, she took her place at Logan's side. She glanced at her, seeing the faint stress lines around her eyes, and barely resisted the urge to glare at the people around her. "Hi."

Logan met her gaze. The tension left her face, and she smiled. "Hi."

"Two minutes," someone yelled.

"Logan." Sharon put her hand on Logan's arm. "Would you—?"

"Excuse us. Could you hold this, please?" Dale plucked the cup out of Logan's hand and pressed it into Sharon's before she could protest. She grabbed Logan's hand. "Come on."

Logan followed her lead without question.

As they stepped away, Dale couldn't resist quirking a smile at a scowling Sharon. *Never happening.*

They ducked out of the room.

Dale led them far enough down the hall to be out of sight but close enough that they could still hear the countdown from the television. She glanced around the deserted hallway. Suddenly unsure, she met Logan's gaze. "Is this okay?"

"This is good. The crowd was getting a little much."

Dale gently rested a hand on Logan's shoulder. She had every intention of explaining about the promise she had made to Casey.

Logan's topaz-brown eyes darkened, making the golden starbursts surrounding her irises appear to glow.

Dale was lost. Drawn by a force too strong to resist, she moved closer to Logan as the countdown to the new year began.

The stroke of midnight found them face to face, mere inches separating them.

"Happy New Year," they whispered simultaneously.

Dale wasn't sure who moved first, but at the first touch of Logan's soft lips against hers, she didn't care.

Long ignored, the passion between them flared brightly.

Logan groaned and pressed close.

The feel of Logan's lush body against hers sent Dale's arousal soaring. She wrapped her arms around Logan and pulled her tightly against her.

Logan took control of the kiss, nipping at Dale's lower lip, urging her to open to her.

When Logan's tongue slipped into her mouth, heat rushed through Dale, pooling low in her belly.

"Friends, my ass!"

Dale and Logan jerked apart, both panting for breath.

Sharon stood several feet away. "Put a lid on it. There are patients around." She turned on her heel and stomped away.

Dale had been so lost in Logan that she had completely forgotten where they were. Sharon was right about that; anyone could have walked up on them, including a patient. She glanced at Logan, who looked away guiltily.

"I'm sorry. I shouldn't have done that." Logan turned to walk away.

Her body still humming from the kiss, she captured Logan's arm before she could leave. "Wait. You didn't. I was the one who started it. Don't go."

Logan shook her head. "We can't... I can't. I'm sorry." She pulled away and fled down the hall toward the elevators.

Dale started to follow her, then stopped. *What were you thinking?* She sighed. Clearly, she hadn't been. It was for the best. She could never be the whole person Logan deserved. With a heavy heart, she headed back to the party.

CHAPTER 30

CASEY GAVE BOTH GLASSES OF iced tea to Dale, then levered herself up onto the couch using her hands.

"Thanks." Once she got settled, Dale handed over one of the glasses.

"I'm sorry I ruined things for you," Casey said, picking up their prior conversation.

Dale dropped her head back against the cushion and sighed. "Quit saying that. It's not your fault."

"If I hadn't pushed you to kiss Logan, none of this would have happened."

"We've talked about this already—several times. You've got nothing to be sorry about. It was my choice. I could've said no." In the week and a half since New Year's Eve, she had cursed herself many times for not refusing. Yet, a large part of her couldn't regret it. It was the only kiss they would ever share, and she treasured the moment. Every time she relived the kiss, it never failed to stir her. Not that that had been happening frequently or anything.

She pushed away the memory and focused on the issue at hand. While they still shared a snack together before work in the conference room, as had become their custom, there was a guardedness about Logan that Dale thought them long past. And they had not spent any time together outside of work. Logan always had an excuse, but they were wearing thin.

She missed Logan's friendship, and Dale knew she wasn't the only one, since Logan always came up with an excuse when Casey asked her to bring Drake over for a visit and to have breakfast with her. "I'm just sorry you got caught up in it. I just wish I knew what to do."

"I know what you mean. I barely got a chance to say a word to her when she dropped Drake off at the VA on Wednesday. Same thing when she picked him up. She just blew in and out of there." Casey smacked the couch cushion. "Damn, she pisses me off with that bland, overly polite crap. I just want to grab her and shake her—get some kind of reaction." She blew out a breath. "Don't suppose you want to tell me what she's running from by living in an RV and traveling around doing locums?"

"I only know part of it." She met Casey's gaze. "And what I do know I don't feel comfortable sharing. That's up to Logan." She knew Logan was running from the pain of her sister's murder. What she couldn't understand was why she was working so hard to keep them both at arm's length again after finally letting them in. No matter how ill-advised the kiss had been, there had to be more to Logan's current behavior.

"Yeah. I hear you." Casey raked a hand through her hair. "The whole situation is just frustrating. I mean, I get it. The thing with Drake was only temporary. But I sure do miss the big guy. Would it kill her to bring him over for a little while?"

"I'm sorry."

"Don't you start." Casey shoved Dale's shoulder.

"Hey." Dale held her glass of iced tea high to keep it from spilling. Settling down, she glanced around the living room. It did seem empty without Drake. Despite her earlier discomfort with him, his gentle manner and calm demeanor had managed to win her over. "Have you ever thought about getting a dog?"

Casey's eyebrows arched. "A lot, actually, since Drake left. But I can't see myself chasing after a puppy." She ran a hand along the foreshortened prosthetics she was wearing. "Even with these, it's not like I can just slip them on like a pair of shoes when a puppy needs to go out. Having a puppy in the house is a lot like having a small child. They need constant attention."

"There must be lots of adult dogs that need homes—right?" Dale didn't know much about dogs, but even she had seen the commercials done by local animal shelters.

"Yeah." Casey nodded, her expression brightening. "Yeah, there are."

"If you're ready for a dog, we could go check the nearest animal shelter."

Casey turned and stared. "We? You want to go with me to an animal shelter filled with barking, rowdy dogs?"

Dale shrugged. "I was the one who got you involved with Drake. It's the least I can do. Besides, I figure after Drake, how intimidating can they be?"

"You are something else, my friend." She squeezed Dale's shoulder. "I'll take you up on that." She set her glass on the end table before using her hands to push off the couch and slide down until the feet of her stubbies reached the floor. "Let me put on my long legs and change, then we'll head out. Just to look, mind you."

Dale smiled as Casey waddled away. *Just to look... sure.* The smile dropped from her face as the reality of what she had just committed to sank in, and she gulped. She couldn't help wishing Logan was there to go with them.

When she spotted Casey coming back down the hall, Dale rose from the couch and went to meet her. "Ready?"

Casey grinned, looking happier than she had in over a week. "Let's go."

Dale peered into the conference room through the partially open door. Upon seeing Logan sitting at the table reading a journal, she blew out a breath, more relieved that she cared to admit. She was never sure that Logan would continue to show up for their pre-shift snack. Every day that went by, it seemed as if Logan was working to solidify the barriers that had come up between them after the kiss. Dale had worked so hard to knock down those barriers the first time, she was determined to not let Logan erect them again. For a lot of reasons, she might not be able to have the type of relationship with Logan that she longed for, and clearly Logan felt the same way, but Dale still wanted to remain her friend.

As she pushed open the door, she forced a carefree-looking smile onto her face. "Hey, Logan."

"Good evening."

Dale stifled a grimace. Logan's expression and tone of voice came across as if she were greeting someone she barely knew. She set the tray on the table. "I picked up some muffins from Maurine's."

Logan's eyes lit up, and she smiled. "Cranberry-orange?"

"Of course." This was more like it. Knowing they were Logan's favorite, she had made a special trip to the bakery, even though it had added forty-five minutes to her commute. Dale slipped into the chair at the head of the table. She always chose that spot so that she could be near Logan and easily see her face without having to turn in her chair.

As they ate, Dale racked her brain to come up with something to talk about that would keep Logan from giving one- or two-word answers. Some days it felt as if she would never reach her and get back that easy interaction. She smiled to herself when inspiration struck.

"Do you know you have to get interviewed and fill out an application to adopt a dog?"

"What?" Logan's eyes went wide. "You're adopting a dog?"

Dale laughed. "No, not me. Casey." She met Logan's gaze. "She really misses Drake."

Logan's shoulders slumped, and she glanced away.

Maybe Logan wasn't as unaffected by all of this as she portrayed.

"Casey has wanted a dog for a while but didn't think she was up to chasing a puppy around. And I can see her point." It was Dale's turn to look away. She still hadn't gotten to the place where she could easily discuss anything that might remind Logan of Dale's own amputation.

She started when Logan placed a hand on her arm and gave it a brief squeeze. The warmth and understanding in Logan's eyes helped hold her insecurities at bay.

"A puppy needs a lot of care. Like Casey said, her prosthetics aren't a pair of shoes that she can quickly slip on in the middle of the night when the puppy needs to go out."

"So if she wanted a dog, why didn't she adopt an adult before now?"

"She kept her brothers' dogs at her place occasionally, and I think she had convinced herself that she could get her," Dale grinned, "'fix' that way."

Logan's eyes narrowed. "Are you insinuating that dog people are addicts?"

Laughing, Dale shook her head. "I'm not insinuating anything."

"Hey!" Logan poked her in the side.

Elation filled Dale at the sparkle in Logan's eyes. This was what she had missed. "But taking care of Drake reminded her how great it was to have a dog in the house full-time. So we went to an animal shelter this morning. I thought you just went in and picked out a dog, but that's not the case. You have to—"

"Wait. You went with her?" Logan's eyebrows rose. "Into the kennels?"

"Yep. I sure did." Dale couldn't help puffing her chest out a little. "Hey, after being around Drake, all those other dogs didn't seem like such a big deal." Well, that wasn't quite the whole truth. Dale's thoughts went back to the first moment they had stepped into the kennel area filled with rows of jumping, barking dogs. The din had been incredible. Talk about immersion therapy. Drake might be huge, but he was always calm. But she had persevered.

"I'm really proud of you." Logan laid her hand back on Dale's arm. "That couldn't have been easy."

Dale struggled not to lose herself in the depths of Logan's eyes. Her gaze dropped to Logan's lips. She started to lean forward, then caught herself. *No. Don't ruin things.* She pushed her chair back, breaking the contact and putting some additional distance between them.

"Anyway, we looked at a lot of dogs, but Casey insisted none of them were 'the one.'"

A frown flashed across Logan's face, quickly replaced by her normal placid expression. "Well, I'm sure she'll find the right one."

Relief washed over Dale that Logan hadn't noticed her momentary slip. This morning had proven that their friendship was salvageable; she just needed to do a better job of keeping her misplaced desire under wraps.

"We're going to go to a different shelter on Friday. How about you come with us? I know Casey would appreciate your help."

Logan visibly hesitated. "I guess I could..."

"Great. We'll meet at Casey's at ten," Dale said, making it sound as if it were a done deal.

Glancing at her watch, Logan said, "We better get out there." She stood and gathered up the remains of their snack. "Thanks for the muffin and coffee."

"You're welcome." She followed Logan out of the room, her mood lighter than it had been in days.

Dale had a spring in her step as she headed for the staff lounge at the end of the shift. For the first time since the ill-fated kiss, things had gotten almost back to normal with Logan. There had been a few times that she'd caught what looked like a sad expression on Logan's face, but as quickly as it had appeared, it was gone and Logan was back to normal. Dale wondered if she was just imagining it because she was so hypersensitive to Logan's reactions.

Pushing open the door to the lounge, she smiled when she spotted Logan at her locker.

Logan glanced her way.

"Hey. I'm starving." She tugged open her own locker. "How about joining me for breakfast? I never did get a chance to introduce you to the food at Gina's Café. You'll love the place."

"Sorry. I've got to drop Drake off at day care, then I have an appointment to get my hair cut." Logan shut her locker and turned toward the door. "See you tomorrow."

So much for things getting back to normal. Struggling not to let her disappointment show, she waved in Logan's direction. "See you."

The door to the lounge swung open just as Logan reached it. She caught the door with her hand.

"Sorry." Jess stepped into the room. "I'm glad I caught you. Listen, if you change your mind, just let me know."

Logan darted a glance at Dale. She nodded to Jess and made a quick exit.

Dale frowned. "Change her mind about what?"

"Leaving at the end of the week."

What! Feeling as if she had been sucker punched, Dale gasped for breath.

Jess was instantly at her side. "Are you all right?"

She was barely aware of Jess. Had Logan planned on waiting until the last minute to tell her that she was leaving? A harsher thought hit. Or was she not going to say a word and just disappear? Anger waged a brief battle with hurt and won. Her hands clenched at her sides.

She glanced at a worried-looking Jess. "I'm fine. Excuse me. I need to go." Determined to confront Logan—right now—she took off after her.

CHAPTER 31

HAVING MISSED LOGAN AT THE hospital, Dale had immediately headed for the campground where Logan was staying. She pulled up near Logan's motor home only to find her SUV missing from its usual spot.

"Where the fuck are you?" Dale slammed her hand repeatedly against the steering wheel. Pain coursing up her arm helped clear her head. That's when she remembered. Logan had said she was taking Drake to day care, then going to get her hair cut.

Undeterred, Dale parked her Jeep in a visitor's spot and marched back over to Logan's RV. No longer completely trusting Logan, she rapped sharply on the door. When there was no answering bark, she plopped down on the top step leading into the motor home to wait. "Well, at least she told the truth about that."

By the time Logan pulled up forty-five minutes later, Dale's anger hadn't cooled one iota. In fact, the more time she had to think about it, the angrier she got. When had Logan decided to take off? After the kiss? Her hands fisted on her thighs. Or before?

As Logan approached, Dale rose from the steps like a raging bull ready to charge. "Were you even going to tell me?"

Logan stiffened. She jammed her hands into the front pockets of her pants. "Don't do this. I have to leave."

"So it's true." She stomped toward Logan. "You were just going to run away!"

"Is everything all right, Dr. Logan?" a quavering voice asked from nearby.

Dale whipped her head around.

An elderly man was standing at the front of Logan's RV.

Blowing out a breath, she took a big step back from Logan, realizing that not only had she been yelling, but she was right in Logan's face.

"Everything's fine, Mr. Kelton."

"Are you sure?" He shot a glare at Dale. "I have my phone." He brandished the small flip phone as if it were a weapon.

"I'm sure. Thank you for checking."

After throwing one last challenging look at Dale, Mr. Kelton walked away, but not without looking back several times.

Once he was out of sight, Dale confronted Logan again. "Well?"

"You should go," Logan said.

Dale kept her voice low and forced a calmness to her tone that she really didn't feel. "I'm not going anywhere until you tell me the truth."

Without a word, Logan stepped around her and walked over to the door of the motor home. She unlocked it and went inside but left the door standing open.

Dale followed her in and closed the door.

They faced off across the tiny living area.

Her lips clamped into a thin line, Logan crossed her arms over her chest.

Dale waited several moments for her to speak, but Logan just stared at her. "So it is true. You were just going to leave without saying a word." She mirrored Logan's position, arms across her chest.

"I would have told you... I just... I didn't..." Logan rubbed her chest above her breast. "I have to go. I can't stay here. Not now." She clamped her hand over her mouth as if she had said too much.

"Tell me why." Dale stepped closer until barely a foot separated them. The hurt she had been trying so hard to smother with anger broke through. Repressed tears stung her eyes. "Does my friendship mean nothing to you?"

"That's not—" Tears lurked in the corners of Logan's eyes too. She shook her head roughly. "I can't stay here!" Her voice rose with each word.

Dale moved closer, crowding her. "Why?"

She backpedaled two steps and hit the door that closed off the back of the motor home.

Dale stayed right with her, pressing even closer, but not touching. "Tell. Me. Why." A single tear trailed down her cheek. "Please."

"Don't make me say it."

Their gazes locked.

Like a living thing, the passion between them flared.

"Damn you." Logan grabbed the front of Dale's shirt and with surprising strength, spun her around until her back was pressed against the door. She closed the distance between them in a flash. "Damn me," she whispered.

Then her lips were on Dale's, rough and demanding, ravaging her mouth. Logan released Dale's shirt and cupped both her breasts in her hands.

Dale's arousal skyrocketed at the unexpected but wholly welcomed turn of events. She clutched Logan's hips, trying to anchor herself.

Logan pulled away from her mouth to kiss down her neck, alternating between sharp nips and licks. She pushed her leg between Dale's thighs and pressed hard against her center.

The seam of Dale's jeans rubbed against her clit, making her hips buck.

"I need to touch you," Logan whispered. "Please."

"Yes." Her blood roaring in her ears, Dale whimpered in relief when Logan unbuckled her belt and opened her pants.

Logan slid her hand inside Dale's underwear and groaned as her fingers eased into the heat between her thighs. "So wet."

She grabbed Logan's ass in both hands and used her leverage to shift enough so that Logan could ride her thigh.

The breath hissed from Logan. As she stroked Dale's clit with firm pressure, her own hips began to thrust, hard and fast.

Dale squeezed Logan's ass in rhythm with her thrusts, struggling not to climax on the spot.

"Oh fuck." Logan panted, her breath hot against Dale's neck. "I'm going to..." Her hips surged against Dale, and she cried out.

The feel of Logan climaxing against her set off the fire coiled in her belly and triggered her own orgasm.

Shuddering with the aftereffects of her powerful release, Logan sagged against Dale.

Dale's arms wrapped around her, holding her close.

Her breath sawed in and out, and it took several moments for her pleasure-soaked brain to start working again. As soon as it did, guilt swamped her. Just as she had feared, once close to Dale, her resolve had wavered, and her long-held promise had gone up in flames. She pulled her hand from Dale's pants and broke their embrace.

"What's wrong?" Dale asked as Logan backed away.

When Logan came up against the pedestal table, she gripped the edge. No matter how much it hurt, she had to do this. Emily could never be with anyone; she didn't deserve to either. She met Dale's gaze. "I'm sorry. I shouldn't have done that. It can't happen again."

Dale stared openmouthed for a moment, then snapped her jaw closed. She jerked her pants shut and righted her clothes. "I understand."

The pain on Dale's face pierced Logan deeper than any arrow could. Regardless of her promise to Emily, she longed to pull Dale back into her arms and never let her go. "No. You don't."

Dale looked away. "It doesn't matter." She ducked her head and made for the door.

Logan stepped directly into her path. "Yes, it does. Please. I need you to understand."

Dale refused to look at her.

"I made a promise to Emily that I would never be with a woman again. I just...I touched you and..." She brought her fingers to her chest and pressed on the permanent reminder of her promise. "I'm sorry. I can't let that happen again."

Dale's head whipped up, anger sparking in her steely gray eyes. "No one, no matter who they are, has the right to demand something like that of you."

She had to make Dale understand. "What happened to Emily was all my fault. I didn't show up on time. We were supposed to go together to drop off the gifts at the women's shelter that night." Logan's hands latched on to her thighs, and she squeezed—hard. "Instead, I was busy having a quickie with some nurse while my sister was being murdered. I swore I'd never touch another woman again. And I haven't—until today."

Dale's expression softened. "What happened to Emily was terrible. But it wasn't your fault."

Logan shook her head. She turned to the picture on the wall that Dale had commented on previously and touched the image. "She wasn't just my sister; we were identical twins."

Dale gasped. Her gaze darted back and forth between the photograph and Logan. "I'm so sorry." She reached out to touch Logan, then hesitated. Her arm dropped before she could make contact. "But that doesn't change the fact that what happened wasn't your fault. Even if you'd been there, it doesn't mean you could've stopped it.

The person who killed Emily is the only one responsible. Not you."

She skirted past Dale and slumped onto the couch. "Emily was robbed of so many things. She never had a chance to marry her girlfriend, have a family..." Logan rubbed her chest. "The list goes on and on. How can I do any of those things knowing she never will?"

Dale sat down next to Logan, leaving a gap between them. Her gaze swept the small space as if she were seeing it for the first time. When she turned back to Logan, a new understanding showed in her eyes. "This place. The way you live your life. It's your prison. Your punishment."

There was no use denying it. Logan ducked her head. "It's more than I deserve. At least through my job, I help people."

"Oh, Logan. No." Dale put her fingers under Logan's chin, urging her to look up. When she did, Dale cupped her cheek.

Unable to stop herself, she leaned into the touch.

"I can never know what it was like to lose your twin. But I do know about survivor guilt; it's very common among vets. You can't let it rule your life."

Logan pulled back, breaking the contact of Dale's hand on her face. "It's not that simple. It's not just that the guilt is always there. I don't know how to explain but—"

Dale stopped her with a touch on her arm. "You don't need to. I know firsthand how hard it is to fight against."

What? Realization dawned. Other people must have been killed when Dale lost her leg. But that couldn't possibly be Dale's fault—could it? She had only thought about the physical injuries Dale had suffered. Was it possible that Dale really understood what she was going through? "Will you tell me what happened?"

Dale swallowed heavily and looked away.

She held back a sigh and briefly stroked Dale's arm. "I'm sorry. I shouldn't have asked you."

Visibly squaring her shoulders, Dale turned back toward Logan. "I want to tell you." She put her hands on her thighs and kneaded the material of her jeans. "We were with a convoy of four vehicles returning to the combat support hospital where I was assigned in Afghanistan."

Logan couldn't help wondering why a member of the navy was assigned to someplace in the desert. Shouldn't she have been on a ship? But she didn't want to interrupt to ask.

"We were just a few miles from the base when the lead vehicle hit an IED. I was in the third vehicle back, and the explosion was so strong, debris from the Humvee hit us. I could see the burning hulk of the vehicle, and I knew they were all dead." Dale's gaze grew distant as if she were seeing it all over again. "That's when the bastards opened up on us with RPGs. We were a bunch of medical personnel, for God's sake; we were helping people. The vehicle in front of us took a hit and caught fire. The people inside started bailing out—right into small-arms fire. Our marine driver told us to stay put, that help was on the way. But there were victims out there, lying bleeding in the sand." Haunted eyes met Logan's. "I couldn't just sit there and do nothing. Bruno...God, Bruno... He was a nurse I'd become friends with during my tour. I told him to stay in the Humvee. There was no reason for both of us to take the risk. He had a wife at home and a baby on the way. But the damn stubborn jerk wouldn't listen. We managed to pull the wounded to the other side of the vehicles, away from where the snipers were. The marines returned fire and protected us as best they could." Dale fell silent as the memories seemed to overwhelm her.

Logan watched her struggle but was hesitant to touch her, fearing she might make things worse. Finally, unable to stand it, she carefully touched Dale's back and stroked up and down slowly. "It's okay. You don't have to tell me anymore."

Blowing out a breath, Dale raked her hands through her hair. "I need to."

Logan nodded and continued with her gentle touch as Dale resumed her story.

"There was a second IED that by some fluke our vehicles had missed detonating." Her expression turned storm-cloud dark. "Or who knows, maybe the bastards planned it that way. Just as the helicopters arrived to drive them off, the sons of bitches set it off. Vehicle behind ours took the brunt of it. I don't remember much after that. But I'll never forget the sight of Bruno, with the side of his head caved in, bleeding out into the sand."

When Logan met Dale's eyes, she saw for the first time the pain of the memories that Dale lived with every day. *Oh, Dale.* Logan pressed her hand to her queasy stomach.

Unlike Logan, Dale had made something of her life after the horrible attack and injuries. Logan felt sick with remorse. *You're a coward.* What Dale had accomplished took real strength and courage. It reminded her once again what an amazing woman Dale was.

"I don't know what to say. 'I'm sorry' seems so inadequate."

"It's okay. You don't need to say anything. I accept now that it wasn't my fault. Bruno made his own choices, and I have to respect that. But that acceptance didn't come easy." She met Logan's gaze head-on. "I blamed myself for a long time and engaged in some pretty destructive behavior. I didn't think I deserved to be happy or have a good life. But I was wrong. The best way I could honor Bruno and the other people who died was to do exactly that. You owe it to Emily to live your life to the fullest."

Was Dale right? Logan wanted so badly to lay down the burden of her guilt, but she didn't know if she could.

As if sensing her struggle, Dale entwined her fingers with Logan's. "A very wise, stubborn woman that we both know once asked me a question."

It only took a moment for her to realize Dale was talking about Casey.

"Let me ask you a similar one. What if it had been the other way around and Emily was the one who survived? Is this the life you would expect her to live?"

She thought of the last two years and pictured Emily with her kind, gentle spirit and her love of people shut off from the world. "No." The word burst from Logan.

Dale cupped her face and traced her thumb over Logan's cheek, brushing away the tears Logan hadn't even realized were there. "If she could see you now, would she be happy with the life you've chosen to lead? Is it really what she would have wanted for you?"

Logan closed her eyes. She could almost see Emily sadly shaking her head. Emily had always faced things head-on. How had she let herself get to this place? She'd not only run from the pain of Emily's death but from life. Her shoulders slumped. *Oh, Em. What have I done?*

The warmth of Dale's palm against her cheek never wavered. Logan opened her eyes and gazed into dark gray irises filled with compassion and understanding. "I don't know what to do."

Dale gripped her hand. "You start by vowing to make the most of every single day. Not just with work but everything in life. Let people in." She smiled. "You've already made a start with me—and Casey."

It was true. As much as she had fought against it, she had come to care for Dale and Casey. But in Dale's case, her feelings went much deeper than friendship. *No more hiding.* Determined to make a fresh start here and now, Logan cradled Dale's face in her hands and placed a soft kiss on her lips. "Thank you for not giving up on me."

"Never." Dale returned the kiss and lingered.

She slid her hand into Dale's hair at the base of her neck and licked at Dale's lower lip, begging entrance. When Dale opened to her, she groaned into her mouth and deepened the kiss.

The sound of a cell phone startled them apart.

Dale growled. "It's mine." She jerked the phone out of her pocket and glanced at the screen before stabbing the connect button. "What!"

Although Logan was perturbed as well by the interruption, she was taken aback by Dale's greeting.

Grimacing, Dale flopped back against the couch. "Yeah. I'm sorry. I'll be there as soon as I can." She rolled her eyes. "Yes, Mom. Everything's fine. No. I'll be there soon."

Logan grinned when she realized Dale was talking to Casey.

"Sorry." Dale pushed off the couch. "I have to go." She glanced at her watch. "I was supposed to be at the VA an hour ago."

Logan opened the door, and Dale slipped past her. "I'll see you tonight. And thank you—for everything."

Dale stepped down onto the first step, then turned back to look up at Logan. Anxiety flashed across her face. "You're staying...after this week—right?"

An unexpected jolt of nerves struck. Taking a deep breath, she said, "I'm staying." Logan grabbed Dale's sleeve before she could walk away. "This is all kind of scary. Just be patient with me...okay?"

A smile that could have lit a city spread across Dale's face. "You've got it. I promise." She tugged Logan down and placed a quick kiss on her lips.

Logan leaned back out of temptation's range. "You better get going. I'll bring the snack tonight."

"Sounds great. See you later."

Logan stayed in the doorway until Dale was out of sight. So much had happened; she still hadn't processed it all. But there was one thing she knew for sure: it felt as if a weight had been lifted from her shoulders. She felt lighter than she had in years.

CHAPTER 32

As Dale neared the conference room door at the beginning of the night shift, anxiety gripped her, but for a totally different reason than it had for the last week and a half. Everything had changed between her and Logan after the events that morning. Logan had opened up to her in a way she never had before. And the mere memory of Logan's hands on her sent arousal skittering down Dale's spine. Despite her fear of Logan's reaction once she fully exposed her physical defects, she was determined to make this relationship work. She pushed open the door.

Logan looked up and smiled. "Hey there."

Dale ran her hands down the front of her scrubs as she approached the table. Should she kiss Logan hello? Keep things professional at work?

Logan solved her dilemma by reaching for her hand and giving it a firm squeeze.

Okay. So professional it was. That was comfortable and familiar. Dale felt some of her anxiety wane.

"How did things go with Casey at the VA?"

Grimacing, Dale said, "You know Casey. She gave me the third degree."

Logan frowned.

"But I didn't tell her everything," Dale blurted, her face going hot. She had a vivid sense memory of Logan's hand down her pants. "I said we had a fight about you leaving and that you were going to stay. And that I told you about Bruno." She laid her hand on Logan's arm. "I didn't say anything about Emily. I wouldn't betray your confidence."

Logan put her hand on top of Dale's. "You could've told her."

Dale shook her head. "That's your story to tell. If you want to."

"Yeah. I do." Logan swallowed heavily. "I need to take Drake for a visit. I'll talk to her then."

"I know she'll appreciate that."

Although Logan had taken a huge first step, survivor guilt was tenacious. It wasn't something she was going to get over in a day. Dale still struggled occasionally with guilt over Bruno's death. As Casey always said, it was important to pay help forward. And knowing that others understood because they had been there themselves had helped Dale. Now she could help Logan.

But it was more than just sharing her experiences; if there was any chance of this working between them, she had to let Logan into other parts of her life. The upcoming basketball game was the perfect opportunity to do so. Could she really let Logan see her like that?

A warm hand on her arm brought Dale back to the here and now.

"Is everything okay?"

The warmth and concern in Logan's eyes soothed her. "Yeah. Sorry. I was just thinking." Dale blew out a breath. *You can do this.* "A group of us get together and play wheelchair basketball once a month. It falls on a day we're both off. I was wondering if you'd be interested in going to the game? Afterward, I'd like to take you out to dinner."

Logan's eyes went wide for a moment, then she smiled and squeezed Dale's arm. "If you're sure, I'd like that. Just tell me when and where."

"Great. I'll pick you up. It's a date."

Logan's expression dimmed before she visibly squared her shoulders. "Never thought I would hear those words again."

Was it too much too soon? Dale tried not to let her disappointment show. "If you're not ready, we don't have to—"

Logan stroked Dale's arm. "It's fine. More than fine. I just... It's a big adjustment."

Tension leaked from Dale. "I understand that. Whatever you need. We'll take it slow." It was a relief for her too as she didn't know how she was going to handle Logan seeing her without her leg and in a wheelchair. Or for that matter, how Logan was going to react. And truth be told, Dale never thought she would be asking a woman out on a date again.

"Thank you. I look forward to it."

"So what did you bring us?" Dale motioned toward the bag next to Logan.

"A new bakery opened just down the street from the campground. Check these out." She pulled a large pecan-covered sticky bun from the bag.

"Oh. Gimme."

Logan laughed. "Yes, ma'am."

Dale settled in to enjoy her treat. For the moment, at least, all was right with the world.

Logan leaned back against the counter at the nurses' station and sipped her coffee. She'd had a hard time keeping her mind on the job tonight, and that never happened to her. She kept thinking of Dale. Not only about what had happened between them that morning, but also about their impending date. Guilt had swamped her several times, but she resolutely fought to vanquish it.

When she spotted Molly approaching, she forced away the distracting thoughts for the umpteenth time. She beckoned her over. At first, she hadn't been very impressed with the resident, but Molly was really putting out an extra effort of late. "How did it go?"

"All set. I did the exam and got the name of her boyfriend."

"You did a really good job. I thought I was going to have to street her. I couldn't convince her to let me do a pelvic exam or even admit she was sexually active."

Molly beamed. "Thanks."

"Make sure you get all the correct forms submitted to report—"

The doors to the ambulance bay banged open.

Jess McKenna strode into the ER and grabbed a nearby gurney. "I need some help out here." She pushed the gurney out the doors.

Logan sprinted for the ambulance bay.

Riley Connolly, a staff trauma surgeon, stood on the running board next to the open door of an SUV. When she turned her head at Logan's approach, Riley looked pale and shaken.

What was she doing here? Logan pushed aside the useless speculation and focused on the patient. She did a double take when she got a look at the woman in the passenger seat. Did Jess have a twin?

The woman clutched her huge belly and groaned.

"Hang in there, Sis. We're going to get you inside," Jess said.

Together, they got Jess's sister out of the vehicle and onto the gurney.

Riley took up a position right next to her. "Everything is going to be okay, Sam. I promise." She brushed back Sam's sweat-soaked hair and placed a tender kiss on her forehead.

"This is my sister, Sam," Jess said as they made their way into the ER and a treatment room. "Thirty-five years old, gravida one, para zero, thirty-one weeks gestation with twins. Onset of periumbilical pain twenty-four hours ago with nausea. No emesis at that time. Afibril. Escalation of the pain in the last hour with migration to the right upper quadrant. Continuing nausea with a single incident of emesis thirty minutes ago. No contractions. No vaginal bleeding. Suspected appendicitis."

Logan was taken aback by Jess's unemotional, clinical recitation. This was her sister. She took a closer look.

Jess had her hands so tightly clenched around the railing of the gurney that her knuckles were blanched white. Stress lines framed her eyes. Riley didn't seem to be fairing any better, but they were both working hard to present a calm demeanor in front of Sam.

Logan's respect for both women rose. She couldn't imagine handling things this well in a similar situation. She did her own quick assessment.

Nancy, one of nurses, arrived with Patty, another nurse, right on her heels.

"Patty, go up to OB and tell them we need a twin fetal monitor," Jess ordered before Logan could. "If they give you any hassle, tell them Dr. Childress is on her way and ordered it."

"I'm on it." Patty took off.

Logan frowned, not familiar with the names of all the doctors from different departments.

"Helen Childress is Sam's OB," Riley said, apparently having caught Logan's expression.

They got Sam transferred to an ER bed and positioned on her left side.

Logan glanced at her boss. Was Jess going to insist on taking care of her sister? She thought it was a really bad idea but wasn't in a position to protest.

After a visible struggle, Jess stepped back from the bed. "I'm here as family. Do what you need to. Helen should be here shortly, but I'm convinced this isn't about the pregnancy. I'll go get her checked in." She gave Sam's toes a squeeze. "I'll be back soon. You're in good hands with Dr. Logan."

When Sam nodded, Jess made her exit.

Logan met Riley's eyes, silently asking what she was going to do.

"I'm her wife. Not her doctor."

Logan nodded. Conscious of Riley's gaze on her, she set to work. She gave Nancy the orders for the necessary labs, then motioned for her to go ahead with what she needed to do.

As Nancy took Sam's vitals, hooked her to a monitor, and prepared to start an IV, Logan grabbed a clipboard with the intake sheet on it and moved to the head of the bed. "Hello. I'm Dr. Logan." Pain-filled blue eyes met hers. "It's Sam, right? Is that okay?"

"Yeah. That's fine."

"Let's start with your medical history." She took down Sam's medical history and double-checked the information Jess had given her, not because she didn't trust Jess but because it needed to be verified and documented.

"Okay, I need to do a physical exam, then I'll get you some pain med onboard. I'm sorry, but this isn't going to be pleasant."

Sam clenched her teeth and nodded.

Logan did a basic exam before baring Sam's large belly. As she examined her, she distracted her by repeating some of her earlier questions.

When Logan palpated the right upper quadrant of her belly, Sam let out a pained yelp.

Riley grabbed the bed rail and looked as if she was about to pass out.

Logan had never seen the talented trauma surgeon so much as break a sweat, no matter how intense the situation. As quickly as she could, Logan finished the exam and covered up Sam's belly. She had felt at least one of the babies move during the exam, which was a relief. She met Sam's gaze. "Since your OB is on the way, I'm going to forgo a pelvic exam. I know she will want to examine you herself. I don't want you to have to go through that twice."

"I appreciate that." Sam glanced over her shoulder at a pale, clammy-looking Riley. "I've had so many women's fingers down there lately, it felt like I was single again."

Riley gasped, her face flushing with color. "Samantha Connolly! You are so bad."

Sam shook her head. "It's the pain meds."

"You haven't had any yet."

"Oh yeah. Okay, it's the pain talking."

Riley mock-scowled at her wife. "Is this what it's going to be like when you deliver?"

A little half smirk twisted Sam's lips. "Maybe."

Logan bit her lip, then, unable to hold it in, she laughed. She darted a glance at Riley.

Riley shook her head at her wife's antics, but she looked calmer.

Ah, well done. Clearly, that had been Sam's intent. Logan couldn't help being impressed with her, especially considering how much pain she must be in.

Patty pushed the cart with the fetal monitor into the room. Jess was right behind her.

After sending Nancy for the pain medication she had promised, Logan chose to set up the fetal monitor herself instead of having Patty do it. It was nerve-racking to work under the eyes of Jess and Riley. Nevertheless, Logan refused to rush. It took several minutes to get the sensors correctly placed with Sam lying on her side. Monitoring two babies simultaneously was difficult. The tension in the room built with each passing moment.

When the dual graphs appeared on the display screen, showing both babies' heart rates in the normal range, indicating that they weren't in distress, Logan breathed a silent sigh of relief.

She turned the monitor around so that Sam and Riley could see it.

"Look, Sam. Look at our boys," Riley said, gripping her wife's shoulder. "They're doing fine."

Sam offered a tremendous smile.

The tension in the room plummeted as if a pressure valve had been released.

Nancy returned with the requested pain medication and injected it into the port of Sam's IV.

Logan weighed her options. For a moment, she wished Dale had caught this case, then chastised herself for the thought. Normally, she would just inform the patient what test she was ordering. It always complicated things when family members of the patient were medical professionals. And in this case, that was doubly so.

She glanced at Jess and Riley across Sam's bed, then addressed Sam. "I agree with your sister that it's most likely acute appendicitis. I feel it's important to get an ultrasound now to confirm that diagnosis rather than wait for your OB to arrive. You're not having contractions, and the babies aren't in any distress at this point. If it is appendicitis, the quicker we get you to the OR, the better it will be for you and the babies."

"Do the ultrasound now," Sam said before Jess or Riley could respond.

That settled it in Logan's mind. "All right, then. One of the nurses will bring in the machine, and I'll be back shortly."

"Thanks," Sam said.

Logan nodded and quickly made her exit.

When the lounge door swung open, Logan glanced up. An automatic smile formed at the sight of Dale. It was nearing the end of shift, and everything was quiet. She hoped to get out of here on time.

"Any word?" Molly asked.

Now that the staff knew the situation with Jess's sister, they had all been anxiously awaiting word on how Sam was doing. She had gone to the OR two hours ago.

Dale shook her head. "Nothing yet." She slipped into the seat next to Logan at the round table in the middle of the room.

Logan returned to her questioning of Molly. While she understood the resident not wanting to be actively involved in a case with a family member of their boss, it was still a good teaching opportunity. "So tell me why a pregnant woman would present with periumbilical and/or right upper quadrant pain instead of the classic right lower quadrant pain with appendicitis?"

Molly's forehead wrinkled, and she worried her lower lip between her teeth.

"A baby sure takes up a lot of room in the abdomen, especially later in the pregnancy," Amber said from her spot on the couch.

"No help from the peanut gallery," Dale said.

Logan hid a smile. It wasn't something she would have been comfortable saying to the resident, no matter how appropriate.

Molly's face lit up. "As the uterus expands, all the organs are pushed out of position. In this case, they are pushed up, so the position of the appendix changes and rides higher in the abdomen."

"Correct. Half a point for that one since you had help."

The lounge door swung open again, and Jess strode into the room. She glanced around. "I didn't know it was ladies' night."

"Yeah. The PMS squad is all here," Amber said. "Just ask Fred."

Everyone laughed. The lone male nurse on duty had been whining all night about the excess of estrogen flooding the department.

"How's your sister doing?" Logan asked the question on all their minds. Although from how relaxed Jess looked, she figured things must have gone well.

"She's doing great. And so are the babies. They all came through the surgery with no problems. Thank you for taking such good care of her."

"You laid it all out for me. I just confirmed it."

Jess moved to stand next to Logan and put a hand on her shoulder. "I'm glad you've decided to stay and help us out until Gretchen comes back. You're an asset to the department."

Logan flushed. "Thanks." She glanced at Dale, surprised to see her frowning. What was that about?

The arrival of the day shift staff distracted Logan.

"All right, let's get this turnover done so these people can go home," Jess said.

The lounge cleared quickly once the transfer of the patients was complete, and the residents headed for morning conference.

When they were the only two left at the table, Logan smiled over at Dale. "How about I pick up Drake and we go barge in on Casey? I'll even make breakfast."

Dale rubbed her hands together. "Oh. You know I'd never turn down your cooking."

"Good. Let's go."

CHAPTER 33

Logan growled as a third step brought her up short again. It wasn't possible to pace satisfactorily in the small confines of the motor home, although that hadn't stopped her from trying.

Drake lifted his head and grumbled softly. Every return trip took her across his bed.

"I know, boy. Sorry." She flopped down on the couch. She was having second and third thoughts about going on a date with Dale tonight. It wasn't that she didn't want to go, she did. But her guilt was trying to get the best of her.

As it once more threatened to overwhelm her, she thought of Dale. Dale sharing the story of her injury and her own struggle with survivor guilt had really hit home. *You owe it to Emily to live your life to the fullest.* Dale's words echoed in her head.

"Emily wouldn't want me to spend my life alone, isolated from everyone." Saying it out loud helped. Blowing out a breath, she pushed off the couch. "I can do this."

Now all she had to do was find something to wear. A fresh wash of anxiety hit. Maybe she should have bought something new. After all, everything she had was several years old. Her clothes were serviceable, and that was all that had mattered. She frequently wore scrubs at work, so that helped prolong their life.

Drake poked her thigh, making her aware that she was pacing again.

Logan reached down and patted him. "Sorry. Okay, no need to freak out. It's a basketball game. Probably at some rec center or something. I can just wear jeans—right?"

Drake remained mute on the subject.

"You're not helping."

Logan scowled and made her way into the back of the motor home. She pulled a pair of black jeans from the closet and held them up. Her thoughts went back to an incident a few weeks ago. She had been bent over rummaging in her locker and glanced over at Dale. She could have sworn that Dale was staring at her butt. At the time, she'd thought she was mistaken, but now she knew better. Heat rushed through Logan's body at the unexpectedly vivid memory of Dale grabbing her ass and squeezing in rhythm with her thrusts against Dale's thigh. She fanned herself. "Black jeans it is."

The choice of the shirt was easier. She still remembered Dale's gaze on her cleavage on New Year's Eve. Logan grabbed the shirt she wanted and laid both items on the bed. Now thoroughly flustered with thoughts of Dale, she headed for a shower—a very cold one.

A glance at her watch made her curse. Her anxieties and trip down memory lane had taken more time than she realized. Dale was due in forty-five minutes.

The headlights of Dale's Jeep pierced the gloom and illuminated the rain-swept street. An occasional gust of wind struck with enough force to rock the vehicle.

"Everyone keeps talking about the drought. But it doesn't seem like much of one to me," Logan said.

"I know what you mean." Dale turned into the parking lot of the community center. "This is the rainiest January I've seen during my six years in Southern California. Two years ago, when I was still in San Diego, we barely got any rain at all that whole winter." She glanced at the clock on the dash and cursed under her breath.

"What is it?"

"We're running late." She pulled into a parking space. "The storm hitting halfway here and messing up traffic played havoc with my timing."

"Sorry. If you hadn't had to pick me up—"

"Hey. No." Dale turned as far as she could in her seat and put her hand on Logan's shoulder. "I wanted to pick you up. You didn't make it rain." She peered out the windshield. "Looks like a slight lull. Come on, let's get inside."

When they reached the double glass doors to the community center, Dale pulled open one of them. A sudden gust of wind almost jerked it out of her hand, knocking her off balance.

Logan grabbed the door with one hand and Dale's jacket with the other. Together, they stumbled inside and pulled it shut.

"So much for the lull. It's getting nasty out there." Dale stopped just inside the door, pulled off her jacket, and shuffled her feet on the thick rubber-backed mat. Logan followed suit.

Now that they were actually here, Dale's earlier nervousness reasserted itself. Her grip tightened on the duffle bag holding her toiletries and clothes for later. She glanced over at Logan.

Stress lines framed her eyes. Clearly, Dale wasn't the only one who was nervous.

"We should go in," Dale said. As they walked down the hall, Dale tried to ease Logan's concerns. She realized this had to be a challenge for her too after having spent the last two years cut off from social interactions for the most part. "There won't be a big crowd. This is a community outreach program for vets. Not a formal league or anything like that. So it will be mostly family and friends of the players from the VA and a few players from a local wheelchair basketball league. And with this weather, the crowd will probably be smaller than usual."

Logan nodded as they stepped into the gym.

The sound of thudding footsteps drew Dale's attention. Dana was barreling down on them like a freight train at full throttle. *Damn it.* The volatile woman was definitely not the first person Dale wanted Logan to meet this afternoon. *No help for it now.*

"Where the fuck have you been?" She got right in Dale's face. "You're late!"

When Logan stiffened beside her, Dale clasped her hand and gave it a quick squeeze, hoping she got the message. She didn't take her gaze off Dana. "I'm not late. I'm on time. It's just now five o'clock." She calmly pointed at the clock on the far wall until Dana turned and looked that way.

She whipped back around. "You should'a been here sooner. We need to—"

"Dana. We'll do whatever we need to, but only if you're calm. You know the rules. Now back up and take a couple of deep breaths."

Dale waited until Dana did as instructed. Only then did she put a hand on Dana's shoulder. "Good. Please bring a chair for me over to the end of the bleachers."

"Okay. Sorry," Dana muttered. She glanced at Logan and scowled as if just noticing her for the first time. "Who are you?" Her eyes narrowed.

Shit. Dale had never brought anyone to a game and had forgotten how suspicious Dana was of strangers. "This is my friend, Logan. I invited her to the game." She kept her voice even. "Logan, this is Dana. She's one of my teammates."

Logan stood her ground and met Dana's hostile gaze with calm certainty. "Hello. Nice to meet you."

Dana glanced at Dale before nodding sharply to Logan. She spun on her heel and marched away.

"I'm really sorry about that," Dale said as soon as Dana was out of earshot. By now, Logan probably regretted coming to the game. "She's had a tough time—"

"You don't need to apologize or explain." Logan pressed her hand. "I know that not everyone's wounds are physical. I have nothing but compassion for Dana."

Logan's understanding and empathy touched Dale's heart. "Thanks." She hefted her duffle bag. "I should get over there."

"Lead the way."

As they made their way across the gym, a number of people called out to Dale. She waved but kept moving.

Dana had left the specialized wheelchair next to the end of the bleachers, just as she had requested. Dale put her duffle on the floor.

"Have a seat." She motioned Logan toward the stands. Taking a deep breath, she pushed her sweatpants down before joining Logan on the bench so she could work them off over her shoes. Her prosthetic exposed, she glanced at Logan, to find her staring at her legs. She barely resisted the urge to drape her pants over her damaged leg.

Logan chose that moment to look up. Her gaze met Dale's, and she blushed.

What the heck?

"Dale! Move your ass," Rob, a fellow player, yelled from farther up the bench.

Dale leaned past Logan and glared. "Chill out. I'll be right there."

Now came the hard part. She couldn't play while wearing her prosthetic. It was one of the rules, as another player could get injured or the prosthesis could get damaged. And it put everyone on a level playing field, with no artificial help. *She's seen you without the leg,* she reminded herself. After pressing the button to release the prosthetic, Dale started to pull it off, then hesitated and glanced up at Logan.

Their gazes met.

Logan's expression dimmed. She turned on the bench until her back was to Dale.

The understanding gesture on Logan's part only served to make Dale feel as if she had failed Logan and herself. *Damn it.* She jerked the prosthetic off. The liner had to go as well, as the locking pin that protruded from the base of the liner could easily injure another player. She rolled it down and off, exposing her residual limb. Unable to help herself, she darted a glance at Logan.

Her back was still turned.

Dale grabbed a compression sock and quickly covered her stump, then shoved both the prosthetic and liner into the duffle bag and sealed it shut. After getting herself strapped into the wheelchair, she put the duffle on her lap and rolled over to Logan. "Would you hang on to this for me, please?"

"Sure." Logan took the bag and set it next to her on the bench.

"Come on, Dale. You're holding up the game," Dana hollered.

Dale scowled. "Sorry. I need to go." She had planned to introduce Logan to some of the other players' families so she would have someone to keep her company during the game. Getting delayed in traffic had really screwed things up. "Why don't you move over there so you're close to the action?" Dale gestured toward the spectators sitting ten feet away. She berated herself for not sitting down closer to everyone to start with. She still struggled with the ingrained habit of retreating away from the crowd to remove her prosthetic.

"I'm fine. Get going. Your team is waiting."

"Are you sure?" Dale hated leaving her here by herself.

"Dale!" Dana, already strapped into a chair, wheeled toward her.

"Go." Logan smiled and gave her chair a little push.

"I'll be back." She sketched a wave before heading for Dana and her teammates.

As Dale rolled away, Logan took the opportunity to look around. About forty people filled the bleachers on one side of the room. Wheelchairs unlike any Logan had seen before, with their wheels canted out at an angle, were filled with players waiting to take the court.

She had been surprised to see Dana in one of the wheelchairs. She had assumed when Dale said she was a teammate that it was as an assistant, not a player and that the game was for disabled players. Then again, from just her brief exposure to the woman, she fit that criteria; she just wasn't physically disabled. Logan had to admit she had been a bit taken aback during her brief encounter with Dana. Foremost was the hostility radiating from her, but that wasn't all that made her daunting. Logan had never met a woman with such extensive tattoos. Dana sported full-sleeve tattoos on both heavily muscled arms as well as ones on her chest and back, exposed by her tank top. Her purple, clipper-cut, spiked hair added to her arresting appearance. But under it all, what Logan saw was a woman trying desperately to cover up her pain.

The sharp sound of a whistle brought her attention to the game. Ten players took to the court, Dale among them. The play was fast and furious.

Logan had assumed that since they were playing in wheelchairs, the game would be slower and less physical. The exact opposite was true. They played with an intensity that was sometimes frightening. The specialized wheelchairs were incredibly fast and maneuverable. She winced when another player slammed into Dale's wheelchair.

"It sounds worse than it is."

Logan started at the sound of the woman's voice.

Standing at the end of the bleachers was a woman who appeared to be in her early thirties. She tucked her dripping hair behind her ears and pulled off her rain-soaked jacket. A younger man stood next to her. He looked vaguely familiar, but Logan couldn't place him.

"Damn it. The game has already started." He tossed his jacket next to the woman's and quickly stripped out of his running pants exposing a pair of shorts and a below-the-knee prosthetic. Plopping down near Logan, he doffed the leg and liner. "Here. Hang on to this." He shoved the prosthetic into the hand of the woman accompanying him. Without another word, he hopped away.

The woman shook her head. She started to offer her hand to Logan, then seemed to remember the leg she was holding. She grinned and put it down before offering her hand. "Hi. I'm Lark."

"Hello. I'm Logan."

They shook hands.

"Nice to meet you." She sat down next to Logan. "And that rude person," she motioned toward the young man settling into a wheelchair, "is my brother, Jeff."

The sight of Dale surrounded by other players as she fought to take a shot distracted Logan.

"First time at a game, huh?"

What? Logan turned her attention back to Lark. How did she know that?

Lark laughed. "You just had that look. I remember the first time I saw a game. I was petrified that Jeff was going to get seriously hurt before the game was over." As if to punctuate her words, several players crashed together. Dale's chair tipped over when she overbalanced while grabbing for the ball. She used her hands to stop herself just in time to avoid doing a face-plant on the hardwood floor.

The action moved away from her as the play continued.

Dale managed to flip her chair onto its side but was trapped in place.

Why wasn't anyone helping her? Logan surged to her feet. Lark's hand on her arm made her start.

"It's part of the rules," Lark said. "If the player is in no danger, the play in progress continues."

Dale worked to release the straps across her thighs and ankle that were holding her in position and keeping her from using her good leg to right the chair.

The ball landed out of bounds, and the referee blew the whistle. Dana and another teammate immediately headed for Dale. Dana said something to Dale, who shook her head. Her teammates watched as she righted herself and refastened the straps.

Logan slumped down onto the bench.

"You're here with Dale?"

"Yeah." She wanted to ask why Lark sounded so surprised, but she held her tongue.

"Can I give you some unsolicited advice?"

Logan met Lark's gaze and read nothing but an honest attempt to be helpful. "Okay."

"Don't intervene or even show too much of a reaction to any injuries. I know it bothers you to see Dale get hurt, and you just want to help. I feel the same way about my brother. But that's not how they see it." Lark tipped her head toward the court.

Logan nodded. Even Dale's own teammates allowed her the chance to get up on her own first. And she'd seen before how much it bothered Dale when she thought she was being perceived as anything other than fully capable. "Thanks for the advice."

"No problem. I learned the hard way, and for a while, Jeff refused to let me come to his games."

Would Dale do that if she felt Logan embarrassed her in front of her friends? She couldn't picture her reacting that way. But then again, she had thought after the time they spent together on Christmas Day that Dale would be more comfortable about exposing her prosthetic and amputation. That had clearly not been the case tonight. The thing was, she hadn't even looked at the prosthetic. Instead she'd stared at Dale's ass and muscled thighs so beautifully displayed in the shorts she was wearing.

"How do you know Dale?"

Logan was startled out of her thoughts. Never one to give out personal information, she thought fast. How much did Lark know about Dale? "We work together." That was benign enough.

"At the VA?"

Logan shook her head. "No. We work together at LA Metro."

"Are you an ER doctor too?"

Apparently, Lark knew several things about Dale. Logan relaxed a little. "Yes."

Lark glanced out onto the court. "I owe Dale more than I can ever repay. Until she stepped in, I thought I was going to lose Jeff too. And not to his injury." She met Logan's gaze, her own filled with remembered pain. "He's the only family I have left."

Logan's heart went out to Lark. "I'm glad Dale was able to help your brother. She's an amazing woman." Lark's comments about Dale didn't surprise her in the least. In just the short time she had spent at the VA, she had seen what a role model Dale was for other injured vets.

"Yes, she is. And it was more than just helping him adjust. She really went out of her way to help him with his PT, not only when he was first hurt but just recently when he had a setback with an infection."

At the mention of PT, it hit Logan where she had seen Jeff before. Heat rushed through her as the memories of watching Dale work out with him flooded her mind. She resisted the urge to fan herself. No wonder she hadn't recognized him. She'd only had eyes for Dale.

Another memory of that day flashed through her mind: Dale had her prosthetic off, not even covered by a protective sock, and seemed perfectly at ease as she worked with Jeff. And she'd clearly helped Jeff become comfortable with his amputation. Logan glanced at his leg lying on the bench. Was she the only person Dale didn't want seeing her without the prosthetic on? The thought hurt.

The crash of metal on metal and the sound of the referee's whistle brought their attention back to the game.

While Logan would have been just as happy to watch the game by herself, Lark had remained next to her and had filled her in on some of the rules specific to this form of basketball. She also talked more about the things Dale had done for her brother.

By the time the end of the game approached, Logan had seen a completely new side of Dale, and she wasn't sure quite what she thought of it. Dale's demeanor during the game had been totally at odds with the gentle woman Logan had come to know. It wasn't the fact that Dale was fiercely competitive; that hadn't surprised her. What had was her aggressive style of play. Logan had never considered basketball a contact sport, but you would've never known that watching this game. The play was so rough, they should have been wearing protective pads. After watching the chairs smash together, she understood why most of the players wore padded, fingerless gloves.

She glanced over at Lark, who hadn't seemed at all surprised by the rough play, so today's game clearly wasn't anything out of the ordinary.

The buzzer sounded, ending the game. A cheer went up from the crowd.

"Let's go congratulate the winning warriors," Lark said.

"You go ahead. I'll just wait here for Dale."

Dale was surrounded by her teammates as they celebrated their win. She looked over and waved. Before Lark could walk away, Dale broke away from the crowd and rolled over. Her hair was plastered to her head. Sweat dripped down her face, and her shirt was soaked.

Logan worked to keep her gaze on Dale's face and off the shirt clinging to her chest. "Congratulations."

Dale grinned and pumped her fist. "Thanks!" She peered up at Lark. "Hey, Lark. Good to see you. Thanks for keeping Logan company."

"My pleasure. Great game." She leaned down to hug Dale.

Dale put a hand on her shoulder to hold her off. "I'm all sweaty."

Lark brushed her hand aside. "Like I care." She gave her a hug.

"Jeff's really getting good."

She looked toward her brother. "I should go congratulate him and say hi to everyone." She turned back to Logan. "It was nice to meet you. See you at the next game."

Would Dale invite her again? Not wanting to put Dale on the spot, Logan settled for a noncommittal nod. "It was nice to meet you too."

As Lark quickly gathered her and her brother's belonging, Logan tried to surreptitiously scan Dale for any injuries.

After Lark walked away, Dale met her gaze with a challenging glint in her eyes. "I'm not hurt."

Damn. Apparently, she hadn't been as stealthy as she thought. But Dale wasn't being truthful. She not only had scrapes on both knees from hitting the floor, but a large bruise was forming on the back of her right hand. And Logan couldn't help wondering what other injuries were hidden beneath her clothes. While she wanted to insist Dale take care of it immediately, she hadn't forgotten Lark's advice. "Looks like your hand could use some ice."

Dale shook her head adamantly. "I'm fine. It's my own damn fault for forgetting my gloves." She rolled closer to Logan and snagged her duffle bag off the bench. "Let me go grab a quick shower and change, then we'll head for the restaurant. Okay?"

Worries of Dale's injuries were sidetracked by thoughts of Dale, a shower, and hot, soapy water. She shook away the erotic images. "Yeah. Sure. I'll be waiting."

"Okay. I'll be quick."

As she watched Dale roll away, she barely resisted the urge to follow her. Just to check and make sure she didn't have any other injuries. *Yeah. Right!*

CHAPTER 34

LOGAN GLANCED UP AT THE clear evening sky as they crossed the parking lot. The storm had vanished as quickly as it had appeared. Dale hurried to open the door before Logan could. She smiled her thanks. As they stepped into the small restaurant, Logan checked out the interior. It was decorated with a map of Europe as well as a myriad of photographs of Italy. On closer inspection, Logan realized that the majority of the patrons were same-sex couples.

"Do you have reservations?" the hostess asked as they approached.

"Yes. For Parker. I requested a booth."

The woman checked her book, then led them past tables covered in checkerboard tablecloths to a small U-shaped booth in the back corner. A candle flickered inside a glass globe on the table.

The low lighting and soft music made for an intimate and romantic atmosphere, bringing home the fact that she really was on a date with Dale. Butterflies fluttered in Logan's stomach.

Dale slid into the booth first, then once Logan sat down, moved over next to her. Their thighs touched beneath the table. Logan repressed a shiver at the contact.

Dale rested her arm on the back of the booth above Logan's shoulders. "This okay?" Dale asked low-voiced.

Logan met her gaze and felt some of her own anxiety wane at the realization that Dale was nervous too. "It's good."

"Would you ladies like to start with some wine?"

"Not for me. I'll have a Pellegrino," Dale said. She glanced at Logan. "I need to rehydrate after the game. Please, have some wine if you'd like."

"No thank you." Dale's close proximity was intoxicating enough. She needed to keep a clear head. "I'll have a Pellegrino as well."

The hostess handed them menus. "Your server will be with you shortly."

When Dale flipped open her menu, Logan caught sight of her hand and the bruise she had seen earlier. She gently stroked her fingers across the back of Dale's hand. "Are you sure that you don't want to put some ice on this?"

Dale pulled her hand away and hid it under the table. "I told you. It's fine."

Logan tried unsuccessfully to keep from scowling. Despite her resolve, it had been hard to watch Dale play. "I didn't realize basketball was such a contact sport. Are the games always that rough?"

"We're a pretty competitive bunch."

It had appeared to Logan that a lot of the aggressive play was an over-compensation for the players' assorted physical deficits, but she kept that opinion to herself. The game had definitely shown her a different, fiercer side of Dale.

"Sorry you didn't enjoy the game." Dale's shoulders slumped.

Logan cursed herself. She hadn't meant to make Dale feel bad. She clasped Dale's arm. "That's not true. I was just worried about you." Hoping to lighten the mood, she added, "I don't like seeing you get a boo-boo."

Dale grinned, the light returning to her eyes. "Well, if you're really worried, you could always kiss my boo-boo and make it better."

Jumping at the chance to touch Dale, she grasped her wrist and tugged Dale's hand from beneath the table. "Okay."

Dale's eyes went wide.

Keeping eye contact, she brought Dale's hand to her lips and placed a soft kiss on the bruise. As soon as her lips touched Dale's skin, Logan realized she'd made a mistake. The soft skin only served to remind her of how soft Dale's lips were. She lingered, kissing the bruise a second time.

Dale's pupils dilated as her irises became streaked with blue.

Arousal skittered down Logan's spine. Her gaze darted to Dale's lips, and she leaned in close, intent on tasting those soft lips again.

"Are you ladies ready to order?"

They both started at the sound of the server's voice.

Logan moved back but didn't release Dale's hand. She couldn't believe how close she had come to kissing her senseless despite the fact they were in the middle of a restaurant. She darted a look at Dale, hoping she wasn't upset.

Dale looked more flustered than upset. She gave Logan's hand a brief squeeze. "Give us a few more minutes, please."

The server nodded and walked away.

Logan released Dale's hand and picked up her menu. "Sorry about that. Didn't mean to get carried away."

Dale laughed. "I started it. But maybe we better save any more boo-boo kissing for later." She leaned in close for a moment. "I have a few others...that I can't show you here."

Logan gulped, then nodded; her thoughts immediately went to other spots that might need kissing.

Dale glanced away and cleared her throat. "So ah... What sounds good?"

You. Suddenly she wasn't hungry at all, at least not for food. She had fought her attraction to Dale for months. It was the reason she had convinced herself that she had to leave. But that had all changed. Now that she didn't have to deny it anymore, keeping herself from acting on her feelings had become even more difficult. The longing to touch her, to be with her, was growing with every passing moment. And seeing the same emotions in Dale's eyes wasn't making things any easier.

"Logan?"

She shook her head roughly, pushing away the distracting thoughts. "Um, let's see." She scanned the menu. "I think I'll have the three-cheese ravioli."

"Good choice. They make their own pasta here. I think I'll have the ravioli too." She motioned for their server.

While Logan had enjoyed the food and their conversation as they talked of work and about the possibility of her volunteering at the VA, now that their dinner was drawing to a close, her thoughts were once again turning in a more arousing direction. She forced her gaze away from Dale and the torture of watching her lick the filling from her cannoli.

"So have you had a chance to think about where you want to get an apartment?"

What? Logan almost choked on a bite of tiramisu. She swallowed hastily. "Apartment?"

"I just figured if you're staying permanently, you'd want get a place—right?" Dale's expression was a mixture of hope and insecurity. "You wouldn't need to stay in the motor home anymore."

"Honestly, I hadn't considered moving into an apartment. We're used to the motor home." Anxiety made her stomach ache. Could she make that leap? She had been on the run for so long, it was a daunting thought to give up her means of escape.

Dale's brows furrowed and her eyes went dim. She looked away.

Fear greater than that caused by the idea of moving out of the motor home hit Logan hard. *No more hiding,* she sternly reminded herself. If she was truly serious about starting a new life and pursuing a relationship with Dale, things had to change. She couldn't expect Dale to live with the uncertainty that she might disappear at a moment's notice. And there was Drake to consider as well. He was getting older, and travel was becoming harder for him.

Logan laid her hand on Dale's arm. "But you're right. I do need to see about getting an apartment. It's just a lot to take in, and these are really big changes for me. Please, just give me some time."

Dale smiled and laid her hand on top of Logan's where it rested on her arm. "You've got it. I'll help in any way I can."

After a quick glance to make sure their server wasn't about to interrupt again, Logan placed a soft kiss on Dale's cheek. "Thank you."

Dale captured Logan's lips in a quick kiss. She pulled away before things could escalate. "Are you ready to get out of here?"

Logan nodded eagerly. Her lips were tingling from the brief touch with Dale's.

Dale flagged down their server. "Check, please."

Dale stopped her Jeep in front of Logan's motor home. Would Logan invite her in? While seeing her without her leg and in a wheelchair earlier clearly had not dimmed Logan's ardor, getting up close and personal with her scars and stump was something totally different. She longed to make love with Logan, but at the same time, her fears held her back.

"Thank you for tonight." Logan turned in her seat. "I really enjoyed our dinner."

"Me too. I'm sorry the game wasn't—"

"Stop. It was fine. Now that I know more about it, I'll know what to expect next time."

Dale smiled at the mention of next time. Her thoughts went back to their earlier conversation, and her heartbeat sped up. "Well...I do still have those boo-boos that need some care." She held up her bruised hand.

Logan cupped Dale's hand in her palm and placed a soft kiss on the bruise. She pushed up the sleeve of Dale's shirt and turned her arm over to kiss the tender skin of her wrist. "Where are the rest?"

The husky timbre of Logan's voice made Dale swallow heavily. She turned toward Logan as she pushed aside her shirt with trembling fingers and tugged down the collar of her T-shirt underneath to expose the bruise over her clavicle on the undamaged side of her chest. "There's one right here."

Logan leaned across the console and pressed her lips against the spot. Trailing a line of kisses up Dale's neck, she left goose bumps in her wake. "Where else?" she whispered close to her ear.

Arousal washed over Dale, and she struggled to find her voice. She pressed a finger to her own lips.

Logan wrapped her hand around Dale's and kissed her finger before capturing her lips in a searing kiss.

Opening to her, Dale moaned when Logan's tongue slipped into her mouth. Logan's hand threaded through her hair and cradled the nape of her neck. She clutched Logan's shoulders as the world around her faded away and all her senses lit up with the sensations rushing through her.

A sharp rap on the window behind her shattered the moment. They jerked apart, both panting for breath.

Dale turned to find a petite, older woman glaring at her.

The woman motioned for her to open the window.

"Oh, great," Logan muttered.

Dale glanced at her. Did she know the woman?

"You can't park here," the woman said before the window was even halfway down. "Have you checked in? What space are you assigned?"

"Sorry, Bernice. She was just dropping me off."

Bernice peered inside the vehicle. "Logan?"

Logan leaned across the console so that the nearby security light shone on her face. "Yeah. It's me."

The woman's gaze darted to Dale, and her eyes went wide. "Oh!" She shuffled her feet. "Well...I umm...I just took Drake out."

Dale could feel the tension radiating from Logan. Clearly, Bernice hadn't known she was a lesbian. She cursed herself for her stupid boo-boo comment that had started their mini make-out session. Would Bernice stop caring for Drake now that she knew?

"Thank you for looking after him."

Bernice's gaze bounced between them, and the silence stretched to the point of being uncomfortable.

Logan blew out a breath. "Bernice, I—"

Bernice held up a hand to stop her. "If you need anything just let me know. I'm always here—for you and Drake."

"Thanks, Bernice. That means a lot."

Bernice smiled. "Have a good evening. Oh, and don't forget you promised Danny that you'd let him help you bathe Drake next time." She waved and walked away.

Logan flopped back into her seat.

"I'm really sorry." Dale gripped the steering wheel until her knuckles blanched white. "That was all my fault," she said, feeling like a fifteen-year-old who had gotten caught by her girlfriend's mother.

"I sure as hell wasn't protesting, and I'm the one who escalated things." Logan raked her hands through her hair. "At least she took it well. She wouldn't have reminded me of my plans with her grandson if she had an issue with it."

Dale couldn't help feeling guilty about outing Logan, no matter how inadvertently. It had certainly put a damper on things. "Well, I guess I should get going."

"You don't want to come in?"

Dale didn't miss the sudden uncertainty in Logan's voice. "Yeah. I do, but I thought after what just happened..."

Logan placed a quick kiss on Dale's lips. "Go park your Jeep in a visitor's spot. I'll be waiting for you."

Her lips tingling from the kiss, Dale didn't need any other convincing. She lingered long enough to enjoy the sight of Logan's ass as she walked away, then drove to the front of the park.

As she headed back to Logan's motor home, her earlier anxiety resurfaced. Just the memory of Logan touching her was enough to send her pulse pounding. Yet at the same time, the thought of seeing a look of discomfort or, God forbid, pity in Logan's eyes when she exposed her scars made her stomach burn. She shook her head, forcing the worries down. One step at a time.

Logan opened the door of the motor home as Dale approached. She moved back to allow Dale inside.

Dale stepped into the narrow stairwell and tugged the door shut behind her.

Drake stuck his big head past Logan to greet her.

She petted his neck. "Hey, big guy."

Logan pointed at his bed. "Park it, Drake." When he turned to get in his bed, his butt banged against Logan's legs and knocked her off balance. She stumbled into Dale.

Still standing a step below Logan, Dale found herself with her face pressed against Logan's full breasts. She groaned as arousal flared. Her hands came up, and she grabbed Logan's hips to stabilize her.

Logan caught hold of the handrail next to the door and pushed away from Dale. When their gazes met, a bright blush suffused her face. "Sorry about that." She moved back, stepped over Drake, and sat down on the small couch.

Dale wasn't the least bit sorry. But she refrained from saying so to avoid looking like a horny teenager, although she sure felt like one at the moment. She wanted Logan with a passion she had thought long dead.

As she moved into the motor home more fully, Dale realized the limitation of Logan's RV. While the small space had been tight but workable with just the two of them, with Drake present and taking up the lion's share of the already tiny space, there was nowhere to go.

She settled for slipping into the passenger seat behind the small pedestal table, where she had sat during her last visit. She would have liked to join Logan on the couch, but with Drake occupying the floor space in front of it, that wasn't feasible.

Logan looked at Dale, then glanced down at Drake. A frown briefly marred her face. "Hang on a sec." She rose and stepped over Drake again.

When Logan opened the trifold door and went into the back of the motor home, Dale peered after her. What looked like a double bed filled most of the space with only a narrow aisle next to it. Cabinets lined the walls above the bed.

Logan grabbed the end of the bed and lifted. It opened on large, piston-type hinges to expose a storage compartment underneath. She pulled out a blanket, lowered the bed back into position, and spread the blanket over the bedding already in place. "Drake. Come," she called.

Drake trotted into the back. When Logan patted the bed and urged him onto it, he readily hopped up and settled down with a sigh loud enough for Dale to hear.

Logan chuckled. "Good boy. Stay."

When Logan closed the trifold door and shut Drake into the back of the motor home, he let out a loud woo-woo.

"Stay," she repeated through the door.

"Is everything okay with him?" Dale had grown accustomed to the vocalization; it no longer sounded threatening as it once had, but it did mean that Drake had an issue with something.

"Don't mind him. It's dog logic. It's one thing to be let up on the bed, which I normally don't allow, and quite another to be told you have to stay there. Guess it takes the 'I'm getting special treatment' pleasure away from it."

"Are you sure? I don't feel right banishing him because I'm here." Dale was struck by the realization of how much her feelings had changed. There was a time when she would have been thrilled if Logan had put Drake in another room.

"Don't worry about him. He's fine. My bed is a lot more comfortable than his." She patted the couch. "Come sit down."

The last time she had sat on the small couch, Dale had kept a space between them. This time, she sat down close to Logan so that their thighs touched along their length.

"Much better." Logan draped her arm across Dale's shoulders.

Unable to resist Logan's nearness, Dale turned slightly and kissed her.

Logan took control of the kiss and slid her tongue into Dale's mouth.

Dale groaned and brought her hand up to cup Logan's breast as her tongue tangled with Logan's in an erotic dance.

Logan broke away from her lips and tugged down the collar of Dale's T-shirt to kiss the bruise as she had earlier. She kissed up the side of her neck. "Where else are you bruised?"

The husky tone of Logan's voice made Dale shudder. "On my side." She reached to pull her T-shirt from her pants on the undamaged half of her body.

A high-pitched repetitive sound broke the moment. "What was that?"

The sound came again. Drake was whining.

Logan pulled away and shot a glare at the closed door. "Drake. Quiet."

The whining stopped abruptly.

As soon as Logan's lips touched hers again, Drake whined.

Logan pulled away and blew out a breath. "Damn it." She scrubbed her hands over her face. "I'm sorry."

Dale would be lying if she claimed she wasn't frustrated by the interruption, but she also understood it wasn't Logan's fault. "It's okay. He's not used to sharing your attention."

"Well, he's going to have to get used to it."

"Yes, he is. I'm going to be around—a lot."

That brought back Logan's smile. "Thank you for understanding." Her gaze locked onto Dale's lips. She leaned forward.

The moment their lips touched, Drake sounded off.

Dale glared at the closed door. How the hell was he doing that?

"Drake. Be quiet."

Drake let out a booming woof in response to Logan's command.

Logan shot off the couch. "Drake. You are in so much trouble."

Dale rose from the couch and caught her arm. This wasn't going to work. "Wait. I guess I should get going."

"I don't want you to go."

"I don't want to, but I don't want you to be mad at Drake either."

Logan slumped into Dale's arms. "I'm not mad at him...just frustrated."

Dale held her close, enjoying the feel of Logan's lush body against hers. "Do you want to try and let him out?"

Glancing around the small space, Logan shook her head. "He'd be right in our laps." She blew out a breath.

"Just proves you're right. I need an apartment." Her gaze dropped to Dale's lips. "Sooner rather than later."

Unable to resist the temptation, Dale pressed her lips to Logan's.

Drake sounded off on cue.

This time it was Dale's turn to growl.

Logan pressed her forehead to Dale's. "I'm sorry."

She wanted to ask Logan to come home with her, but it didn't seem right to ask her to leave Drake here alone after he'd been on his own since early afternoon. And once she got Logan to her apartment, she knew she wouldn't want to let her leave. Why couldn't Logan have had a cat? As soon as the thought crossed her mind, Dale regretted it. She knew they came as a package deal. It was her frustration talking. She really had come to like the big dog.

"It really is okay. Could I interest you in breakfast tomorrow? Afterward, we could pick up Drake and take him to the park or something?"

The smile that lit Logan's face took Dale's breath away.

"Yeah. I told Lark right. You're an amazing woman."

She had? Dale flushed with pleasure. "I'll pick you up at nine tomorrow."

Logan shook her head. "Nope. My turn to pick you up."

"It's a date." As much as Dale would have liked to linger, she knew it was time to go. There was a cold shower with her name on it waiting for her at home. "I'll see you in the morning." She pressed a quick kiss to Logan's lips and left while she still had the willpower to do so.

CHAPTER 35

DALE PUSHED OPEN THE DOOR to her apartment and motioned a grinning Logan inside. "It wasn't that funny."

"It was. There you were standing next to a hundred-and-fifty-pound Great Dane, and a tiny six-pound Chihuahua had you scurrying to get away from him."

Scowling, Dale pulled off her jacket. "He kept giving me the evil eye. I've seen that bug-eyed crazed look before. My grandmother had a dog that looked just like that. Pepe was always waiting for a chance to ambush you the second you let your guard down."

Logan laughed and hung her jacket next to Dale's on the hall tree. She kicked off her shoes. "I would have protected you."

Dale crossed her arms over her chest. "Drake didn't like him either." It had been embarrassing to have her bravado slip in front of Logan. She'd done so well with all the dogs until that evil little Pepe incarnate arrived.

"Well, that settles it, then." Grinning, Logan patted her arm. "I'm sorry. I shouldn't be teasing you. It was really nice of you to not only find a restaurant where Drake could go with us to breakfast but then suggest the dog park afterward. Thank you."

"You're welcome." They'd had great fun playing with Drake. "Have a seat." Dale motioned toward the couch. "I'll make us that hot chocolate I promised." While the sun was out, the morning had been breezy and cool. "If you want, I can turn on the gas fireplace?"

"I'm fine. Unless you're cold?"

Dale was anything but cold. After their bout of "canine interruptus" yesterday, her dreams last night had been of a much different ending to their evening. All morning, she had been aware of Logan's proximity; the urge to touch her had been a constant temptation. "No, I'm good. I'll be right back."

After returning with the hot chocolate, Dale settled on the couch next to Logan. Although she longed to do so, a part of her still hesitated to start something physical, knowing Logan would want to touch her as well. The thought of baring her scars and her stump weighed heavily on her mind. While Logan had already seen her scars, that had been in a clinical setting, not as a lover.

"What's wrong? You seem a million miles away all of a sudden." Logan ran her hand down Dale's thigh.

Dale tensed when Logan's hand approached the knee of her damaged leg. She cursed herself for having sat down with that leg closest to Logan.

Logan's brow furrowed and she pulled her hand away.

Dale caught Logan's hand in hers and brought it to her lips to kiss her palm. "Sorry. Just a little nervous."

Logan tipped her head, then looked pointedly at Dale's leg. "You don't have anything to worry about as far as I'm concerned. You know that—right?"

The understanding in Logan's gaze made Dale's throat tighten. Tears prickled at the backs of her eyes. *Damn it*. She turned away.

"Hey." Logan took Dale's mug and set it and her own on the table next to the couch. She cupped Dale's chin and urged her to turn back toward her before placing a soft, almost chaste kiss on Dale's lips. "Nothing will happen that you're not ready for. This is a big step—for both of us."

Dale sighed, mentally cursing her nagging insecurities. She was screwing this up, just as she had with Glenda. "That's just it. I'm more than ready. I want you so much, I just..." Gazing into Logan's caring eyes, she gathered her courage. She cradled Logan's face in her hands and kissed her long and deeply. The repressed passion between them flared brightly, burning away Dale's anxieties—at least for the moment.

When the need for breath broke them apart, Dale pressed against Logan. The feel of Logan's breasts against hers sent Dale's arousal soaring. She kissed down her neck, nudging her shirt aside as her kisses moved lower. When the shirt impeded her progress, Dale leaned back, breaking the connection between them so she could work the buttons of Logan's shirt.

Logan dipped her head and placed openmouthed kisses along her neck.

Dale groaned and fumbled with the buttons. "I can't think when you do that."

After nipping at her pulse point, Logan asked, "You want me to stop?"

She kissed her hungrily in answer. Too frustrated to deal with the buttons, Dale tugged Logan's shirt from her pants and slipped a hand underneath to caress warm, soft skin. She moved her hand up to cup Logan's breast through her bra.

Logan sucked in a breath and pressed herself into Dale's hand.

Dale shifted, urging Logan down and onto her back on the couch.

"Wait." Logan grasped Dale's shoulders.

Struggling to calm her buzzing body, Dale looked into Logan's passion-glazed eyes. "What's the matter?"

"Not like this. Take me to bed."

Images of Logan naked beneath her made Dale's heart beat double time. She offered her hand and tugged Logan off the couch.

It wasn't until they were standing next to the bed that her anxiety once more reared its ugly head.

The sudden apprehension radiating from Dale was unmistakable. It wasn't as if Logan didn't have her own body image issues. But she refused to let her insecurities ruin this moment. She had faith that Dale wanted her just the way she was—as she wanted Dale.

Hoping to lighten the mood, she lifted Dale's bruised hand and kissed it. "Our chaperone isn't here. Want to show me the rest of your boo-boos?" She placed a second, openmouthed kiss on the darkened skin.

Dale's fingers trembled in hers. She used her free hand to tug down her Henley and the collar of her T-shirt, exposing the bruise below her clavicle.

It hadn't escaped Logan's notice that no matter what type of shirt Dale wore, she always had a T-shirt underneath. As she leaned in close and kissed the bruise, she lingered, placing soft kisses on Dale's throat along the edge of her shirt. She worked her way up her neck. "Show me the rest."

A shiver rippled through Dale. After pulling her shirt from her jeans, Dale bared her side. The smooth, taut skin just above the waistband of her pants was marred by a narrow, finger-long bruise.

Logan traced the darkened skin with her fingertips, then bent and feathered kisses along the same path. Goose bumps erupted in the wake of her touch. When she reached the middle of Dale's belly, she tugged the other side of the T-shirt from her jeans.

Dale's breath hitched, and she clasped Logan's shoulder.

Soothing a hand along the outside of Dale's thigh, she kissed the soft skin just above her belt, then pushed the shirt higher and revealed pitted shrapnel scars. The visual reminder of all that Dale had endured made Logan's throat grow tight. She skated her lips over the scars, not knowing if the damaged tissue would be sensitive to the touch.

Dale flinched. She shifted so that Logan's lips came in contact with undamaged skin.

Logan glanced up. "Does it hurt when I touch them?"

Dale shook her head. She urged Logan to stand and pulled her into her arms.

Logan wasn't sure how long they stood by the bed and kissed. Her hands moved restlessly over Dale's body as the longing to touch her more intimately grew. But she held herself in check, knowing that Dale needed to make the next move.

Panting for breath, Dale drew back and met her gaze. "I have to touch you." She reached for Logan's shirt.

Her own nervousness spiked, but Logan stood passively and allowed Dale to remove her shirt. As the garment slipped off her shoulders, she had to resist the urge to cover her plump belly.

Dale seemed oblivious. Her gaze was riveted on what had been uncovered.

Logan glanced down, already knowing what had garnered Dale's attention. She traced her fingers over the fist-sized heart with a jagged rend down its center separating the two halves that graced the upper swell of her left breast. Dale was the first person, aside from Logan and the tattoo artist, to ever see it.

Dale looked up and held Logan's gaze.

The understanding shining in her eyes helped Logan deal with the reminder of Emily. Despite the emotions stirred by exposing the tattoo, the pulse of her arousal hadn't subsided. She didn't want this moment to become about Emily. Drawing closer to Dale, she kissed her. The rightness of the connection between them filled her. When Dale opened to her, she groaned as she slipped her tongue into her mouth.

Dale's arms wrapped around her back, pulling her against her firm body. The feel of Dale's shirt rubbing against her nipples through her bra brought them back to stiff peaks. Widening her stance, she grasped Dale's ass and pulled her tightly into the space between her spread legs.

Dale's pelvis ground against hers. Panting, she pulled away from the torrid kiss and reached behind Logan to unhook her bra. After freeing Logan from the encumbrance, Dale filled her hands with the heavy breasts. "So beautiful." She lavished the soft flesh with kisses before dipping her head to take a hard nipple into her mouth.

Logan's knees weakened as Dale began to suckle her. She grabbed her shoulders to stabilize herself. If this went on much longer, she was going to embarrass herself and come before she even got Dale's clothes off. "Slow down a minute." She urged Dale away from her chest.

Dale whimpered.

"It's your turn. I want to touch you too." She extended her hand toward the hem of Dale's shirt.

A look of distress flashed across Dale's face and she caught Logan's hand. She quickly recovered and reached for Logan. "Later. Let me touch you."

Logan shook her head and stepped back, crossing her arms over her bare chest. She hadn't missed Dale's discomfort, but she couldn't do this unless they were equal partners.

Dale glanced at the window, where the blinds stood partway open, allowing bright sunlight into the room. "Okay. Hang on a sec." She moved toward the window.

Her stomach sank when she realized what Dale was going to do. There were room-darkening shades behind the blinds that Logan hadn't noticed before. "Dale. Don't do that."

Dale's hand stopped in mid-reach. She turned back to Logan.

"Please come back." Logan held out her hand. She knew all too well that once you hid from something, it gained power over you.

Dale's shoulders hunched, and she wrapped her arms across her belly. She seemed frozen in place.

A sigh escaped before Logan could stop it. "If it's too much, I understand." Feeling exposed both emotionally and physically, she picked up her shirt from the bed where Dale had dropped it.

"Wait!" Dale's gaze darted between the blinds and Logan. "Just this once—"

Oh, Dale. No. If she accepted Dale hiding her body now, it would always be a barrier between them. She loved her too much to let that happen. *Love her.* The stunning realization shook her to her core. *Talk about hiding things from yourself.* Her heart filled to overflowing with the strength of her feelings for this amazing woman. She longed to tell her, but seeing her looking so anxious and vulnerable, Logan knew she couldn't. Not now. She wouldn't put that kind of pressure on her.

"Please. Just this once," Dale repeated.

More determined than ever not to give in to Dale's fears, she shook her head. "No. I can't do that. I meant what I said. Nothing will happen until you're ready. I'll wait for you. You're worth waiting for." She started to pull on her shirt.

Dale crossed the room in several swift strides. "Please don't." She tugged the shirt from Logan's grasp and tossed it aside.

The pleading look on Dale's face almost made her relent—almost. Logan cradled Dale's face between her palms and stared deeply into her eyes, willing her to believe. "I want you. All of you. Just the way you are." She kissed her until Dale began to respond, then stepped back. This had to be Dale's decision.

Dale fisted the bottom of her shirt. Her gulp was audible in the quiet room as she pulled both shirts over her head. After a moment's hesitation, she dropped them onto the floor.

The scars were just as vivid as Logan remembered them, covering half of Dale's chest and side. They made her no less beautiful in Logan's eyes, but she doubted

Dale would believe that—at least not now. "Thank you for trusting me."

Dale took a step forward, but Logan stopped her with a shake of her head. "The bra too. Please."

Her pulse beating visibly in her neck, she locked gazes with Logan.

"I want you," Logan repeated.

That seemed to give Dale courage. She pulled the sports bra over her head in one smooth motion.

Not giving her a chance to withdraw, Logan drew Dale into her arms and pressed their bare upper bodies together. Arousal soared anew.

Dale whimpered and clutched her painfully tight.

Logan held her, gliding her hands softly up and down Dale's back, touching equally the smooth and damaged areas of her skin. After a few minutes, she skimmed her hands along Dale's sides and stroked the outsides of her breasts.

Groaning, Dale rubbed against her. "Feels good."

"I want to make you feel good." She kissed along the column of her throat and up close to her ear. "I've wanted to touch you like this for so long."

Dale drew back. She traced her thumb softly over Logan's lips. Her eyes shone with emotion. "I've wanted you too—for months. Let me make love to you."

Her gaze on Dale, Logan opened her jeans and let them drop to the floor. Her own nervousness about her body, quiet until now, made her hesitate. She ducked her head and spread a hand self-consciously over the bulge of her lower belly.

Dale caught her chin in her hand and urged her head up. "You're beautiful."

Logan flushed at the conviction in her voice. When Dale glided her fingers underneath the waistband of her panties, she shivered. Dale pushed the panties down, and she stepped out of them.

Dale kissed her neck, then moved lower, lavishing her breasts with openmouthed kisses. Her hands stroked Logan's body, sending her arousal higher.

She clutched Dale's shoulders as the throbbing pulse between her legs grew more insistent. Everything else ceased to exist. The feel of Dale's hands and mouth on her became her world.

Dale urged her to sit on the edge of the bed, then, pressing her back, stretched out half on top of her. The rough denim of her jeans rasped against the soft skin of Logan's thighs. She braced herself on one arm, making her muscles stand out in sharp relief. "You're so beautiful." Dale's free hand swept down her body, exploring every dip and curve.

Her arousal at a fevered pitch, Logan couldn't stand it any longer. She needed Dale with a fierceness she had never experienced. She grasped her hand and pressed it between her spread legs. "Please."

Dale's fingers delved into the soaking wetness between her thighs. She dipped her head and took a rock-hard nipple into her mouth.

Logan's body arched at the dual assault. Her eyes squeezed shut as the world narrowed down to the exquisite point of pressure building between her thighs. She struggled to make her voice work. "Inside."

The feel of Dale's fingers deep inside triggered her climax. She clutched at Dale, her body shaking with the power of her release. Panting, Logan forced her eyes open to find Dale staring at her with an intensity that sent aftershocks rippling through her.

Dale leaned down and took her lips in a searing kiss. Her fingers began to move slowly inside her.

Logan groaned into the kiss. Breaking away, she caught hold of Dale's wrist. "I can't again. Not so soon."

Grumbling a protest, Dale gently removed her fingers. She slipped off to the side but remained pressed against Logan. She traced patterns on Logan's sweat-dampened belly, then moved higher to lightly stroke her breasts. "I could touch you all day."

Logan captured her hand, stilling it in place. As her body calmed, it dawned on her what she had allowed to happen. *Damn it.* She'd let her passion get away from her. They had never even gotten fully into the bed. She looked over at Dale, still dressed in her jeans and shoes, with her legs hanging over the edge of the bed.

Dale met her gaze for a moment, then looked away. A sudden tension radiated from her. She moved away and sat up.

Determined not to let things end this way, Logan moved fully onto the bed and knelt behind Dale—close, but not touching.

Dale glanced back at her with wide eyes.

"Relax. Let me love you." Logan leaned forward just enough so that her breasts brushed Dale's back. She bit her lip when her own nipples immediately hardened. Making sure just her breasts touched Dale, she trailed them up and down her back before bending her head and closing her teeth on the tender flesh at the juncture of Dale's neck and shoulder on the unscarred side. She soothed the tiny bite with her tongue.

A throaty growl escaped Dale, and she leaned back.

Logan clenched her thighs together at the erotic sound. She did the same thing on the other side, being extra careful with the damaged skin. It wrenched an even deeper growl from Dale and a buck of her hips.

Bringing her hands into play, Logan traced the sculptured muscles of Dale's upper arms, then her prominent abdominal muscles. After denying the possibility for so long, it was incredible to finally be able to touch Dale.

Dale's breath hitched. "Please." Her hands covered Logan's.

Not absolutely sure whether she was asking her to stop or keep going, Logan continued to kiss along her neck but stilled her hands. "It feels so wonderful to touch you. Let me touch more of you." She nestled her face close to Dale's. "I need to touch more of you."

Dale's grip on her hands tightened. Drawing a deep breath, she slowly guided Logan's hands to her breasts.

Stroking the pliant flesh, Logan felt not only the difference in texture of the skin but the disparate size of Dale's breasts. Her heart ached for all that Dale had suffered. She forced the thoughts aside. This was about pleasure, not pain. She gave each breast equal attention while taking extra care on the side that had been injured. "Is this okay? It's not hurting you—right?"

"Feels so good." Dale pressed hard against Logan's knees.

"You feel good. I love touching you." Logan spread her legs and drew Dale back between them, cradling her body against hers. She continued to pleasure her breasts until Dale began to squirm in her arms. When Dale reached between her own legs to stroke herself through her jeans, Logan caught her hand. "Ah-ah. No touching."

Dale whimpered. "Please. Touch me."

"Open your jeans." Dale complied with alacrity, making Logan smile. At least for the moment, she'd managed to make her forget about her scars. She slid her hand down Dale's abdomen and into her underwear to gently cup her sex. "The jeans have to go."

Dale froze in place.

She slicked her finger a single time across Dale's engorged clit, then withdrew.

Dale's hips jerked. "You're killing me."

Tell me about it. Logan ached to do what they both so desperately wanted but held herself back. There could be no half measures here. "Take off the jeans." She stroked Dale's clit again with a little firmer pressure, then quickly retreated, not wanting her to come by accident.

"I can't." Dale's shoulders slumped. "I'd have to take off my..."

Now came the true test of Dale's trust and faith in her. Logan knew full well that she couldn't take off her jeans without removing her leg first. She slipped her hand from Dale's underwear. "Then do it."

Dale stiffened in her arms.

Logan caressed Dale's shoulders, then allowed her hands to drift to her breasts. She put her mouth next to Dale's ear. "I need to touch you. All of you. Please." She trailed a hand down to the top of Dale's open jeans and stroked the soft skin of her lower belly.

A shudder rippled through Dale's body.

Logan nipped the tender spot on her neck hard enough to make Dale jump. "Do it now." She released her hold so that Dale could sit up.

Dale pulled her pant leg up. Her hands around the prosthetic, she hesitated. She looked back at Logan, her expression pleading.

Logan met her gaze head-on. She wasn't budging on this. "Off." Leaning forward, she pressed her breasts against Dale's back. She captured Dale's breasts in her hands and repeatedly brushed her thumbs across her hard nipples.

"I can't think—"

"Good. I want to touch you everywhere. Stroke you. Make you come." Logan gave her breasts a firm squeeze. "Hurry."

Groaning, Dale released the prosthetic and dropped it.

Logan kept her chest against Dale's back, lightly stroking across her arms and breasts, never losing physical contact as Dale removed her remaining clothes.

When the liner covering her residual limb hit the floor, Logan wrapped her arm around Dale's waist and urged her between her spread knees. She scooted back, drawing Dale with her until Dale's legs were completely on the bed. She cradled Dale against her chest. "Oh, yeah. So much better." She skated her fingers down the tops of Dale's bare thighs. "This is just perfect. You're perfect." She caressed every inch of skin she could reach, building Dale's arousal higher, touching her everywhere except where she most wanted to be.

"Please." Dale guided Logan's hand between her thighs.

As her fingers slid into the drenched folds, Logan bit back a groan. Her legs tightened around Dale. Sliding up to stroke Dale's clit, she felt it pulsing against her fingertips.

Dale's breath hissed from her. "Yes." She clutched Logan's knees.

Applying firm pressure, Logan worked her closer to release. The sight of Dale, as she neared orgasm, the light from the window bathing her body in a soft glow, took Logan's breath away. *So beautiful.*

Dale's body arched as an incoherent cry was torn from her lips.

Logan continued to caress her, drawing out her pleasure as long as possible. When Dale's body went limp, she wrapped her arms around her and held her tight.

Her breathing returning to normal, Dale stirred. She turned her head to gaze at Logan, her eyes filled with emotion.

Logan kissed the tear lurking in the corner of her eye. "That was so beautiful. Thank you for trusting me."

Dale burrowed deeper into Logan's arms.

By the time Dale woke, the clouds had returned, obscuring the late-afternoon sunlight and throwing the room into deep shadow. She savored the feel of Logan's naked body pressed against her back. So much had happened; she still couldn't process it all. Inexplicably, her thoughts were drawn to the past. Suddenly restless, she slipped from beneath the covers, careful not to disturb Logan, and sat up on the side of the bed. She shook her head at the sight of the scattered clothes and her prosthetic on the floor. She pulled her forearm crutches from beneath the bed. After propping the prosthetic in the corner, she quietly padded over to the dresser and pulled on a T-shirt and a pair of flannel pants. The chilled hardwood floor beneath her bare foot made her toes curl. She glanced at the bed to make sure Logan was still asleep, then slipped from the room.

As she settled on the couch, her thoughts turned to her ex, Glenda, and the few times they had tried to make love again after her injuries. Glenda had always bowed to her need to douse the lights. Although it had been at Dale's insistence, a part of her had wondered if it was easier for Glenda too, not having to see her scars and stump. Those insecurities had driven a wedge between them and remained with her after they split up.

Her mind's eye filled with images of lying in Logan's arms, the sun streaming in the window, every scar and her stump vividly on display. Yet through it all, there had been no hesitation in Logan's touch—on any part of her body. And never once had she seen anything but desire in Logan's eyes.

Logan's adamant refusal to enable her fears allowed her to see that she had been projecting her own insecurities as to her desirability onto Logan.

It was humbling, and something she never thought she could ever have—someone who accepted her just as she was: scars, stump, and all.

It made her love Logan that much more. She sucked in a breath. *Love?* Of course, she cared deeply for Logan. She had for quite some time. But love her? Her chest grew tight with the strength of her emotions. "I love her," she whispered to the empty room.

The realization galvanized her into action. She needed to be with Logan—to tell her. After grabbing her crutches, she padded back into the bedroom.

Logan had turned on the bedside lamp and was sitting with the covers drawn up around her chest.

Dale's heart gave a startlingly hard thump at the sight of her. *Oh, yeah. I love her.* How had she not realized it before now?

"Hey. I was wondering where you disappeared to. Is everything all right?"

At the uncertainty in Logan's voice, Dale mentally cursed herself. Of course she would worry when she woke up alone. "Yeah. Everything's great." She propped her crutches against the nightstand and sat on the side of the bed facing Logan. She stroked her fingers along Logan's cheek before leaning in to kiss her.

Logan smiled as the kiss broke and the tension left her body. "I'm glad to hear that."

"Scoot over." Dale lifted the edge of the covers.

Logan held the blanket firmly in place. "Lose the clothes."

The husky timbre of her voice sent all the moisture in Dale's body south. She stood and automatically reached for the lamp switch.

"Don't you dare."

Dale jumped and jerked her hand away. Her gaze darted back to Logan.

"Don't ever hide yourself from me."

Under Logan's watchful eyes, she pulled the T-shirt over her head, then pushed the flannel pants down and let them drop to the floor. Although there was a part of her that wanted to scurry under the covers, she understood now that it was her own irrational fear talking. Clearly, it would take some time to get completely comfortable with exposing her scars and stump. But she was confident that Logan would be there by her side to help if she faltered.

"Just perfect." Logan held up the covers.

Dale joined her in the bed. Her heart pounding, she couldn't hold it in for another second. "I love you."

Logan's eyes went wide. She pulled Dale into her arms and held her tight. "I love you too."

Elation washed over Dale. In more ways than one, Logan had given her back things she had never dared hope to have again. She pulled back until she could look into Logan's eyes. "Love me," she whispered.

"Always," Logan said before taking her lips in a searing kiss and pressing her back onto the bed.

CHAPTER 36

LOGAN LEANED AGAINST THE DOORFRAME in the physical therapy department and watched Dale work with a new patient on the low padded table. The last month had been the happiest she'd spent in over two years. Dale had brought love and a hope for the future back into her life. While there were still times when her guilt over Emily's death threatened to swamp her, Dale was always there to pull her out before she went under.

Dale's laughter drew Logan from her thoughts. When Dale lay down on her back and spread her bent legs wide open, Logan bit her lip. Her mind filled with images of the last time she had been between those muscular thighs. Arousal swept through her.

"Still get your kicks watching, huh?"

Logan started. She crossed her arms over her chest to cover her hard nipples. No sense giving Casey any more ammunition. She turned her back on the PT room and faced Casey. "I'm observing her technique."

"Oh, sure. I believe that." Casey snorted. "So where did you park your motor home?"

"Huh? Why would I bring it here?"

"You said you were bringing Drake." Casey's brows lowered. "You left him in your SUV?"

"Of course not. You know me better than that. We came in with Dale."

"But you don't have clearance to enter the building with him. How did you get him past security?" Casey's jaw dropped open. "Dale brought him in?"

Logan grinned. "Yep, she sure did." She was learning firsthand how slowly the bureaucratic wheels turned in the VA. After four weeks, she was still waiting to receive her clearance so that she could take over handling Drake as he went about his therapy work.

"Wow."

"Hey. She's getting really good with him." That Dale had stepped up and volunteered to bring Drake today meant so much to Logan.

"So where is he?"

Logan turned back to the PT room where Dale was working and pointed.

Drake lay stretched out on his side on the other side of the room in front of a wooden rack filled with free weights.

"Is he okay?"

"Yeah. He's just saving his energy for his therapy work." Logan let out a low whistle.

Both Drake and Dale turned to look at her.

Casey laughed. "Got them both trained, I see."

Logan elbowed her. "Don't you have patients waiting to see Drake?"

Slapping her thighs, Casey called Drake, who jumped up and trotted toward her. She snagged his leash. "Fine, we know when we're not wanted. I'll just keep my good news to myself."

Logan grabbed her arm before she could walk away. "What good news?"

"I'll tell you when we come back."

"Casey." Logan growled.

"Okay. Okay. I found you and Drake a place to live."

"You've been looking for a place for us?" Logan shook her head at the obvious question. As happy as she had been, the one lingering frustration was not being able to find a decent place to live. She had discovered that rentals were hard to come by in LA; add to that finding somewhere that would accept a Great Dane, and it had become seemingly impossible.

"So what is it? And where? Will they accept Drake?" Where not long ago the thought of moving out of her motor home had been daunting, now she couldn't wait to get into a new place.

Casey grinned at the rapid-fire questions. "Well, I put out some feelers to the community two weeks ago. A friend from my old squadron has a buddy who's also ex-military that has a small house that he rents out. Whenever possible, he gives preference to a vet or military family. The house will be move-in ready in three weeks."

Logan's shoulders slumped. Why was Casey even telling her about this place? "But I'm not either of those things."

"I told my friend Herschel about you and Drake. And the good work you're both doing here at the VA." Casey gripped her shoulder. "You're part of our family now. And we look out for our own. He talked to his buddy Al, who said if you want it, the place is yours."

A lump formed in Logan's throat, choking off her voice. The camaraderie and sense of family among the former military people she had met was something she had never experienced before. To be accepted into that family was totally unexpected.

Drake let out a soft mournful woo-woo.

Looking worried, Casey said, "Uh...I thought this would make you happy?"

Logan soothed Drake. "It does. I—"

A pair of warm hands landed on her shoulders. "What's wrong?"

Logan smiled and put her hands over the top of Dale's. "Nothing. Casey found a place for me and Drake."

"That's great." Dale wrapped one arm around her waist and hugged her from behind. She propped her chin on Logan's shoulder. "Thanks, Case."

"Well, Logan's got to see the place first. But from what Herschel told me, it sounds like it is just what she's been looking for. Small, two-bedroom ranch with a fenced backyard in Westchester."

Dale's whoop echoed through the PT department, drawing the attention of several patients and staff.

"I thought you'd like that," Casey said.

Logan couldn't believe it. Not only had Casey found a house for her and Drake, but in all of Los Angeles, it was in an area directly adjacent to the city where Dale lived. Talk about all the stars aligning. She stepped away from Dale and wrapped Casey in her arms, giving her a warm hug. "Thank you."

Looking flustered, Casey moved back. "You're welcome." Drake head-butted Casey's hip. She bent and hugged him. "You're welcome too." She picked up his leash that she'd dropped when Logan hugged her. "Hey, I was wondering since you're working tonight, would it be okay if I took Drake home with me? We could all have breakfast together when you come get him tomorrow morning."

Opposing wants tugged at Logan. Having Drake with Casey meant she could spend the day with Dale, which she longed to do. At the same time, she felt guilty not spending time with Drake. *Three more weeks,* she reminded herself. Once she had a place of her own, it would solve the problem and allow her to spend time with both of them.

Casey threw her a pleading look. Despite checking out multiple animal shelters, Casey had yet to find a dog she was willing to even give a trial home visit. It hadn't escaped Logan's notice that they hadn't seen any giant breed dogs at any of the shelters. She thought of the rescue place she had seen online and smiled to herself. There was one phrase she'd heard often in her short time at the VA: pay it forward. Maybe she could help Casey in return for her help with the new place.

"Sure. You can take him home with you."

A brilliant smile blossomed on Casey's face. "Great! Come on, we've got work to do." She waved as she walked away with Drake.

Logan turned to Dale. "I should let you get back to your patient."

Dale inclined her head toward the woman who was working with the free weights. "We were pretty much done anyway. Just let me give her some instructions for next time, then I'm all yours."

Logan lowered her voice. "Oh, you're going to be mine, all right. Repeatedly."

Dale gulped as all the moisture in her body headed south. The desire in Logan's eyes drew her in and sent her senses reeling. She leaned in, intent on tasting Logan's sweet lips.

Before Dale could close the distance between them, Logan stopped her with a hand on her chest. "Not here. You touch me, and you're going to end up on that table over there—with me on top of you."

It took Dale's passion-hazed brain several moments to figure out why that was a bad thing. She growled and pinched Logan's side, making her yelp. "You expect me to work on that table after you put that image in my head?"

Appearing completely unrepentant, Logan grinned.

"You can help me back over there since you're the one that made it impossible for me to walk." Despite having her prosthesis off, she didn't really need Logan's help, but she wasn't going to pass up a chance to be pressed against her.

Laughing, Logan wrapped her arm around Dale's waist and assisted her to the low-slung workout table. She moved away and leaned against the wall to wait for Dale to finish up.

Dale sat down on the far corner of the low platform and motioned Keisha over.

Keisha rolled her chair over and parked near Dale.

"I want you to work on the exercises I showed you. It's really important to keep the hip flexor and adductor muscles loose. They can get really tight from spending too much time in the chair. You need to get up and use the forearm crutches. You'll need to be proficient with them even after you get your first prosthesis."

Keisha looked away.

Dale laid her hand on Keisha's arm. "I know it seems overwhelming right now, but it will get better. I promise you. And I'll be here for you. Every step of the way."

"It's just, you seem so comfortable and everything." She sighed and traced her fingers over the pink scars on her thigh and knee that stood out sharply against her dark skin, stopping short of touching the compression dressing around her stump.

"Believe me, I didn't get that way overnight. It takes time."

Keisha met her gaze. "Can I ask you a personal question?"

"Sure."

She tipped her chin toward Logan. "That's your girlfriend—right?"

An automatic smile tugged at the corner of her lips. "Yes."

"Did she know you before you got hurt?"

Dale wondered where this was going. "No. We met five months ago."

"Oh. Well...doesn't it bother her?" She ducked her head. "Your leg, I mean." She touched her own leg again, and her shoulders slumped. "And the scars. My boyfriend says it doesn't, but..."

The defeated posture was so familiar that Dale's throat grew tight. "Keisha, look at me." When she finally looked up, Dale continued, "I'm going to be honest with you. I had those same concerns, and they almost stopped me from having a wonderful woman in my life. You need to understand that those body image fears are our own. Make sure you're not projecting them onto someone who cares about you and driving him away. If you really care about the man, you need to take him at his word." She motioned for Logan to come over.

Logan pushed off the wall, picked up Dale's prosthetic, and carried it over with her.

"Logan, I'd like you to meet Keisha."

"Hi, Keisha." Logan started to reach out, then seemed to remember the prosthetic she was holding. She extended it to Dale with a smile before offering her hand to Keisha.

Dale glanced at Keisha to see her looking wide-eyed at Logan. Clearly, Logan's ease with the prosthesis had surprised her despite what Dale had said. That comfort level hadn't come easy, at least not for Dale. But Logan had refused to accept any hiding on her part.

"Nice to meet you." Keisha shook hands with Logan. She looked at Dale. "Thank you." Her gaze darted back to Logan. "For everything. I'll see you on Thursday."

"See you then," Dale said. "Keep after those exercises."

After Keisha rolled away, Logan settled onto the padded platform next to Dale. "What was that about?"

"She's worried that her boyfriend isn't being honest about being okay with her scars and amputation. She wanted to know if you were bothered by my leg. You couldn't have done a more perfect thing than walking over and handing me my leg like that." Dale leaned over and brushed a soft kiss across Logan's lips. "I love you."

Logan smiled. "You love me because I brought you your leg?"

"Yep. That's one of the many reasons."

"I love you too. Now put the thing on so we can get out of here."

"Yes, ma'am." Dale plucked the liner from inside the socket of the prosthesis and rolled it into place over her residual limb. *What the heck?* She propped the knee of her injured leg on top of the good one and adjusted the liner. She grumbled and did it again, then twisted her leg at an awkward angle and looked at the locking pin where it protruded from the base of the liner.

"What's wrong?"

"Something's the matter with the liner. It's not lying right at the bottom edge."

"Let me see."

Dale was struck again at what an amazing woman Logan was. While Logan made a point of touching the stump during lovemaking, Dale had never expected her to be willing to deal so directly with her amputation. Dale turned sideways and held out her stump.

Logan ran her hands along the liner, then down to the base that held the locking pin in place. Holding Dale's stump firmly in her hand, she bent to get a closer look. "Ah. I see it. The fabric is worn here, and it's allowing the base that holds the pin to shift, and it won't lie flat."

"Damn. I felt it pinching earlier, but I thought I just hadn't gotten it seated right. I adjusted it a little, and it stopped."

Logan rolled the liner down and pulled it off. She carefully checked every inch of Dale's stump. "I don't see any rub spots. Do you have a spare liner?"

"Yeah. In my bag."

Logan snagged the bag off the floor and handed it to Dale.

Dale put on the liner, stood, and donned her prosthetic. After shifting her weight several times, she smiled. "I'm good." She held out her hand to Logan and tugged her to her feet.

Her thoughts turned to Logan's earlier teasing. "Let's get out of here." She glanced over her shoulder to make sure no one was in sight, brushed her hand down Logan's ass, and gave it a firm squeeze. "Someone promised me repeated ravishing."

Logan's eyes darkened. "Oh, you're going to pay for that."

"Promises. Promises."

Logan grabbed her hand and pulled her toward the door. "Come with me."

Dale grinned. *Oh, I plan to. Repeatedly.*

CHAPTER 37

LOGAN STRETCHED AND ROLLED OVER in the bed. A moment of disorientation swept over her at the unfamiliar surroundings. She had to remind herself that this was her bedroom. While her new home was modest by most people's standards, after two years in a tiny motor home, she felt a little lost in all this space. She sighed. It hadn't felt quite so empty when Dale was here. She turned on the bedside lamp and sat up on the side of the bed, automatically ducking to avoid a cabinet that wasn't there. Her gaze swept the sparsely furnished room. Maybe a rug on the floor or some pictures on the wall would help. The thought wasn't the least bit appealing. She'd done more shopping in the last two weeks than she had in the past few years combined.

The click of nails on the hardwood floor alerted her to Drake's arrival. "Hey, boy."

He trotted over and tried to climb into her lap.

Logan straight-armed him in the chest. "Off."

Huffing, he backed away.

"You want to go outside?" Logan laughed at his enthusiastic woo-woo. While she might be uncomfortable with all the space, Drake had reveled in it, especially having access to a yard and not having to be on a leash. She slipped on her shoes and snagged her robe from the foot of the bed. "Outside."

He headed for the bedroom door.

Logan followed him to the sliding glass door in the living room. Although it was only five thirty in the evening, it was already twilight. It took her a moment to find the switch to the exterior lights. Drake butted her hip. "Hold your horses." She flipped the switch and slid open the patio door.

Drake charged out.

Leaning against the doorframe, Logan smiled as he gamboled about the yard. She wrapped her arms around herself and pulled the robe closed as the evening air chilled her. "Hurry up. Do your dog business," she called out to him. While she hated to cut his fun short, she still wasn't comfortable leaving him in the yard alone even though she had checked every inch of the fence line to make sure he couldn't get out. She promised herself that she'd try leaving him in the yard alone for a little while during the day. That way she could keep an eye on him out the window.

Drake trotted up.

Logan shook her head at the sight of grass hanging out of his mouth. "I told you before. You're not a cow."

The doorbell rang.

Drake raced for the front door; his booming bark echoed through the house.

While she normally would have shushed him, Logan let him bark. She wasn't expecting anyone, and they had been in the house only a few days, so she didn't know any of the neighbors yet. Dale had called earlier. She had gotten hung up at the VA with a patient she was mentoring and planned on heading home to get some sleep before their shift tonight. And she doubted Casey would drop by without calling. Wishing that the door had a peephole, she tugged the belt of her robe tight. "Drake. Quiet."

With Drake standing close to her side, Logan opened the door just enough to see out. Her breath left her lungs in an audible whoosh. "Dale! What are you doing here?" She pulled the door open wide.

Dale caught hold of Drake's collar as he tried to bolt out the door.

"Drake. No." Logan's voice stopped him in his tracks. "You know better than that." She hauled him back into the house. "We're going to work on that, bud."

He pulled away from Logan and went straight to Dale.

Dale greeted him, then turned to Logan with a smile.

Logan mock-scowled at her. "Really? You greet the dog first?"

The stunned look on Dale's face was priceless. "But he—"

Laughing, Logan pulled Dale into her arms and kissed her soundly. When the kiss broke, she stepped back, having learned that she couldn't think clearly wrapped in Dale's arms. "Not that I'm complaining, but what are you doing here?"

Dale shifted, and a blush dusted her cheeks. "Couldn't sleep."

Logan drew Dale back into her arms. "I missed you too. I woke up and this place seemed so big and empty."

Dale's arms tightened around her. "Are you sorry you gave up your motor home?"

Hearing the worry in Dale's voice, Logan leaned back in Dale's arms so she could gaze into her eyes. This was about more than just moving into a new place. So much had changed. She was in love with an amazing woman—something she had thought she would never experience. And she had a permanent place to live, as well as a family at the VA. While it was a lot to take in, she was happier than she'd ever been—happier than she deserved.

She could feel the tension radiating from Dale at her delayed answer. "No. I don't regret it. Not for a second." She stroked her fingers across Dale's cheek. "I like this place. And Drake loves it here. It's just going to take some getting used to."

"I understand. I'll do anything I can to make it easier for you."

Her heart filled to overflowing with the love she felt for Dale. She kissed her long and lovingly until the press of Dale's body became too much to ignore. "You could take me to bed." She nipped at Dale's pulse point. "But I can't promise how much sleep you're going to get."

A sexy growl rumbled through Dale's chest. "I've got no problem with that. No problem at all."

Her heart feeling as if it were going to beat out of her chest, Dale gripped the sheets and held on for dear life as Logan's tongue plunged repeatedly inside her. Her second orgasm was rapidly approaching. Logan's lips closed around her clit, triggering her climax. Her body arched as pleasure blasted through her, blowing away all coherent thought.

After the aftershocks subsided, Logan moved up next to her and gently stroked her body.

Dale's muscles were too limp to even lift her arms. She opened her eyes and peered up at Logan. "Love you."

"Love you too." Logan leaned in and kissed her.

The taste of herself on Logan's lips made Dale groan. "Give me a few minutes to recover, then it's your turn."

"We need to get some sleep. Rest now."

Logan's gentle touch was lulling her to sleep. She shook away her drowsiness and made her sated body move. "No fair." Dale shifted and pressed Logan onto her back before settling down next to her. "Don't deprive me of the pleasure of getting to touch you."

She traced the tattoo above Logan's left breast, then leaned down and placed a lingering kiss in the center. Goose bumps broke out in the wake of her touch. Unable to help herself, she dipped her hand lower and stroked Logan's breasts, brushing her thumbs over Logan's already hard nipples.

Logan's hand captured hers and held it in place, allowing Dale to feel the rapid beat of her heart. "We should sleep."

Undeterred, Dale shook her head and straddled Logan's thighs. She rose up on her knees and took her time visually surveying all the delights laid out before her.

"Dale." Logan's gaze flickered to the nightstand, where a lamp illuminated the bed in a soft pool of light.

While she knew that Logan still harbored some insecurities about her weight, just as she did about her scars, Dale loved Logan's body exactly as it was. Logan had given her the gift of total acceptance, and she offered Logan nothing less in return. "You're perfect." She gazed deeply into Logan's eyes, seeing the restrained passion lurking just below the surface. "Please. Let me love you."

A soft whimper escaped Logan's lips.

Dale leaned down and kissed her deeply, sealing her surrender.

She filled her hands with Logan's full breasts, then captured a taut nipple and rolled it between her fingers.

Logan's body arched beneath her.

Dale began her quest to love every part of Logan's body. She explored every inch of her, first with her fingers and then with her mouth. "I could touch you all night."

Logan's head thrashed, and she squirmed as Dale stoked her passion higher. "God, Dale. Please." She wrapped her arms around Dale and pulled her down on top of her.

Dale groaned at the feel of Logan's lush body beneath her. When Logan shifted and pressed her thigh against Dale's soaking wet sex, her clit twitched warningly. *So much for being sated.* Logan had a way of stirring her passions as no one else ever had.

Trying to ignore her own arousal, Dale slipped her hand between Logan's legs. She bit her lip as she buried her fingers in slick, heated folds. Her own hips rocking against Logan's thigh, Dale stroked Logan ever closer to orgasm.

"Go inside," Logan said, her voice low and husky.

Dale pushed deep inside in a single thrust. At the feel of Logan's internal muscles clenching around her fingers, a moan was torn from her lips. She stroked her deep, her own hips following the rhythm of her fingers.

Logan grabbed Dale's ass and squeezed, matching Dale's thrusts.

It was too much for Dale. Her climax struck with stunning force.

Logan's hips arched beneath her, lifting them both from the bed. "Dale!" Her shout echoed in the room.

They collapsed back onto the bed, panting for breath.

Dale tried to move off Logan, only to have her tighten her arms around her.

"Stay."

Not having the willpower to resist, Dale relaxed against her.

When Logan shifted under her, she wasn't sure how much time had passed. Dale moved off to the side. The chilly air quickly took its toll on their sweaty bodies. Shivering, Dale tugged the covers over them and cuddled against Logan, who ran her fingers through Dale's shaggy hair.

Sated and content in Logan's arms, Dale felt the sleep that had eluded her earlier overtake her.

Dale stifled a yawn as they headed for the staff lounge. "It's going to be a long night."

Nudging her in the side, Logan said, "Whose fault is that?"

Another yawn cut short Dale's grin. She waggled her eyebrows. "It was worth it."

Logan's eyes went dark. "Yes, it was."

Unexpected arousal skittered down Dale's spine. She shook a finger at Logan. "Behave."

"Me?" Logan's attempt to look innocent totally failed.

"Yeah, you." Dale pushed open the door to the lounge and stopped short.

Jess was sitting at the round table in the center of the room.

"What's going on?" Dale asked as they strode in. The intake board had been full when they passed the nurses' station, but no alerts had been issued that would account for Jess's presence at this time of night.

A grimace flashed across Jess's face.

Uh. Oh. That's never a good sign.

As if realizing she had allowed her feelings to show, Jess donned the professional expression she normally wore. "Carlton called in sick at the last minute. With Karen on vacation and David on temporary disability, we were short staffed. So I pulled a double."

While Dale had not worked with him, she'd heard through the grapevine about some of the stunts Carlton pulled: calling in sick right before his shift was due to start, claiming to be sick in the middle of a shift and leaving, as well as dodging the difficult patients. She didn't understand why Jess put up with it.

"Well, Logan and I can take it from here. Why don't you head out?"

Jess glanced at the clock. It was forty-five minutes until the end of shift. "Actually, I need to talk to Logan before I leave." She turned her attention to Logan. "Would you prefer to go into my office?"

What's going on? Dale glanced at Logan, who looked just as startled and clueless.

"Uh. No. We can talk here," Logan said.

"Okay." Jess motioned for her to take a seat at the table. She glanced between them, then said, "Dale, why don't you join us? This affects you too."

Dale shared a worried look with Logan as she slid into a chair next to her at the table.

Jess steepled her hands. "I didn't want to say anything about Gretchen until it was official."

Panic flashed through Dale. Why was she coming back early? She couldn't imagine Gretchen returning to work two weeks after the birth of her little girl. While she was holding her own, the premature baby was still in the neonatal unit. Did Gretchen need the money? Although Dale knew that she and Logan would eventually no longer work together, she wasn't ready to face that yet.

Logan's hand on her thigh calmed her runaway emotions. She forced herself to smile at her, then focused back on Jess.

"Gretchen decided that working nights isn't a viable option for her any longer. She won't be returning to the night shift."

Dale's gaze darted between Jess and Logan. Did that mean what she thought it meant? *Oh please, offer her the job!*

Jess smiled. "Before I open the position to applicants, I wanted to officially offer you the job, Logan. You've been a great asset to the department, and I'd be pleased to have you on my staff permanently."

Equal parts fear and hope coursed through Dale. This was the moment of truth for Logan. Deciding to give up the nomadic life she had been leading and actually taking that final step by accepting a permanent position were two very different things.

Logan's hand tightened on Dale's thigh, and a look of fear chased briefly across her face.

Dale's stomach sank.

Her eyes met Dale's, and their gazes locked. A thousand unspoken words passed between them.

The stress left Logan's face, and she smiled before turning to face Jess. "I'll take it. And thank you."

She's staying! Dale barely resisted the urge to pull Logan into her arms and kiss her senseless.

Jess reached across the table and shook Logan's hand. "Great. Glad to have you. Personnel will contact you in the next few days to work out all the contract details." She tipped her chin in Dale's direction, and a little half smirk appeared. "I take it this meets with your approval?"

Dale grinned. "Oh. Absolutely."

"I thought that might be the case." Jess pushed back her chair. "Well, then, I will leave you ladies to it. Good night."

When the door swung shut behind Jess, Dale turned in her chair and pulled Logan against her. Uncaring who might walk in, she kissed her with all the joy in her heart.

When the kiss broke, Logan rested her forehead against Dale's. "Thank you for not giving up on me. I love you."

"Never. I love you too." Dale didn't know what the future held for them, but she had faith that whatever came their way, they would face it—together.

ABOUT RJ NOLAN

RJ Nolan lives in the United States with her spouse and their Great Dane. She makes frequent visits to the California coast near her home. The sight and sound of the surf always stir her muse. When not writing, she enjoys reading, camping, and the occasional trip to Disneyland.

CONNECT WITH RJ NOLAN:
Website: www.rjnolan.com
E-mail: rjnolan@gmail.com

OTHER BOOKS FROM
YLVA PUBLISHING

www.ylva-publishing.com

IN A HEARTBEAT

The L.A. Metro Series - Book #2

RJ Nolan

ISBN: 978-3-95533-159-7
Length: 370 pages (97,000 words)

Officer Sam McKenna has no trouble facing down criminals but breaks out in a sweat at the mere mention of commitment. Trauma surgeon Riley Connolly tries to measure up to her family's expectations and hides her sexuality from them. A life-and-death situation at the hospital binds them together. But can there be any future for a commitment-phobic cop and a closeted, workaholic doctor?

BLURRED LINES

Cops and Docs - Book #1

KD Williamson

ISBN: 978-3-95533-493-2
Length: 283 pages (92,000 words)

Wounded in a police shootout, Detective Kelli McCabe spends weeks in the hospital recovering. Her only entertainment is verbal sparring matches with Dr. Nora Whitmore, the talented and reclusive surgeon.

Two very different women living in two different worlds. When the lines between them begin to blur, will they run from the possibilities or embrace the changes they bring to each other's lives.

ALL THE LITTLE MOMENTS

G Benson

ISBN: 978-3-95533-341-6
Length: 350 pages (132,000 words)

Anna is focused on her career as an anaesthetist. When a tragic accident leaves her responsible for her young niece and nephew, her life changes abruptly. Completely overwhelmed, Anna barely has time to brush her teeth in the morning let alone date a woman. But then she collides with a long-legged stranger...

FRAGILE

Eve Francis

ISBN: 978-3-95533-482-6
Length: 300 pages (103,000 words)

College graduate Carly Rogers is forced to live back at home with her mother and sister until she finds a real job. Life isn't shaping up as expected, but meeting Ashley soon begins to change that. After many late night talks and the start of a book club, the two women begin a romance. When a past medical condition threatens Ashley, Carly wonders if their future together will always be this fragile.

COMING FROM YLVA PUBLISHING

www.ylva-publishing.com

CROSSING LINES
Cops and Docs - Book #2

KD Williamson

Despite all the upheaval around them, Nora Whitmore and Kelli McCabe found their way...together. Unfortunately, little by little, things fall apart around them. Can they navigate through seemingly impassable obstacles? Or will the lines they cross keep them part?

REWRITING THE ENDING

hp tune

A chance meeting in an airport lounge and a shared flight itinerary leaves Juliet and Mia connected. But how do you stay connected when you've only known each other for twenty four hours, are destined for different continents and each have a past to reconcile?

Wounded Souls
© 2016 by RJ Nolan

ISBN: 978-3-95533-585-4

Also available as e-book.

Published by Ylva Publishing, legal entity of Ylva Verlag, e.Kfr.

Ylva Verlag, e.Kfr.
Owner: Astrid Ohletz
Am Kirschgarten 2
65830 Kriftel
Germany

www.ylva-publishing.com

First edition: 2016

Credits
Edited by Sandra Gerth & Michelle Aguilar
Cover Design & Print Layout by Streetlight Graphics